HAYLEE

and the

Traveler's Stone

an illustrated, paranormal, adventure

by

Lisa Redfern

Little Mountain Publishing, California

Published by
Little Mountain Publishing
P.O. Box 1038
Nevada City, CA 95959

Edited by Erica Ellis, ericaellisfreelance.com

HAYLEE Haylee Custom Font Design by Megan Greene,
megangreenedesign.com

Nymphette Font by Lauren Thompson

ISBN-13: 978-0-9655998-7-0

Version 1.1

Library of Congress Control Number: 2014921386

Printed by CreateSpace, a DBA of On-Demand Publishing, LLC
in the United States of America

This book contains an excerpt from the forthcoming title **Haylee and the Last Traveler.** This excerpt has been set for this edition only and may not reflect the final content of the final work.

for

Elisabeth Ann

1921-2013

Contents

Illustrations

Many thanks to my first string readers

Kevin Melton, who formed that first writers' support group.

Gary Redfern, whose promise of a green Smiley was the carrot in front of the cart.

My grandma, Betty Wrysinski, who believed in the project.

My mom, Dianne Peterson, who "couldn't put it down."

…to the more recent readers.

Kamara Garcia who worked to find oopses and whose smile and encouragement kept the energy alive.

Peggy and Megan Greene, who helped to tighten the straps and tie the bows.

Ashley Votaw who requested more details and Scott Welch whose careful notes and comments improved the believability of many of the scenes and characters.

Robert Heirendt who sparked the 'ah ha' moment with the comment, "I don't know why there aren't as many illustrations in books as there used to be."

Todd Frantz who helped polish the project during its final stages.

A hearty thank you to my freelance editor Erica Ellis. I loved your comments and rewrite suggestions. All of it was spot on! You took this project and gave it a professional refinement.

Thank you to my Home Team

My husband, cheerleader, and plausibility sounding board, Gary Frankel. Thank you for being the wind under my wings and helping me to see that I really can fly.

To my son, I thank you for believing in me and being such an enthusiastic promoter of my work.

Thank you both for your patience while I spent all that time thinking and pounding away at the keyboard instead of doing other things…

Finally, to our furry family members, thank you for keeping me laughing!

1

OUTING

Present since planetary formation, Star beings slumber in repose. Located in the far reaches of the deep Mother blood, their state would be very close to what one might think of as hibernation. However, if the strict definition of the word were taken into account, it would not accurately describe it.

Summer, 1972

To spend a day in town was a treat for the Garrett family. The 120 acre walnut farm that they owned and worked on took up more than a significant amount of their time.

Five-year-old Haylee sat on a cool plastic chair. The air-conditioning raised bumps on her exposed arms and legs, but it felt refreshing after coming in from the heat outside. With her hands pressing flat on the table, she swiveled her chair from left to right then back the other way again, repeating this over and over. She liked how the skin below her shorts stuck to the seat.

Mommy is getting napkins and ketchup, Daddy is waiting for our food, and I am saving our table!

"Haylee, sit still." Her mom scolded gently, as she

returned. Doris unfolded several napkins and arranged them in the shape of a placemat in front of her daughter.

"Will I get to sit on the Hamburgler statue like those kids over there?" Haylee pointed.

"Sweetheart, that's not polite." Doris reached over to push Haylee's arm down. "Yes - after we've eaten lunch." She looked up as her handsome husband approached carrying a plastic tray loaded with cups and neatly wrapped packages. A smile formed on her face as she watched female heads turning in his direction.

"This sure smells good!" Eugene commented, oblivious to the attention he attracted.

Doris and Gene busied themselves with removing the items from the platter. A small box of fries, a hamburger and a soda were arranged on Haylee's napkins.

Her parents chatted amicably as Haylee began to sample a few fries and unwrap the paper that covered her hamburger. Suddenly the expression on her face grew serious. She lifted her knees up one at a time, unsticking her legs and tucking her hands beneath them. Haylee looked down at the floor so that her hair made a curtain around her face.

It took the adults a few moments before they realized that their daughter's demeanor had drastically changed.

"Hay, Hay what's the matter?" her dad asked.

Her mother, sitting beside her, placed a comforting hand on her back. "Honey, tell us what's wrong."

Haylee's eyes brimmed with tears as she looked up to meet her mother's gaze, then dropped to the table.

"I can hear them." she whispered.

For a brief moment, with eyes wide, Doris remained unmoving. Then she went into action, rewrapping the offending object.

"What on earth are you doing D? She needs to eat that."

Gene was irritated.

In clipped tones Doris replied, "I forgot to tell you that the last time we went to the pediatrician, Dr. Webber mentioned that red meat may cause stomach aches. Could you go order her a grilled cheese instead?"

Gene huffed but went to fulfill his wife's request.

Doris turned and looked earnestly at her child. "Haylee, what did you mean?"

"I can hear the cows Mommy....."

2

TOGETHER ALONE

1974

Losing a mother at seven had been incredibly painful, but losing a father at the same time, even though he was still alive, had been devastating.

Gene had turned away from Haylee. He barely spoke and would not look at her. Unable to find comfort with a parent who used to be loving, safe and strong, Haylee grew angry. She yelled at the mothers from her class who came by the house. "Stop trying to hug my Daddy! And stop bringing us food! We don't want you! We can take care of ourselves!"

Her friends at school felt awkward, not knowing what to say or how to engage with her anymore. Haylee was mad at them because they still had their mothers.

Haylee, once a happy, outgoing girl, had become a loner. She coped the best way she could, by caring for their animals, cooking their meals, talking to herself, and by staying out of her father's sight as much as possible.

⚜3⚜

AWAKENING CHANGES

Elverta, California
November 12, 1984
4:40 p.m.

She was sure that she had a migraine, even though she'd never had one before. Excruciating pain started at her temples and radiated out like pinpoint pricks of burning sparks throughout her entire body. Haylee, with eyes squinted into slits, had to forcefully refrain from groaning as each step sent waves of nausea washing over her. She drew in deep breaths in an attempt to keep her stomach contents where they belonged. Concentrating only on walking softly, Haylee slowly managed the half-mile walk down the dirt road that led to her house. It felt like it took forever.

The cool interior darkness that enveloped her as she crossed the threshold offered a fleeting sense of relief. Within moments, she was clammy and trembling again.

She held onto the walls to make her way to the bathroom. Once there, she let her book bag drop to the floor and crawled like a suffering supplicant toward the porcelain deity. After twenty minutes of dry heaves, she thankfully welcomed its cool countenance along the side of her face as she crouched there, embracing it for another ten minutes.

When it appeared that her world had ceased its sickening gyrations, she gingerly moved a few inches to test her theory.

OK, I think it's getting better, she thought. Although the prickling pain persisted, the nausea had abated slightly.

Stooping carefully to retrieve her bag, Haylee didn't bother to glance in the mirror as she shuffled toward her room. Returning shortly in her bathrobe, she reached in the shower to turn on the hot water. If she had not been so preoccupied, she would have been shocked by what the mirror revealed. Drenched by sweat, dark hair hung limply around an ashen face. Her lips were gray. A once straight, angular body had become more rounded.

Shakily, she stepped over the edge of the tub. The cascading water soothed her, but only temporarily. Lost in a dull haze of pain, but not knowing what else to do, Haylee stood there, eyes closed, remaining as still as possible.

In her misery, time was meaningless. At some point, her father started knocking on the bathroom door. Feebly, she responded to his questions. She was relieved when he finally left her alone. Long after the shower had turned cold and the house had become silent, she stepped out of the tub.

Laboriously, she put on her robe. The mirror reflected even more startling changes. Her hands and arms had begun to take on more pronounced lines. Her neck, shoulders, hips, and legs had developed a graceful quality. In a few short, painful hours, Haylee Garrett had begun a metamorphosis. The pain she experienced blinded her to all else, but somewhere in the back of her mind, it registered that her robe was too small.

Without turning on the lights, Haylee entered her room. Feeling for the electric blanket controls, she cranked the heat up to high. Crawling under the covers, she curled into a ball and wished that she could die…Anything that would allow her to escape the pain would be welcome.

November 13, 1984
6:24 a.m.

Early the next morning, Haylee became dimly aware of her father moving around as he prepared to go to work. Before he left, he cracked opened her bedroom door. She squinted, turning her face away from the hall light.

"How are you feeling?" Gene asked.

"Better," she mumbled.

She didn't see her father's indecision about whether or not to enter her room. His voice traveled across the distance from the doorway.

"You should stay home from school. Don't worry about your chores; I'll take care of everything." Gene closed her door softly on his way out.

Lying there quietly, Haylee looked around the room as she assessed herself. She felt sticky. *My headache is gone and I don't feel sick to my stomach anymore.* Her electric blanket lay in a warm heap on the floor. Switching off the heat, she leaned over to fling it back onto the bed. Burrowing back in, she contentedly closed her eyes.

Much later, she woke up as a ferocious growl came from her stomach. Throwing back the blankets and swinging her legs over the side in a hurry, Haylee stood up, shaking with such an intense hunger, she almost lost her balance.

"Geez," she said while making a focused effort to remain steady. On wobbly legs, she headed across the floor. As she reached for the door, her eyes met those of her reflection in the full-length mirror. Haylee suddenly pulled back as if the door-knob were on fire. Stumbling, she fell down hard.

The person staring back at her did not look like the person she knew. At first, she thought that sometime during the night she had miraculously turned into her mother. On hands and knees, she crawled closer.

Her eyes had turned a deeper shade of hazel, with golden flecks. Their slight tilt at the outer edges, while noticeable before, was more pronounced, giving her an exotic look. Leaning on her knees, she reached up to pull her hair away from her honey colored face. She took in all of the new planes and angles, as well as the full lips.

A quick glance down revealed full breasts jutting out from the soft material. Astonished, she released her hair to reach down to feel them. Cupping her hands, she tested their weight. She was amazed at how firm and round they were.

Still in shock, Haylee stood up to strip. She wanted to see everything. "Wow!" she muttered as she marveled at this new, very beautiful body. The shapely lines of her legs, hips, and buttocks were pleasing. She turned around so she could see her back, and then faced forward again. Her hands splayed over a tapered waist and once again returned to cup full breasts. Her eyes returned to her face.

The cold air caused goose bumps to rise. Her nipples tightened. Haylee was unprepared for the strength of these simple sensations. It was as if she could feel every hair standing up at attention.

Mystified as to what to do about any of this, Haylee just stared blankly. Just then, Oscar, her fluffy Siamese mix, rubbed himself around the edge of the door as he glided into her room. He stopped suddenly, arching his back, hissing. His alarm, uncertainty, and fear stopped all of the other thoughts in Haylee's head.

"It's just me." She spoke softly as she lowered herself to his level.

His body relaxed slightly, but a low growl began as he stepped back.

Taking a deep breath, Haylee focused on opening her thoughts to him. She visualized a flower with petals unfolding. Feelings of tenderness and love floated from the flower to the feline. Finally understanding that this was his girl, he cautiously approached to verify this with smell.

"See, it's still me," she crooned. He allowed her to stroke him, but he also let her know that he did not like this surprise— he was not going to purr.

Giving and receiving comfort, she responded, "I completely understand."

At the next loud growl from her stomach, Oscar's ears went back, his hair stood on end and he shot out of there like the hounds from next door were after him.

Haylee too got moving. Rushing into clothing, she raced to the kitchen.

⚕4⚕

SLIPPED PAST

April, 1980

More than she ever thought possible, thirteen-year-old Haylee felt alone as she sat on the crowded school bus, morosely staring out the window and desperately trying to swallow past the lump in her throat.

"I will not cry! I will not cry!" she wordlessly mouthed to her reflection in the bus window, hoping it would be true.

For what seemed like the hundredth time that day, she relived the mortifying scene that had made her the laughing stock of the entire school. Every day in English class, there were a few minutes for students to write in their private journals. The teacher promised not to read anything that was written there: she just wanted her students to practice expressing themselves on paper.

As was her custom, Haylee wrote poetry. Today, instead of writing the poem and then naming it as she usually did, she wrote the name of her beloved boldly across the top of the paper.

Curtis Carter.

Engrossed in her efforts to put down her thoughts, she failed to notice Bethany, a classmate, lean across her desk to stare over Haylee's shoulder. She didn't see her eyes grow wide when she spotted the name Haylee had written. Haylee also failed to notice Bethany putting her head together with her friends to share what she had seen. The group shared a snickering laugh.

At the end of class, Haylee gathered up her books with a satisfied smile. She always felt happy when she could write the exact words that she needed. One of Bethany's friends rushed into Haylee, sending her books flying.

"Hey!" Haylee exclaimed.

Frannie casually glanced over her shoulder and flippantly replied, "Sorry," with a shrug as she continued on her way.

Another girl from their group bent down to help, quickly grabbing the journal and passing it to Bethany before it was noticed. With a frown, Haylee squatted down to retrieve her possessions. The girl, nodding in Frannie's direction said, "She can be such a bitch sometimes." She handed over the books, stood up, and abruptly turned to follow her friends.

"Thanks," Haylee replied glumly to the girl's retreating back.

It wasn't until later that she realized that her journal was missing. She retraced her steps, searching for it. A knot of worry formed in the pit of her stomach. *What if someone finds it and reads it?*

At that very moment, Bethany stood in the middle of a small group of laughing teenagers, reading Haylee's words out loud. Curtis, Bethany's 'steady,' was among them.

In her search, Haylee happened to walk by the group. She didn't pay much attention to them except to notice Curtis. Her head snapped around as she heard her words spoken in

Bethany's waspish voice. "Curtis, you can't see me, but if you could, you could read what my heart has written in my eyes." An uproarious laugh went up.

All at once, time seemed to move in slow motion as Bethany glanced up and looked directly at Haylee. The group turned together, as one, to stare at her. Jeering, they pointed.

Mortified and red as a beet, Haylee made eye contact with the object of her affection. His insolent glance took her in from head to toe. "You've got to be kidding," he commented sarcastically.

For a moment longer, Haylee gazed directly at him. She thought she saw a look of shame. And something else—pity. Spurned into action, she rushed forward into their surprised midst and yanked her journal from Bethany's grasp, knocking her down in the process. With book in hand, Haylee ran.

She stopped when she was winded and felt like her lungs would burst. Near an empty baseball diamond, she climbed down into the dugout to hide from the world.

Never one to skip school, Haylee missed all of her classes that afternoon. Her thoughts were concentrated on getting home. She had to ride the bus. Bethany, Curtis, and most of their friends rode the same bus.

By the time the last bell of the day rang, Haylee had pulled herself together. She had levels of strength running through her that still remained untapped. She would get on that bus, ignore them, and get off. Absolutely no emotions would show on her face.

Passing Haylee in the aisle, Bethany snarled, "You're going to be sorry about that little rush and grab stunt."

Haylee worked hard to keep an iron grasp on her emotions when she overheard them say her name over and over again, laughing, as they spread their tale to everyone within hearing distance. Her gentle spirit felt trampled and crushed. She wondered what she had ever done to deserve such cruelty and humiliation.

By the time they arrived at her stop, Haylee was drained. She picked up the books from beside her and plodded down the aisle. The bus was empty; the others had long since departed. As she approached the front, the sad-eyed driver glanced up into the wide rearview mirror. "Haylee, blow them off. They're not worth it."

She met his eyes in the mirror and nodded. Gulping back the lump that suddenly reappeared in her throat, she hurried past him and down the steps. His kind words brought all of her closely held emotions back up to the surface. She did not want Joe, her sometimes confidant, to know that they had gotten to her and that she was about to cry.

The long walk down the dusty dirt road gave her plenty of time to vent. Clutching her books to her chest as if they were her old raggedy teddy bear, she screamed, "How can I possibly hate someone I love so much?"

She talked to herself often. Spending a lot of time alone seemed to have caused this tendency. "Curtis, I don't see how you can like Bethany. She's so mean! I know you're not like that. So why do you hang around with her? I bet ya it's because she has big boobs. Who cares about big boobs? There is a lot more to life than boobs! She doesn't love you, you know. Not like I do."

Anger finally replaced self-pity. Kicking a rock, Haylee yelled, "Someday people will want to hear what I have to say. And they won't be laughing about it either!"

With this said, she felt slightly better. She thought she would probably love Curtis forever, but for now, it was best to try to forget about it.

Walking into the empty house, Haylee went to her bed-room. She tossed her books onto the bed and went to the bathroom to wash her face. The cool water rinsed away the vestiges of her tears. She grabbed the hand towel from the rack, sighing as she vigorously rubbed it over her face. Refreshed, she thought about how she compared to those girls at school.

If she could say anything about herself, she would say she had nice hair. Thick, wavy, chestnut locks fell just past her shoulders. It was usually pulled back into a ponytail. Haylee scrunched up her face as she pulled out the rubber band that always pulled out strands with it. Reaching for her brush, she began running it through her hair. She was satisfied with its thickness and body. Haylee closed her eyes, enjoying the silky feel of the heavy locks as they swished around her face.

She wore no bangs and wondered if bangs would help make her eyebrows look smaller. She had thick eyebrows. At one point, she had decided to attempt to pluck the offending hair and make them smaller, but the exercise had been so painful, she decided that she would live with them the way they were. Large, intelligent, hazel eyes gazed back at her. She'd been blessed with long, thick eyelashes but dismissed them. She noted that her facial features were somewhat angular. Her cheekbones were high and her chin was wide. Shaking her head from side to side, she concluded that her lips were just plain fat!

Tall for her age, she thought she looked gawky, and she did—after all, she was only thirteen. Haylee thought she looked somewhat like a husky football player.

Dressed in straight-leg jeans, a Western, long-sleeved, snap-up shirt, and cowboy boots, Haylee contemplated her wardrobe, which was more of the same. Shopping at Big R Western Wear left a lot to be desired. But that was where her father went for clothes, so that's where she went too. She couldn't bring herself to ask him to go anywhere else. Still, she couldn't help wishing for body suits and bell bottoms. Sighing once again, she pulled back her hair, and wound the rubber band back around it. She headed for the door. The animals were hungry.

Always a solace, the actions of scooping, washing, and filling faded into the background as visions and feelings—not her own—took center stage in her mind. The chickens were delighted with the tasty bug selection today. The goats were busy figuring out how to get to the grass on the opposite side of their enclosure and the pigs were daydreaming about apples as they lounged in the sun. Haylee laughed out loud at her cat Oscar's satisfaction over making the mama cow startle when he performed a surprise pounce from behind a thick clump of grass. To Oscar's continual chagrin, he could never hold his ground when the bovine turned on him, chasing him in the opposite direction.

Haylee giggled as Oscar bolted across the yard, and for a little while at least, she forgot about Curtis and the humiliation she had suffered that day.

᪥5᪥

SOMETHING SPECIAL

1982

Early on, Haylee had learned not to name the animals and to never speak of their silent language or ideas.

She was six-years-old when she first understood that her father meant to have Miss Pebbles Piggy and two of her sisters killed. Haylee'd raged at him and struck out with all of the might her little body could muster. He'd knelt down to her level, trying to explain. All the while, the man who'd arrived with the shotgun waited off to the side.

Furious and frustrated because she could not make him understand that they could speak, she screamed, "I hate you!" and spat into his face.

This was the only time she had ever been struck as a child. Her mother's voice was angry, telling her that she was not to ever—ever!—be disrespectful to her father. Doris dragged a still-kicking-and-yelling Haylee into the house. She forced her to stand in a cold shower clothing and all. Haylee's body jerked as every shot rang out. She screamed until she had no voice left and cried until she had no more tears.

Hours had passed as she sat on her mother's lap in the rocking chair. Her father peeked in on them; his face drawn and tired. Doris shook her head to send him away.

Awakening from a fitful dream, Haylee was surprised to find her mother still rocking her.

Seeing that her daughter was awake, Doris spoke quietly. "Haylee, it's time for you to understand some big girl things. Are you listening?"

She nodded.

"I know that you can understand what the animals are saying. This is something that is very special. In fact, all of the women in our family have unusual abilities. Have you ever wondered why Daddy calls me his Lucky Weather Charm?"

Haylee shook her head.

"It's because if I concentrate, I can change the weather over the northern part of our state. Every time Daddy tells me that he wishes it would rain…or that it would stop raining so much, it happens." Doris smiled with sadness in her eyes. " This is really important—most people can't do the things that we do. People who are not like us don't understand. When people are afraid, they can be mean. This is something that you have to keep secret."

"Even from Daddy?" she rasped.

"Oh honey, Daddy is a wonderful man, but it would make him feel worried if he knew that you really can talk to animals. He just thinks that you have an active imagination."

Haylee began to sob again. "B-b-b-but Mama, the animals feel scared!" she whispered.

Doris cried with her little girl, holding her tighter. "Oh Hay, I know this is hard!"

Once they had themselves under a little more control, her mother continued. "Humans eat animals to survive. We raise them for food."

"But—"

"No! Haylee, this is just the way it is. If you name the farm animals, it makes it harder when their time is over. Every living thing has a time to live and a time to die. Not all of us...." Doris cleared her throat and began again. "Not every life gets to continue until old age. We have to live fully in every minute so that we can get the most out of the time we do have. It's as simple as that."

~ ~ ~ ~

Haylee had wanted to hate her father for slaughtering the pigs. Her mother reminded her often, with casual comments, about what a good man her father was and how hard he worked to take care of his family.

Haylee had chosen to help make their animals as happy as possible. She'd also found a way to modify her dad's procedures so that when the time came for their lives to end, it was not filled with fear. And she learned to respect her father.

She wondered, at times, if her mom knew that she wouldn't be around for a long time. Haylee felt sure that she had gotten the most out of her life while she was here. That thought helped....some.

Haylee was glad, now, that her mother had taught her those hard lessons.

6

FORGOTTEN REMEMBERED

November 13, 1984
6:45 a.m.

Before his wife's death, Gene had been a loving, affectionate man. Since then, he had become quiet and unapproachable. He worked like a man possessed, only hiring help when it was absolutely necessary. On one of the few times he had opened up to his daughter, he'd told her that he had to work all the time to keep himself from hurting.

Something felt strange that morning. It was like the nagging sensation you get when you know you've forgotten something.

On his drive out to the orchards, he mentally went through his list in order of importance. *The walnut trees looked good this year, the harvesting equipment he had been working on was almost ready to go, and Haylee was alright.* Unable to pinpoint the source of his disquieting feelings, he shrugged his shoulders and forgot about it.

At forty-two, Eugene Garrett was handsome and extremely fit. All of the hard work he did to keep his orchards fruitful kept his body lean and hard. His shoulders were broad; the muscles on his arms bulged beneath his short-sleeved western shirts. The skin on his face and torso was deeply tanned to an almost reddish-brown color. Close-cropped, curly, dark brown hair, salted with gray at the temples, framed a weathered face. Sad, light green eyes outlined by thick lashes inspired women's daydreams.

If he shook your hand, you would first notice his strong grip and then his callouses. Sometimes, in the winter, his dry hands would crack and bleed, but that would never stop him. He worked constantly, ignoring the world around him, to keep from thinking about Doris.

Ten years after her death, Gene continued to work hard to keep the memories away. Lately though, some of them would creep up on him when his guard was down. While driving his truck, a memory had inundated his mind and heart. It was so clear, he felt like he was there reliving it.

Doris had decorated the backyard with balloons and streamers and had intricately decorated a cake in a theme from one of Hay's favorite cartoon shows. Kids were running around, screaming and having a wonderful time as he pulled into the driveway. He lifted the new bicycle fitted with training wheels out of the pickup bed. Big white bows that Doris had made streamed from handlebars as he rolled it toward the party. Most of the commotion stopped as the children turned to look at the Red Racer. From across the yard, Haylee spotted her father with the bike and a huge grin on his face. "Oh! Daddy! Daddy!" she squealed as she ran toward him.

He knelt down with arms outstretched to catch her. Clutching his daughter to him, he stood up and twirled her around. He took a moment to hold her close and breathe in the clean smell of her hair. "I love you, my big four year old," he whispered.

She pulled back so she could look into his eyes and stated very seriously, "I love you too, Dear Daddy." His heart constricted as an angelic smile spread across her beautiful face. Sweetly, she asked, "Can I look at my bike now?"

"Whatever the birthday girl wants," he replied as he set her on her feet.

She gave him one last hug. "Thank you, Daddy! Thank you! Thank you!" Then she ran to inspect her bike with her friends.

His gaze met Doris's across the yard as he straightened up. Whenever their eyes met like this, a current of energy passed between them. She smiled a smile that was just for him and started wending her way in his direction. He was proud that after eight years of marriage, he could still be mesmerized just by watching his wife. Her flowered halter dress displayed lovely shoulders and upper arms. He loved her generous curves. Her eyes didn't leave him as she glided through the crowd of children. Thick, shiny blue-black hair coiled at the back of her head. Loose tendrils lightly brushed against the creamy, brown skin of her neck and shoulders. A muscle on the side of Gene's face twitched.

The sparkle in her eyes made his heart expand. A faint waft of gardenia-scented perfume reached him a moment before she did. She placed a hand on his chest and slowly ran it up around the back of his neck so she could pull him down. As he leaned in to fulfill her unspoken request, her low voice and breath caressed him. "You know your daughter idolizes the ground you walk on."

He smiled. "You're the one who makes me look so good," he replied in quiet undertones. Their lips met. At first, the kiss was gentle and soft. Tightening his hold to fit her body more closely to his, it became more demanding. She pulled away with a breathy laugh. "We can't forget that we have an audience."

He leaned his forehead against hers and sighed. "Alright, but I expect you to hold that thought until later."

"You know I will." Giving him quick kiss, she returned to the party.

He spent a pleasurable afternoon entertaining the children and flirting with his wife.

That evening, after tucking in a tired Haylee, Doris sat on the edge of her bed and sang "Happy Birthday" one more time. Doris's voice was lilting and slightly husky. Her face took on a faraway expression as she continued singing, "From the Heart of the Dawn, keys of survival birthed in stone. The smaller travels a straight line, a larger is passed by the hands of the Travelers alone."

Haylee blinked heavily, fighting sleep. Doris stroked her hair as she sang. The combination of her mother's voice and soothing touch quickly sent her into the world of dreams.

Gene came to stand behind his wife, putting his hands on her bare shoulders and caressing her neck with his thumbs.

"What was that song?" he asked.

Absentmindedly, she replied, "Oh, something my mother taught me."

He looked at his peaceful daughter feeling the goodness of the moment wrap around him like a warm, tropical breeze filled with the sweet scent of blossoms.

Leaning down, Gene nuzzled Doris's neck. She could feel his warm breath as he whispered in her ear, "Mrs. Garrett, I think it's later…"

❧7❧

MUNCHIES

November 13, 1984
11:57 a.m.

Haylee raced to the kitchen driven by her fierce cravings. Barely able to contain her desires, she opened the refrigerator and grabbed the first thing her hand landed on—milk. After a half dozen lusty swallows, the empty carton landed with a dull thud in the middle of the kitchen floor. Empty cheese wrappers followed by cold cut wrappers, mayonnaise, mustard and ketchup bottles, an empty pickle jar, Tupperware containers that had held Tuna Helper leftovers, a tray from what was left of a pineapple upside-down cake and an empty egg carton were added to the pile.

Haylee paused to survey the bare refrigerator shelves for anything else of interest. A deep burp burbled up from her throat that tasted like mustard and tuna. *Not a bad combination…* Haylee rejected the horseradish and jalapeño condiments. Resting one hand on her stomach while wiping goo from her face with the back of the other, Haylee thought with surprise, *I don't feel sick or like puking after eating all of that!* A louder burp erupted, followed by another growl from her stomach. Not stopping to question any further, Haylee began riffling through the cupboards. Soon the plinking of empty tin cans sounded as they hit the floor. The contents of the trashcan increased the size of the refuse pile.

With a glassy look in her eyes, Haylee's hunger finally wound down as she licked food remnants from the dirty dishes in the sink. Consciously, she had to stop herself from tossing the Corel plates and bowls into her heap. Although the advertisements claimed that they were unbreakable, Haylee knew this was not true.

What a relief not to feel starved! Haylee took a deep breath and sighed with contentment as she wandered over to the couch. Her head barely landed on the cushion before she was fast asleep.

November 13, 1984
5:38 p.m.

Abruptly, Gene brought himself back to the present, shaking himself. "No!" he rasped in a hoarse voice. His stomach felt tight and queasy. "It still hurts."

Off and on throughout the day, Gene would hear Doris singing "Happy Birthday" in his mind. It was so clear, it was as if she were standing right next to him. Each time he heard it, he would stop what he was doing, frown, look around, shake his head, and go back to work. It wasn't until he was done for the day that it hit him; today was Haylee's birthday.

He couldn't remember when they had celebrated a birthday since Doris died. With a start, he realized Haylee was eighteen. *Where did the time go?* he asked. *I've missed years of my daughter's life,* he thought, feeling a sense of shock.

He shut his eyes, as waves of loss and emptiness washed over his heart. He remained in that spot for a very long time.

Silent tears rolled down his face. He thought about Doris and all of those lost years with Haylee. For ten years, he had treated his daughter as if she didn't exist. All of his pent-up feelings started to unravel. His body shook as mournful sobs let loose. It was hard work, but Eugene finally broke through the shell he'd kept around himself for so many years.

November 13, 1984
7:37 p.m.

The screen door banged against its frame as Gene walked into the house. "Haylee, where are you!" he yelled. It was too late for dinner, but he could still take her out for dessert. His heart constricted with pain as he wished that he had a present for her. He intended to make things right if he could. He hoped that it wasn't too late.

The afternoon's catharsis continued its unpredictable flow. Like bubbles rising to the surface of a fizzy drink, another memory popped into his mind.

Doris, holding their baby in a rocking chair. Seeing the tears streaming down her face, he'd asked, "What's wrong?"

"I was just thinking about how much I missed my own mom growing up and how sad it would be if Haylee experienced that."

"She won't!" he replied adamantly

Doris sat quietly for a moment, staring carefully into his eyes. "But if she does, promise me that you'll find a good woman to be there for her...for both of you."

Gene was offended. "How can you say something like that?"

"Please!" she begged. "If you humor me here, I promise that I'll never bring it up again."

"OK," he said reluctantly.

Silently she regarded him. It wasn't what she had asked

for, but she knew that it was the best he could do.

"Eugene, I love you and trust you. That's why I married you."

He closed his eyes. To him, being anywhere in the world without Doris was unthinkable…as were thoughts of another woman. *Didn't she know that?* But wanting to make her happy, and wondering if it was the baby blues talking, he said what she wanted, "I promise to take good care of her if you aren't here."

True to her own words, Doris never did bring it up again

The memories—yet another reminder of how he'd failed Doris—were like an exquisite arrow piercing his heart. They almost brought him to the brink of going back into that dark place that was infinitely more comfortable than this one.

November 13, 1984
7:43 p.m.

Walking through the house, he called Haylee's name. Reaching her bathroom, Gene found the door locked. "Haylee, are you in there?" he called. There was no answer. A trickle of fear ran down his spine. He pounded louder. "Haylee! Answer me!" All of the concern and love that Haylee had been longing for was in his voice. Unfortunately, she was in no condition to appreciate the change in her father's attitude. "Haylee, if you don't answer me, I'm going to break this door down!"

"I'm sick," he heard her soft reply. Relief flooded through him. "I thought you were feeling better this morning."

"I'm not….I'm taking a bath," she replied.

"I wanted to take you out for your birthday. Do you feel up to getting dressed?" Gene asked kindly. After a long silence, he asked, "Haylee, did you hear me?"

"Thank you, Dad, but I would really like to just be left alone. OK?" Sighing, Gene reluctantly agreed and asked her if there was anything she needed, to which she responded, "No." Wishing her a happy birthday through the door and telling her that he loved her, he waited for some reply. Disappointed when there was none, and feeling like a complete ass, he plodded away.

❧8❧

FAILURE TO THRIVE

1982

Most of the girls her age started getting their periods at thirteen. Haylee was well aware of this because those who were "on the rag" didn't have to shower in gym class. It was almost an honor, and a sign that a girl had moved into womanhood.

When she turned fourteen and was practically the last girl in her class not to have gotten her period, her schoolmates started talking about her behind her back.

When she was fifteen, still periodless, and showing no signs of development, the gym teacher called Haylee into her office and started asking embarrassing questions. Mortified, Haylee stared at the ground as she quietly informed the teacher that the women in her family had always been very late bloomers—she was grasping at straws—and that she was sure that any day now it was going to happen.

The teacher, who was quite fond of the quiet, intelligent girl, looked doubtful. She empathized with Haylee's discomfort, and she knew that Haylee probably had no one to confide in.

"Haylee, I want you to know that if you need anyone to talk to, I'm available. I didn't bring you in my office to embarrass you. I'm just concerned. It may be true that you are a late bloomer, but it could also be that something's wrong, like a hormone imbalance. I've discussed this with the school nurse and—"

"How could you talk about this with someone else? It's none of your business!" Haylee shouted in a strained voice. She felt light-headed and breathless, as if she had just been kicked in the stomach. Tears welled up in her eyes.

"It is my business, Haylee," the teacher replied sadly. "Teachers have a responsibility to look after the welfare of their students. If it looks like the parents are neglecting—"

"What? You're saying my father is doing something wrong because I'm not..."—her brow furrowed, Haylee searched for the right word—"...growing up?"

"This is important, Haylee. If you don't look like you are progressing normally, I will have to call your father and make sure you see a doctor."

"No! Just leave me alone and stay away from my father!" Haylee yelled as she practically jumped for the door. She felt suffocated and trapped and needed air.

Not long after what Haylee thought of as "The Big Period Incident," she ordered herself a bra through a catalog and started stuffing herself. She also became an expert at avoiding gym class.

Through her fifteenth year, she successfully hid her lack of development. She couldn't bring herself to talk to her father about it. He never looked at her closely enough to notice.

Even before her talk with her gym teacher, Haylee had wondered if there was something wrong. At first, she was convinced that she had cancer eating away her insides, keeping her from growing. She had fantasies about how her condition would wake up her father. He would figure out how to save her, and they would be close from then on. As she got older, she worried that she had a congenital disorder that would keep her from ever maturing.

Despite her fears, and through all of the other trauma in her young life, Haylee stayed balanced. Even though she was quiet at school, she enjoyed learning and took pleasure in her classes—except gym—easily outshining her classmates. Her teachers respected her quick thinking.

When all of her chores were done for the day and her father was fed, Haylee would go outside, climb up on the old tractor that sat rusting behind the barn, and watch the sun set. Its beauty always touched her.

The feeling of the cool evening air, as it caressed her face, had her smiling. She thought about how much she loved caring for their animals. The pictures and thoughts that they shared with her made her feel accepted as part of them. They saw her... really saw her. This was something that Haylee desperately needed.

Life would be so much simpler if I were an animal instead of a human. No one would care if my growth was stunted. If I couldn't perform my job, my dad could just put me down.

❧9❧

LIFE'S BLOOD

November 13, 1984
11:59 p.m.

Haylee slept fitfully. A migraine headache had started again. By midnight, she was curled into a ball, feeling nauseous and dizzy. Raw fear coursed through her. *What's wrong with me?* her mind screamed. *What's going to happen this time?* Large, silent tears traveled down her face.

After spending more than three hours in agony and fear, Haylee's body suddenly jerked into a sitting position as a piercing, sharp pain ripped through her abdominal area. With bulging eyes, she opened her mouth to scream and found that she couldn't breathe. Her heart was pounding so hard and fast, she thought it would burst. She panicked and clawed at her throat, leaving angry red marks. Her eyes rolled back in her head; she lost consciousness.

Sometime later, she awoke. The pain was still with her, but she was able to move. She noticed that her legs felt warm and slippery. Slowly, she reached over to turn on her bedside lamp. Looking down, she was horrified to see that she was lying in a pool of blood. Inhaling a shaky, ragged breath, her throat constricted. *Daddy, …please help me, I'm so scared,* she thought.

After a struggle, she managed to get herself onto her feet. She could see thick ribbons of dark red traveling down her legs. "Daddy," she croaked, starting to cry. Holding onto the furniture and swaying, Haylee slowly inched her way to the bathroom. Every now and then, she would try to call her father, but no more than a whisper came out. She left a path of wet, bloody footprints behind her. Eventually, she collapsed unceremoniously into the bathtub. Wave after wave of pain ripped through her. Her breath became shallow; she lost consciousness again, sure that this time she would never wake up.

November 14, 1984
4:00 a.m.

Usually a heavy sleeper, Gene woke with a start. A glance at the clock on his nightstand told him the time. Fuzzily, he wondered what roused him. The strong smell of gardenias in the room brought him fully awake. A sense of urgency overcame him.

He fumbled for the switch at his bedside lamp. Momentarily blinded by the sudden illumination, Gene's eyes squeezed shut. For some inexplicable reason, he scrambled to put on his clothes.

Flipping on the hallway light, his eyes spotted the dark pools of liquid and what looked like dragging footprints on the floor. His confusion cleared as he realized what he was seeing. Gene's heart thudded. "Jesus in Heaven!" he muttered as he ran down the hall. Bursting into her bathroom, Gene's breath was knocked out of his body as he took in the scene before him.

His daughter lay in a heap in the tub, looking as white as a corpse. The bottom half of her nightshirt was soaked with blood, and her legs were smeared with it. "Dear God!" he cried as his body shook. A fresh, steady stream was pooling and dripping down the drain.

Falling to his knees beside her, he grabbed her shoulders. "Haylee! Haylee! Can you hear me?!" he yelled with desperation.

She was limp. Thinking fast, he felt for a pulse. It was there, but it was fast and weak. Reaching for a towel, he stuffed it tightly between her thighs to stanch the flow. Gently gathering her up in his arms, Eugene ran to his truck, saying all the way, "Dear God, I beg you, please don't let her die! Please don't take my daughter away from me!"

Stretching her out on the bench seat, Gene cradled Haylee's head in his lap. With shaking hands, he struggled to put his key in the ignition. He looked at them and saw them covered with blood. It was almost his undoing. Closing his eyes momentarily, he told himself that he had to stay calm to help her. Tears clouded his vision and made driving at full speed difficult. Once out on the paved road, Gene put a hand on his daughter's cheek, telling her in his calmest voice that everything would be alright.

Arriving at the hospital, he raced around the truck to scoop her into his arms. The towel he had used to stop her bleeding was soaked through. "Oh God!" he exclaimed in anguish. Hastily, he ripped off his shirt to replace the heavy towel. He burst through the emergency room door with Haylee in his arms; his eyes were wild and he was beginning to hyperventilate.

Immediately, Haylee was whisked away. Gene made a move to follow, but a nurse blocked his way. He would have fought to get past her but stopped when she told him harshly that if he wanted to help, he would have to stay out of the doctor's way.

Looking down, he saw a petite, redhead with intense blue

eyes standing before him. In a calm, soothing tone she told him, "She's in good hands. Let the doctors do their job."

He nodded. His voice was hoarse and wavery when he spoke. "Please take care of her."

The nurse used a firm voice to direct him into a quiet, empty treatment room where she sat him on a table. Coming back from closing the door, she brought tissues, rubber gloves, and moist towels to clean off the blood. As she reached out to hand him a tissue, she found herself caught in his grasp. He pulled her close, and laid his head on her chest. His large body shook with deep soul-shattering sobs. Within his emotional storm, Gene didn't see the look of concern on her face.

He realized his tears were more than just fear over the danger that Haylee was in. They were self-loathing for ruining their lives—for not being there through Haylee's younger years—and terror that he would never have a chance to tell her he was sorry.

~ ~ ~ ~

Surprised at being so abruptly handled, the nurse stiffened. Direct contact with the blood sent a wave of adrenalin through her, knowing that she would now have to be tested. However, the gut wrenching sobs coming from the big man touched her and brought out softer instincts. Slowly, as if of their own volition, her arms came up and wrapped around him. She stroked his back and thick, wavy, hair while murmuring softly. Eventually her words got through. "You have to be strong for your daughter." Gene quieted but still held her close.

Silently, she continued to stroke his hair. She noticed its silkiness and how his bare chest, pressed close to hers, radiated a great deal of heat. Her eyes widened in surprise when she realized that she was feeling attracted to this man!

At the same moment, Gene became aware of the smell and

feel of the woman in his arms. A conflict between feelings of comfort, pleasure and disloyalty caused him to become tense.

~ ~ ~ ~

Keenly aware of the change in his demeanor, Nurse Glori Ridgeway abruptly stepped out of his embrace. She busied herself with cleaning the dried blood from his hands and arms. He asked what was happening with Haylee. Telling him to stay put, she went to find out.

₰10₰

BREAKING FREE

November 14, 1984
7:00 a.m.

Haylee emerged from the blackness that engulfed her. The beeping sounds around her were confusing. Feeling euphoric, she noticed a light, floating sensation. Hearing muted voices, she struggled to become fully conscious.

Her vision was fuzzy at first but cleared after a few moments. Her dad's face came into view. She wondered why he looked so tired and unshaven. There were deep lines on his forehead and around his eyes.

He reached out to brush hair off of her forehead. Seeing her eyes grow clearer, he turned his head to speak to someone. "I think she's coming around."

A woman's face appeared. A bright light was directed in one eye and then the other. The woman turned to Gene. "I can't explain it. She seems to be stronger."

The faces left her line of vision. Haylee could hear soft voices. Then her father was back. His hand felt warm and strong when he reached out to take hers. "Haylee, do you know where you are?"

Frowning, she moved her head slightly.

"You're in the hospital. I brought you in early this morning."

She closed her eyes. His words brought her memory back; she nodded.

"You are going to be just fine." He rubbed her hand. "You need to rest. Try to go back to sleep, OK? I'll be right here."

Although she didn't say a word, Haylee noticed that he was holding her hand. She liked that.

~ ~ ~ ~

Sitting in a chair next to her, Gene watched his daughter close her eyes again. Her dark, wavy hair was a stark contrast to the white pillow. Each time he looked at her, he thought her face looked rosier. It was amazing. Earlier this morning, he was so afraid that she'd die. Now her color was almost back to normal.

Shaking his head, he was confused by the events of the morning. After he brought her into the hospital, Haylee continued to lose blood. By all accounts, the amount she'd lost should have killed her.

Gene could tell that the doctor felt uncomfortable informing him that. "The only thing we can determine at this point in time is that she was having an unusually heavy menses."

Dr. Lester was a tall, dark-haired woman in her fifties. "Her bleeding has stopped on its own. She appears to be out of danger, but I'd like to keep her here for observation for a few days."

Gene pushed the doctor for answers. With a few short, icy words, she told him that they would do everything they could.

Feeling unsettled but relieved to have made it through the crisis, Gene returned to Haylee's bedside.

November 14, 1984
8:00 a.m.

Nurse Ridgeway brought Gene something to eat and a cup of coffee. She smiled tentatively as their eyes met.

"Thank you," he said in hushed tones as he accepted her offering.

A delightful blush spread across her freckled face. "If Haylee feels like eating when she wakes up, buzz me and I'll bring her some breakfast." She pointed to the button at the side of the bed.

"I will, Nurse...?"

"Ridgeway," she supplied. "You can call me Glori."

For the first time, Gene fully noticed how attractive she was.

Glori Ridgeway, although diminutive, had a "no nonsense" attitude that made her appear taller than she actually was. She kept her straight, red hair with its blond highlights cut close to her head. This hairstyle displayed a long, graceful neck and opalescent skin. Large, expressive blue eyes revealed a variety of emotions. She wore no makeup; *she didn't need any*, Gene thought.

Her lips were a lovely shade of pink, and she had a cute habit of biting her top lip when she was concentrating, which made her lower jaw jut out just a bit.

"Thank you, Glori," he said tiredly.

Feeling magnanimous, she leaned a little closer to confide. "Doctor Lester isn't known for her bedside manner, but she is one of the best doctors on our staff. Haylee is in good hands."

Cocking his head, he looked at her with keen eyes. A slow smile spread across his face, and he noticed that she caught her breath. Still speaking softly, Gene said, "It seems like the only two words I know right now are 'thank you.'"

Returning his smile, she commented over her shoulder quietly as she left the room, "I never get tired of hearing that."

November 14, 1984
9:00 a.m.

When Haylee woke up, she felt tingly and fresh. Smiling broadly, she threw her arms over her head while tightening her legs and pointing her toes so she could stretch her whole body. The IV stuck in her hand was a nuisance. She glanced over and saw her dad rousing from a doze. While pushing up on the bed and arranging the pillows behind her, she joked, "Hey! You're not supposed to be sleeping!" Her voice sounded strong and amused. Looking sheepish, Gene rubbed the kink in the back of his neck. "Sorry. I'm sure glad you're feeling better."

"I feel great! Except I'm starving! Is there any way to get some food in here?" Giving her an odd look, Gene leaned over to press the call button. "Are you feeling hungry, like normal hungry? Or ravenously hungry like you were yesterday?"

Haylee became perfectly still, and fixed a stare on him.

~ ~ ~ ~

The hairs on the back of Gene's neck pricked to attention.

"What do you mean?" she asked very quietly.

"When I got home last night, I saw that the refrigerator was completely empty."

That look on her face disappeared so quickly that Gene wondered if it had been his imagination.

~ ~ ~ ~

Haylee knew it would be a mistake to tell the truth, "Normal hungry—I guess…"

Her dad seemed to relax at her statement.

"So what's wrong with me?" Reaching out and taking her hand in both of his, Gene raised his eyebrows and shook his head.

"It's the darndest thing; all they could tell me was that you had an unusually heavy period."

"What?" she burst out, looking surprised, embarrassed, and more than a little pleased. "You lost a lot of blood, so much so that under normal circumstances, we could have lost you."

He squeezed her hand and continued. "They can't explain how you recovered so quickly. We're going to keep you here for testing."

"Dad," Haylee complained, "if you think about it, it does make sense. If my body is producing a lot of blood, it must need a lot of food to replace it."

They looked up as Nurse Ridgeway came in with a tray. The smell of the food instantly drew all of Haylee's attention. Glori efficiently placed it in front of her and removed the cover. Haylee picked up a spoon and shoveled in huge mouthfuls of scrambled eggs. Barely chewing, her swallows were audible. Gene and Glori regarded her with expressions of concern and mild repugnance.

Finishing every speck on her plate in too short a time, Haylee looked up. Their faces must have shown their surprise. Haylee took a moment to put down her spoon. With an exaggerated slowness, she wiped jam off her chin. "I was really hungry! Do you think they might have a little more left in the kitchen?"

Glori momentarily looked shocked, but then she shook herself and reached for the empty tray. "Certainly, but it will take a few minutes." She glanced at Gene. He shrugged his shoulders while mouthing the words, "Thank You," to her. Blushing again, Glori left the room.

Gene's gaze followed her through the doorway. A slight smile lingered around his mouth. Haylee caught this small, intimate exchange; it made her curious. Deciding to leave it for now, she asked, "How long did they say I had to stay here?"

He brought his attention back to his daughter. "They didn't."

Pursing her lips, she looked down. "Hmm."

Letting him think what he would, she remained silent.

When Nurse Ridgeway brought in the second tray, Haylee knew that the adults were trying not to make it obvious that they were watching closely. Instead of inhaling the food, as was Haylee's desire, she forced herself to eat slowly. They seemed to relax. Haylee looked at the nurse, and commented, "I know he's been sitting up all night and must be really tired. Can you convince him that I won't die if he goes home to get some rest?"

Gene balked, but Haylee assured him that she would feel better if he wasn't exhausting himself. After giving his daughter a long, searching look, he kissed her on the cheek before leaving. Glori followed him out. Finally left to herself, Haylee quickly dispatched her second helping and started thinking about a third.

Not being able to satisfy her hunger made her jittery. She knew that if she asked for still more, she would have a whole bunch of people asking her a lot of questions to which she had no answers.

Sliding out of bed, she tested her legs. Relieved, she found that they were strong. Pulling the IV out of her arm, she crept over to the door and closed it quietly. She paced the room. Thoughts whirled through her brain; her heart rate increased. Her strides became long and quick. Every now and then, she would stop suddenly to stare out the window while her body became unnaturally still. Then the pacing would begin again.

November 14, 1984
11:25 a.m.

Haylee reached up to massage her temples, realizing that another headache was coming on. A self-preservation instinct took over. She knew she had to get out of there…NOW! Racing to the closet, she checked to see if she had any clothes. Seeing nothing, she slammed the door while thinking about what to do. Her headache grew worse. She noticed that the palms of her hands were sweaty. Wiping them on her gown, she made her way to the door. Opening it a crack, she looked out into the hallway. Seeing her opportunity, she slipped out.

With movements that were quick and panther like, she walked down the corridor, her ears tuned for any sound of alarm. She walked quickly toward the staff locker room.

Entering, she stood motionless, listening. With the tension involved with concentrating on her escape, Haylee hardly noticed the headache. Her heart leapt when she heard a movement across the room. She flattened herself against a row of lockers and waited until whoever it was left the room.

Hearing the exit door swish, Haylee poked her head around to make sure that she was alone. Systematically, she went down each row, trying the locks on every door. Her hands shook as the minutes clicked by. Each consecutive locker was locked. Desperately, she whispered, Shit! Shit! Shit! There must be someone left in this world who doesn't lock their stuff! The clicking resistance sounded loud in her ears. She could feel sweat from her underarms trickling down her sides. Her hands were so damp that her fingers kept slipping as she tried to grasp the handles. Inside her mind, the phrase, *I gotta get outa here! I gotta get outa here!* kept repeating.

When her stomach growled loudly, Haylee glanced down. Remembering how hungry she was, she wiped her clammy hands on her gown again and resumed her search.

Her agitation increased tenfold as she started down the last row. Haylee considered the possibility of having to escape wearing only a hospital gown. It would make her much more conspicuous.

There were only three lockers left to check when one of them finally gave way under her hand. She let out a relieved breath and realized that she had been holding it for the last few seconds. Opening the door, she surveyed its contents.

It was full of men's clothing. *Oh well,* she thought, *it will have to do.* Quickly, she put on the shirt and jeans, rolling up the sleeves and legs. She removed the drawstring from of a pair of hospital pants and used it as a belt on the jeans. She found a cap, put it on, and stuffed her hair inside.

For a moment, she contemplated the shoes. They were obviously too big and would probably be more of a hindrance than a help. She put on a pair of shoe cover booties so that it would not be apparent that her feet were bare. Without thinking, she slammed the door shut. A male voice from across the room commented, "Bad day, huh?"

Fear immobilized her. In her rush to dress, she hadn't heard anyone enter.

She looked around, calculating an escape route, and realized that whoever had spoken wouldn't be able to see her. She grabbed her cast off gown and wadded it up into a ball. Speaking in a low voice, she replied, "Yea," as she walked boldly toward the door. Haylee cast a glance over her shoulder to make sure she wasn't being followed. She noticed a clothes hamper nearby and tossed her gown into it before slipping out.

Haylee ran down the last few feet of the empty hallway to the staff entrance. The fresh air and the feel of the afternoon sun gave her a fleeting sense of freedom.

Trying to move with confidence, Haylee walked away from the building with her head held high. The farther she got, the faster her heart beat. At the edge of the parking lot she thought jubilantly, *I made it!*

She continued moving, putting distance between her and the hospital. It was a thirty-mile trip home, but this didn't bother her. She started running. She ran down alleyways, crouching down behind cars when someone came her way. She probably wouldn't be recognized, but she couldn't be too careful. She saw a pair of cloth tennis shoes hanging on someone's laundry line and pulled them down. They were almost a perfect fit.

She felt a powerful surge of energy. Running for miles was effortless. Now that she'd felt successful in her escape, her first priority was to satisfy her hunger.

She found a dumpster behind a school and immediately jumped into it. Must be pizza day, she thought. Haylee started digging through the refuse and froze when she heard voices approaching. 'Did you hear something?' one of them asked. 'Probably rats in the dumpster again,' said the other. 'Don't have time to deal with it now. Gotta get back to cleaning up the lunch room.' After a few minutes, they wandered away.

Grateful for the abundance, Haylee brought large handfuls of the mixed, wet, gloppy discards to her mouth. As she buried her face in the slop, a part of her brain noticed that she was making sounds not unlike her pigs. She didn't care. Eventually, Haylee felt satiated and was relieved to be rid of the hunger pangs.

In one graceful movement, she leapt out of the dumpster. She brushed as much of the offal from her as she could. With her hunger no longer distracting her, she realized that her headache was getting stronger. Soon it would immobilize her.

Not knowing what would happen this time made her more than a little anxious, but she realized that she had no choice in the matter. Sadly, she also knew that there was no one she could go to for help.

Knowing that her time was growing short, Haylee set off on her flight. More alleyways flew by as she ran and ran, keeping out of sight as much as possible.

November 14, 1984
1:45 p.m.

As Head Nurse on the floor when Haylee decided to make her hasty exit, Glori had been the one to call the girl's father when the security officers had been unable to locate her.

Gene had been pale and quiet when he arrived back at the hospital to speak to the police. Looking into his troubled eyes, Glori had to forcefully hold back her emotions at the thought of letting him down.

Naturally, he wanted to join the search. Upon learning that there was no one to keep watch at home, Glori volunteered to keep a vigil at the Garrett house in case Haylee showed up while others were out.

If anyone from administration found out that she'd offered to personally help the family, she could lose her job. It was a lot to risk. *There is something about these two that I can't stop thinking about. Besides, it feels like the right thing to do,* Glori thought.

November 14, 1984
8:30 p.m.

When Haylee reached the edge of the city, she was relieved but still continued to run. She noticed that she could still see clearly, even though it was dark. As her legs continued to pump and her strides elongated, Haylee's hair floated on the wind behind her. It was invigorating to feel so strong and to run so fast. Under normal circumstances, Haylee would have wondered how it was possible for her body to maintain such an abundant supply of energy. Why, after hours of running, didn't her muscles cramp or her breathing grow labored? But today, running like this just felt right. Just one more mysterious change in her body to add to the rest.

Crossing the boundary of her father's property relieved her sense of urgency somewhat. Suddenly, she knew where she had to go and headed in that direction.

Approaching a tight clump of bushes, Haylee got down on her hands and knees and crawled underneath them. She was satisfied that no one would be able to see her. She sat down to rest.

Sitting quietly brought the pain in her head into sharp focus. Her eyes throbbed in their sockets. Every joint in her hands ached. As the agony began to wrap her more tightly in its clutches, fear caused her breath to catch in short bursts. Trying to relax, Haylee lay down, and resolved to ride it out or perish.

It came on as before, in throbbing waves. She felt as if her head would split apart. Her teeth hurt. Drenched in sweat and writhing on the ground, Haylee didn't notice when the ache in her head subsided and the stinging in her hands began. Every joint felt as if it were on fire. Her bones were so hot she thought that they would scorch her skin. Cracking her eyes open, she saw that all of her fingers were bright red. They were bent and claw like; she couldn't move them.

She let her hands drop, which sent a jarring wave of pain through her. It was more than she could bear. As her eyes rolled back into her head, consciousness slipped blissfully away like a wave pulling back from the shore before vanishing into the sea.

Sometime later, through a haze of agony, Haylee felt as if her head were cradled in someone's lap. A cool hand brushed the hair back from her face. A woman's voice murmured soothing words. The gentle ministrations helped. The soft voice crooned, "That's right, dear, try to relax. The pain will pass."

Haylee nodded and mumbled, "I will, Mama."

November 15, 1984
2:00 a.m.

With still no sign of Haylee, Gene returned home. Glori poured a steaming cup of coffee as he dropped his weight heavily onto one of the kitchen chairs. Noticing the bags under his eyes and the grim line of his mouth, she placed the mug on the table in front of him.

Glori, like the doctors, was intensely curious about the medical miracle they'd witnessed at the Garrett girl's recovery. The staff had all assumed her case would be post mortem by the end of that shift. Glori had felt more than the normal amount of relief that Gene didn't have to hear the words that no family member ever wants to hear. Her consternation at the thought of losing a patient had been replaced by curiosity about Haylee. "She's going to turn up, Gene. I just know she will."

He nodded then took a sip. "She has to. Glori, I don't know how to thank you for…"

"No…no…you don't need to thank me."

"I realize this"—he waved his hand to encompass the kitchen—"goes way beyond the job description."

Sitting down at the table in front of him, she reached out to place a hand on his arm. "I care," she stated simply.

He placed his hand over hers, and their eyes met and held. "Me too," he whispered. He leaned back, removing himself from her touch.

With arms crossed over his chest, he regarded her. It was nice to have someone to talk to. Someone who shared the burden of his worry. She was easy on the eyes….

Gene was surprised and perplexed by these feelings. Yet he knew that without a doubt, if something happened to Haylee, he'd be finished. He wouldn't care if he saw another human face again—ever.

When the time grew close for her next shift at the Hospital, Glori said a reluctant good-bye, promising to check back periodically to see if there had been progress.

The miserable look on his face, prompted her to offer reassurance. "Gene, when we last saw her, she was well physically and there was no evidence of a struggle. The fact that a staff locker was broken into, suggests that she left of her own free will. I think she had a reason for leaving, and we'll find out what it is once she decides it's time to come home."

Gene's mouth made a grim, straight line, "I hope you're right—"

November 15, 1984
4:45 a.m.

It was dark and cold when Haylee finally opened her eyes and sat up. Her breath sent out wispy puffs of steam. She half expected to find someone with her, but she was alone. Shaking her head to clear the grogginess, she reached up to rub the sleep out of her eyes.

At that moment, she remembered the magnitude of the pain she had felt in her hands. Gingerly, she clasped and unclasped her fingers. Everything seemed fine now. Shrugging, she crawled out from under the bushes.

Haylee stretched, feeling extremely strong and powerful. The cool morning air was refreshing. There was another feeling there also, something strange and different. She couldn't put her finger on what it was. Taking a few minutes to get her bearings, she grinned when she realized that she was hungry again.

To the barn! Once she had eaten her fill of cracked corn, Haylee took a few minutes to inspect her hands in the dim light.

They looked normal. She flexed them open and closed again. They felt normal. *I wonder what that burning was all about?*

Just then, a bug landed on her arm. When she moved to swipe it away, she heard a —*thwap*. She stared at her hand in astonishment. There was webbing between her fingers! She wiggled them noticing the increased resistance. She flicked the other hand—*thwap*! Now this hand had the webs too! They glistened and sparkled in the early morning light. When the webs were out, she felt a powerful energy humming just below the surface of her skin, as if it were waiting to burst forth.

Haylee was quivery and giddy.

She flicked both hands at the same time — *thwap!* The webs were gone! She practiced making them appear and disappear until her fingers grew sore.

Flicking the webs away, she massaged the area between her digits, marveling over the fact that there appeared to be no evidence of them.

November 15, 1984
6:00 a.m.

Finally, it registered that she'd been gone for a long time. Her dad would be worried.

A deep fatigue overcame her as she started toward the house. Looking down at her clothes, she made a face. *I'm filthy!* Haylee pulled the shirt away from her body. *I stink.*

These webs are so weird! I am definitely a freak of nature now! Thank goodness they will go away when I don't want them to show... It might be hard to explain why I have duck-feet hands in public. I wonder why they are there at all?

⚜11⚜

EXCUSES, EXCUSES

November 15, 1984
6:10 a.m.

"Sixteen hours! You disappear out of your hospital bed and no one has any idea where you are for sixteen hours!" Eugene was furious with his daughter for having dragged him through hell. Could it have been only yesterday that he'd carried her, heavily bleeding and unconscious, through the doors of the emergency room? Time seemed to have stretched out and warped. Aside from all this, he was extremely relieved to see her looking filthy, but otherwise alright.

"Dad! Calm down," beseeched a raggedy Haylee, who was dressed in an odd assortment of too large men's clothes.

"May I remind you that they couldn't find a thing wrong with me."

What she said was true, but still, Gene couldn't help but feel like she was hiding something.

"I was still hungry! At breakfast, you and Nurse Ridgeway were looking at me like I'd sprouted two heads."

It came to Haylee that for the first time in a very long time, she had her dad's full attention.

Crossing his arms over his chest, Eugene gave her a skeptical look. She continued. "After you left, I realized that I felt perfectly fine except for the fact that I was still hungry. So I borrowed these clothes" — she held out her arms and looked down—"and left the hospital. I walked a few blocks to the fountain in front of the courthouse where I fished out enough money to buy a couple of burgers."

"You 'borrowed' the clothes. And what hamburger place did you go to where you got junk smeared all over the front of you?" He continued. "Did you stop to think that people might be worried about you?" Gene truly had no idea how to handle her. They'd never been in a situation where he'd had to grill her with questions.

She gave him a sheepish look. "Well, yes. But it but felt so good to be outside. I didn't want to go back to the hospital, so I walked home instead."

Still angry, he replied, "Uh huh. Did you forget how to use the telephone?"

Frowning, she snapped, "No!"

She started to pace and calmed her voice. "I knew that you needed to rest so I decided to get home on my own. I got to our property around dusk and started feeling tired myself, so I stopped to rest, and I must have fallen asleep." She gave him a direct look. "When I woke up a little while ago, I came straight home."

He stood there for a moment studying her. Sounding genuinely remorseful, she said, "I am really sorry to have worried you, Dad. Now that you see that I'm alright, do you think we could both get some sleep and finish this when we're fresh?"

Gene considered what a person might do if an intense hunger drove them to desperate acts. As tired as he was, fishing coins out of a fountain seemed plausible. His eyes told him that she wasn't about to keel over.

Watching the emotions play across his face, Haylee reached out a hand to rest it on his arm. "Dad, I'm fine….really. Can I get washed up and go to my room? "

He looked straight into her eyes. "You can go to bed, young lady, but don't ever pull a stunt like that again! Is that clear?"

Haylee looked down, replying with a subdued tone, "Understood."

He nodded and turned toward his own room. "Good. I'll take you back to the hospital later this afternoon," he stated over his shoulder. She stared at the empty space where he'd stood. "We'll see about that," she whispered.

~ ~ ~ ~

When Gene called Glori at work, shortly after Haylee returned, relief flooded through her at the news. Once he'd answered all of her questions about how Haylee was looking and behaving, Glori could tell by the tone of his voice that Gene felt a sense of relief too. She also knew that he was beyond exhausted. "The best thing for both of you right now is to get some sleep." She didn't press for any of the details that nagged at her.

~ ~ ~ ~

To Gene's consternation, Haylee had a million reasons why she shouldn't return for further medical exams.

"I don't want to be poked and prodded! They already said that they don't know what's wrong, so I don't see what going back there will accomplish," she had grumbled. Haylee certainly looked and acted perfectly healthy. Gene wasn't too keen on Dr. visits either, plus, they had a lot of chores to catch up with around the place—so he let it go—at least through the weekend.

Saturday, November 17, 1984

Haylee got up early. She quickly grew frustrated when none of her clothes fit anymore. Resorting to the sweats that no longer needed stuffing, she stomped out of her room in search of breakfast. Haylee smelled the food cooking before she entered the kitchen. Her father was usually gone at this time of the day.

Hearing her approach, he glanced in her direction. The smile died on his lips; his eyes grew wide. Sucking in a breath, he rasped hoarsely, "Doris?"

Unsure about what was going on, Haylee hesitated, "No, Dad, it's me."

Shaking himself, "For a minute there, I thought you were your mom…." He eyed her critically, "Haylee, when did you get so pretty?"

Seeing her eyes widen, he stammered when he realized that his words weren't coming out right. "I mean in a womanly sort of way…and that I didn't see it before." Relief flooded through her as she met his sad eyes.

He still looked a little in awe of her mature beauty. "You're looking well today," he smiled.

Seeing her father as Nurse Ridgeway must, Haylee acknowledged that he was really awesome…kind, handsome, and in good shape.

"Here, sit down," he directed, as he brought over a plate of scrambled eggs and hash browns.

They chatted while they ate. Every chance she got, Haylee mentioned how great she was feeling.

He took his plate to the sink. "Now let's talk about when

we can schedule to go back to the hospital…or at least to the Dr.'s office," he stated.

"No!"

Gene began to protest, but Haylee cut him off.

"I feel fine. Being able to walk home the other day should be proof enough of that." She could see by the look on his face that she wasn't convincing him, so she lied. "You know, I was thinking about it last night. I remember Mom telling me that the women in our family all have a hard time when they first start their periods." She hesitated but then continued, "Plus, my gym teacher told me that my belated period could be hereditary." Her cheeks grew rosy with embarrassment and guilt.

Drawing his brows together, Gene commented, "I didn't realize that your teacher talked about this with you."

"Well, it was a while ago, and it's not something you want to run home to tell your father!" she replied with exasperation.

With just a hint of a smile on his handsome face, he said, "I can understand that. I'll let this slide for now, but if you notice anything that doesn't seem right, I want you tell me immediately."

Realizing she'd won, she smiled and gave him a quick kiss on the cheek. "Thank you Dad!"

Clearing his throat, he reached out to bring her into a gentle hug. "Haylee, I'm sorry I checked out on you…after we lost Mom. I want to make it up to you…if I can."

Tears gathered and her throat constricted as she wrapped her arms around his solid form. Many emotions hovered under the surface of her brave façade. She could have easily sunken into a crying fit, but she kept a tight lid clamped on those feelings.

"Since I am taking the day off from work…and since we

aren't going back to the hospital, I'd like to do a make-up for your birthday....well a lot of them, actually. What would you like for your birthday kido?"

Haylee smiled, looking down at her attire. "I could really use some new clothes…"

The idea of taking her shopping had Gene suddenly feeling very uncomfortable, until a thought popped into his mind. "I know what we can do."

❧12❧

ACCESS

Climbing up the stairway leading to the attic, Haylee was filled with anticipation. Gene reached the top ahead of her to turn on the light, illuminating a large room filled with cobwebs and dust-covered sheets draped over unidentifiable objects. A little nervously, he turned toward Haylee. "Well, here we are." He spread his hands wide and slapped them against his legs.

She raised her eyebrows, contemplating him quietly for a moment. "Dad, if this is going to be too hard, I can look around by myself."

He considered this for a moment, then he shook his head. "No, I want to; it's way overdue." Walking over to a large object, he pulled off the sheet. "Let's see what we have here."

As her father glanced down at the large chest made of oak and iron, Haylee could tell by the sad look on his face that he was remembering her mother. After her death, a year had gone by before he had moved anything. Then one weekend, he had sent Haylee to stay with her cousins in Seattle. By the time she returned, every single thing that had belonged to her mother had been packed away.

Haylee remembered that time. The shock of finding every-thing missing had sent her into a panic. She'd screamed at her dad, begging for something, anything, of her mom's that she could hold onto. With a stony face, he'd regarded his daughter. Turning away from her in more ways than one, he'd chosen to express his pain with his hands and his muscles—fixing machinery, tending the soil, and managing his orchards.

Getting ready to open the chest for his daughter, Gene paused. Haylee saw a look of concern cross his face. She knew he was afraid that the act of cracking the lid would reopen those torturous wounds again. Haylee walked up behind him, touch-ing his arm. "Dad, are you OK?"

He cleared his throat. "Yes, why don't you open it?"

Kneeling, Haylee carefully lifted the lid. She saw sev-eral stacks of neatly folded blouses. A faint scent of gardenias wafted up to her. Inhaling deeply, she closed her eyes and was rewarded with a clear memory of her mother. "Oh Dad! I just remembered what Mom looked like. I....I...had forgotten."

Quietly, Gene nodded as he sat down on a nearby box.

Haylee tenderly removed shirts, sweaters and pants, hold-ing them up to see if they would fit. It looked like she was pretty much the same size as her mom. From time to time, Gene would share some remembrance.

Gathering a stack of clothes to take down to her room, Haylee returned the rest of them to the trunk. As they made their way to the top of the stairs. Haylee took one last look at that attic. "Is it OK if I come up here by myself?"

Gene shrugged his shoulders. "I don't see why not."

"Thanks!" She smiled brightly.

Monday, November 19, 1984

The green sweater Haylee wore draped softly over her torso and breasts, displaying their mature, graceful lines.

Stepping back from the mirror, she viewed her complete attire. Not at all reluctant to cast aside the western wear, her eyes sparkled with satisfaction.

With a Teen magazine open to the "makeover" section, Haylee applied makeup and styled her hair. Looking at the results, she nodded. "I'm ready."

Gathering her school books and shoving them in her book bag, she headed toward the kitchen.

"What do you think?" Haylee asked as she turned around in front of her dad.

Speechless for a moment, Gene cleared his throat, "Right now, Hay, I can't believe that your mom and me made such an extraordinarily beautiful daughter…"

~ ~ ~ ~

Saying nothing in the corridor on her way to her first class, Haylee shyly met many of the eyes trained on her. She saw interest in the boys' faces and looks of scorn on the girls. Eventually, she realized that they had no idea who she was, which made her grin.

When she answered, "Here," to roll call in homeroom, silence fell as everyone turned in her direction. Momentarily, she felt a surge of confidence. Unused to having so much attention paid to her, it dwindled rapidly. She shut her eyes and willed everyone to stop looking.

Regaining his own composure, the teacher cleared his throat, "Well, Haylee, it appears that your illness agreed with you."

"Uh-huh," she responded.

Bringing attention back to the front of the room, the instructor resumed calling names.

Throughout the day, the same scenario was played out again and again.

Four years had gone by since that humiliating incident with Curtis Carter. For the most part, she'd put it out of her mind. Today, she started thinking about it again.

Her stomach dropped to her feet when she saw him waiting outside the door of her last class. His eyes clearly took inventory of her new assets. He acknowledged her with an upward, sideways nod that beckoned her to follow. Her heart raced; she could feel heat radiating from her face. The thought of snubbing him never occurred to her as she headed in his direction. In spite of everything, she still maintained a soft place in her heart for him.

As she came to a halt in front of him, his eyes lingered a little too long on her breasts. Finally, he looked at her face. He smiled when he saw the blush on her cheeks, "Hey."

"Hi," she replied glancing away.

"I heard the whole school talking about how great you look. I decided to come check it out for myself."

Not quite knowing how to respond, she just said, "Oh?"

"Yeah." He let his eyes roam over her from head to foot. "You do look great."

His words and the warm look in his eyes made her breathing difficult. Confused, she looked away again. "Thanks."

"You got a ride home?"

"Uh, yeah, I'm taking the bus. Which reminds me, I've got to be going." She turned to go, he stepped into her path.

"I can give you a lift."

She remembered hearing that he was going steady with Lauren Hosteral, a curvaceous blond with a haughty attitude. "What about your girlfriend? Won't she be mad if you drive me home?"

"Screw her; she doesn't tell me what to do." He moved in so close that his chest was only inches from hers. Again, she had trouble breathing; her skin felt tight. A knowing smile spread across his face as he met her questioning eyes. "If I want to give you a ride home, nobody's going to tell me I can't. How about it?"

Feeling giddy, she said, "Maybe another day, Curtis?"

"Maybe I'll ask you for more than a ride home one of these days." He turned and left, walking confidently back to where his vehicle was parked.

All the way home, Haylee could not keep the Cheshire-cat smile from her face. Curtis had noticed her! He'd practically asked her on a date!

❧13❧

EXPERIMENTATION

The webs—they didn't make sense. Haylee had developed a habit of flicking them out when she was alone. Other than a humming sensation under her skin—it reminded her of high-powered electricity lines—and a slight ringing in her ears, she didn't think anything else about her was different. *When Mom told me that the women in our family have "different" abilities, she didn't say anything about this…*

She'd been experimenting with using the webbing to scoop out larger portions of grain or transporting water into watering dishes.

The animals grew agitated if she had the webs visible in front of them. When the mama pig saw them for the first time, she frantically raced to the opposite side of her pen screaming shrilly. All of the other pigs and nearby creatures joined in the cacophony of fearful cries.

Haylee could barely read their thoughts with all the upset. No amount of her own mental communication could calm them down. She'd had to leave their sight and send multiple assurances and apologies in order for them to accept her presence among them again.

❧14❧

BEES TO HONEY

January, 1985

Haylee had more date requests than she knew what to do with. Curtis was not among them.

Mark Predstrat had been the first boy to ask her out. He was in her Advanced Calculus class. Although he was a year younger than Haylee, she liked him because he was smarter than most of the seniors in the class and he wasn't afraid to show it. About math, they could converse easily.

Not knowing how to go about broaching the subject with her father, she informed him that she had a date for the coming Friday evening.

Gene's first reaction was, "Oh no, you're not! You are too young to date!"

Having had her father's attention for the last few weeks had been wonderful, but now that it was interfering with what she wanted to do, it was a pain. She crossed her arms over her chest yelling, "I'm eighteen AND a senior in high school! Besides, all of the other girls in my class have been dating for years!"

He responded, "I don't care what the other girls do; you are not going to date!"

That eerie stillness came over Haylee. Perfectly motionless, she narrowed her eyes, raised her chin slightly, and held her father's gaze. For an uncomfortable moment, Gene looked worried.

When she spoke next, it was with a quiet dignity. "Dad, how old were you when you went out on your first date? Do you know what it's like to watch everyone around you going out or going steady? Mark is a really nice guy. He's in my Calculus class and I know you'd like him. Please, Dad, let me have him come meet you Friday. If you don't like him, I won't go out with him."

Gene reluctantly agreed.

Haylee soon discovered that dating was not as exciting as she thought it would be. She usually felt nervous and unsure of herself; the boys seemed to feel the same way. Most of them seemed focused on one thing…her body. Haylee would find herself sitting on pins and needles, waiting for a move. When they inevitably reached out and attempted to grope her clumsily, she would struggle, slapping their hands away, and demand to be taken home. Both of them, for their own reasons, would be left feeling angry and cheated.

Eventually, when the general male population at school realized that Haylee would not be an easy lay, the number of suitors vying for her attention drastically declined. This was both a relief and a disappointment.

₰15₰

CURTIS

February 11, 1985

In the months since Haylee had bloomed, she'd matured considerably and gained a certain amount of sophistication. She dressed stylishly and carried herself with confidence. Flirting came naturally; she was a fast learner.

Although she continued to be asked out, Haylee turned most of them down. She decided it was time to go out with someone she really liked—Curtis. A formal Valentine's day dance was a few days away. She wanted to go with him.

Haylee had been watching for him during the lunch break for a couple of days. He usually left campus, but she was hoping to catch him there sometime. With her lunch bag in hand, she scanned the large room where the students were gathered. Spying him sitting with a group of his friends, she made her way toward them. He was sitting with his back to her. A couple of his friends noticed her heading in their direction and leaned over the table to alert Curtis. Sitting up a little straighter, he turned around as she reached the table. "Hi," she smiled.

He looked up at her with a welcoming smile of his own. "Hey, gorgeous."

Witnessing the exchange, Curtis's companions started jibing him with catcalls and mutterings of "gorgeous." They elbowed each other.

Glancing in their direction, Curtis stood up. "I'll catch you later." He put his hand on the small of Haylee's back, propelling her away.

At his touch, a shiver traveled down her spine. He led her to a quiet bench where they could sit. Looking into her face, he said, "I can't believe how much you have changed! It really is amazing."

Feeling the blush that bloomed across her cheeks, she felt like the old tongue-tied Haylee.

Unexpectedly, her imagination conjured up what his muscles might feel like, causing her blush to deepen further. Curtis's sparkling brown eyes reflected his interest. She could smell a faint hint of his cologne. Realizing that the silence between them was lasting a little too long, Haylee said, "I was wondering if the offer for a ride home was still good?"

He smiled. "It is, if you can wait till I'm done with football practice."

"I think I can manage," she returned his smile.

Curtis's eyes were drawn to her full lips. He lowered his voice, keeping the feeling of intimacy between them. "Great. Wait for me in the bleachers. I'll do better at practice if I know you're watching me."

"I'll be there."

"OK, then, I'll see you after school," he said as he got up to leave.

She nodded.

For the next two days, Haylee waited for Curtis after school so he could drive her home. Conversation flowed freely between them; she looked forward to the time they would spend together each day. She found out that he had broken up with his latest girlfriend only a few weeks before. He told Haylee that when he was with her, she made him forget all about Lauren. He also told her that ever since she had written that poem about him when they were thirteen, he had thought she was neat. Haylee was so happy, she thought she would burst.

Turning his pickup onto the dirt road leading to her farm, Curtis glanced at Haylee's laughing face. He was telling her a story about how he and a friend had gotten caught in the act of streaking naked around, what they thought was, a deserted football field.

Stopping in front of her house and turning off the engine, Curtis stretched his arm across the back of the seat. "I've been thinking about the Valentine's dance. You wanna go?"

Taking a deep, pleasurable breath, she leaned back in the seat resting her head on his arm. Quietly she said, "What do you think, Curtis?"

Her smile and bright eyes answered the question. With his free hand, he reached over to pick up some of her hair, letting it brush against her neck as he did so. While fondling the thick, lustrous strands between his fingers, he leaned in to nuzzle her ear. "You smell good."

Feeling his warm breath caress her face, Haylee's heart picked up speed. He was so close. Her chest tightened. *Is he going to kiss me?*

Curtis leaned away. "We'll go out to dinner before the dance," he said.

A little disappointed, Haylee closed her eyes giving him a lovely view of thick eyelashes caressing honey colored cheeks. Her voice sounded husky. "That sounds great."

He pulled away from her entirely so he could turn his key

in the ignition, saying, "OK, I'll see you tomorrow."

As Haylee got out of the truck, Curtis sucked in his breath sharply. His body was taut with the strain of holding himself in check. *Damn, she's hot! I wonder what she'll feel like?* he thought. With a self-satisfied smile, he backed the truck out onto the dirt road.

Curtis had been aware of Haylee's crush on him since seventh grade. He hadn't given it much thought until he'd heard the rumors that she was suddenly the sexiest girl in school. When he had seen her in the hall about a month ago, he'd been shocked. He couldn't believe that she was the same mousey bookworm of a couple of months ago. He had almost decided to go for her right then, but he was having problems with Lauren. They had been fighting like crazy. She'd told him that she thought that she was pregnant and in the same breath declared that they should get married. His first reaction had been to tell her that he was sure that it wasn't his. She threatened to tell his parents.

Since then, he had treated her with kid gloves. He assured her that everything would be alright and that they could handle things on their own. He brought up abortion a couple of times, telling her that they were too young to have a kid. She flatly refused. He had no intention of marrying her, but he let her think what she wanted, to keep her quiet. When she tearfully confided that she wasn't pregnant after all, he told her to go to hell. He turned his back on her and decided that he was through with girls. That was until Haylee sought him out a few days ago.

⚜16⚜

RESIGNED CONFLICT

February 4, 1985

Five days! I've only got five days to get ready for the Valentine's dance! Haylee thought. She didn't stop to consider how easy it had been to get Curtis to ask her. Haylee went to her room to change so she could do her barn chores.

She chatted amiably with the animals as she went about feeding them. She told the cows how handsome she thought Curtis was; she told the goats how much she was looking forward to going out to dinner. She practiced on the pigs how she would ask her Dad to take her shopping for a dress.

Although she and Gene were getting along pretty well, he still worked long hours. Haylee was happy that they were communicating at last; however, she still had things that she felt she couldn't talk to him about. Like how and why she had failed to develop normally and then how it happened all at once. She couldn't talk to him about how she felt when boys tried to touch her in uncomfortable places and attempted to ply her with sloppy, wet kisses. A shiver of revulsion went through her. She knew about the sex act—she'd seen it plenty of times on the farm—and she knew about birth control; they went over all of that in sex education at school. But male/female human relationships were a mystery. And the webs. She couldn't talk about them either—no matter how much she wished she could...

When Gene arrived home that evening, Haylee came running from behind the barn where she had been daydreaming on the tractor.

She yelled excitedly, "Dad! Dad!" She reached him about halfway to the house. A little out of breath, she exclaimed, "Guess what!"

Seeing her animation, the lines of worry that marred his face disappeared. Smiling, he asked, "What?"

Reaching out, she grabbed his hands. "Only the greatest thing possible! Curtis Carter asked me to the Valentine's dance!"

"Oh," was his less than enthusiastic response.

Ignoring that, she continued, "There are only three days till the dance. I need to get a formal dress. Will you take me shopping?" When he remained silent, she begged, "Please, Dad."

He sighed and nodded. "I suppose you want to go into town tonight?"

"If that's OK?"

Resigning himself, he told her that he needed to get cleaned up first and that they'd grab something to eat in town.

Smiling brightly, she leaned up to kiss him, saying, "Thank you!"

~ ~ ~ ~

Trying to pick a formal dress for Haylee was more difficult than he had anticipated.

Haylee had her heart set on a thin, black, strapless sheath.

When Gene saw his teenage daughter looking more like thirty, his eyes bulged. He flatly refused to buy it for her.

"This is not fair," Haylee complained. "Everything you like makes me look like Little Bo Peep!" They were at a standoff, and dinner was tense. Gene asked if there was anything else that wanted to talk about.

Crossly, she responded, "Yes! I want that black dress!"

He sighed heavily. "I sure wish your mother was here."

After uttering these words, Gene's face softened. "Haylee, your mother might be able to help us out here. She had a few formal dresses... They are in another trunk in the attic. Shall we go have another look around?"

"Really?" she asked excitedly.

Gene's offer instantly melted all of her peevishness. On the way home, a nagging worry began when Haylee noticed a headache slowly creeping its way up the back of her neck.

⚘17⚘

DATE NIGHT

Friday, February 10, 1985

The next morning, Haylee woke early. Flipping her hands—*thwap!*—webs appeared between her fingers. *They're weird…and pretty,* she thought as she moved her hands this way and that to observe them. They were translucent and sparkly at certain light angles. She chuckled quietly when she realized that the internal humming sensation she felt when the webs were out sounded sort-of like a Light Saber…at a very low volume.

Once again, Haylee was glad that, with another flick of her hands, the webbing would disappear.

After years of hiding unexplainable physical issues, she accepted this change as yet another odd thing that she'd have to live with.

Her second thought of the morning was about her date for the dance. Pulling the covers up a bit higher to snuggle back into her bed, she sighed with contentment. Haylee lay still to fantasize about Curtis. She imagined being held in his arms while a slow song played. *Will he kiss me when it is time to say goodnight?*

Somewhere during her fanciful musings, she became aware of a new sensation….a buzzing in the pit of her stomach that radiated out through her arms.

A knot of trepidation tightened in her chest. She was so focused on not letting a physical malady interfere with her big plans that it did not occur to her that it could be a problem for someone other than herself…

Need to Feed

Part Two

**From the deep Mother blood
came we...to carry the seed.**

One billion years ago

Fingers of light spread out over the surface of the pristine blue ball floating in space. Insects began to stir. Unfolding and opening their wings to the warmth, they began to chirp and sing.

A rare convergence was taking place. Star beings formed a circle. As one, they mentally projected as close to a voice as could be described.

'We each and all join to establish the will of the Upholders.'

The eldest of their ranks manifested a form in the center: a naked human male. With his odd sense of humor, he made the figure strut around, gesturing grandly as he spoke. "Of the possible life forms that may develop in this environment, I foresee that this one will be the greatest cause of concern." A covering appeared on the man, white folds of cloth hanging from the shoulders to well below the knees. A belt of gold cinched the material at the waist. "This humanoid"—the man clenched his fist, banging it on his chest—"will seek dominance. It will consume all within its grasp, spitting out vileness in its wake." The man came to a rest, spread his feet wide, and clasped his hands at his belt. "As a potential threat, it must not be allowed to develop."

Grunts sounded around the circle to indicate that the statements had been heard.

A naked female then appeared with a diaphanous covering draped over her body. As she began to walk counterclockwise around the outer edges of the circle, the material waving in her trail gave her a bird-like quality. "I disagree," she said. "These creatures have the ability to build and create." The woman stepped next to the man, affecting a similar stance. "They can learn. They must be allowed to proceed."

Grunts sounded out again.

Two identical children appeared, one wearing animal hides, the other in a body conforming suit that covered all but head, hands, and feet. They walked toward the center, speaking in unison. "We propose a compromise." The children spread apart, one stopping to stand in front of the grown humanoids, the other behind them, both facing outward. "We can create a monitoring system that will give us the ability to make repairs without interrupting our slumber."

Grunts and a series of short, high-pitched whistles sounded out, indicating that an agreement had been reached.

❧18❧

CHECK-UP

Glori hung up the phone and started packing her nurse's bag. She had been delighted to get Gene's call asking her to come check on Haylee, but was surprised to hear that it had been Haylee's idea. Glori knew that Gene and his daughter had been having disagreements for weeks over Haylee's refusal to return for a medical check-up. Gene was concerned because he'd witnessed Haylee suffering from more and more headaches recently. He had wanted Haylee to cancel her date for tonight but Haylee had suggested that Glori come over to confirm that she was healthy enough to go. *That Haylee was one smart girl.* Glori hadn't hesitated to agree to Gene's request when he made it, but now that she had to perform it, she felt uncertain. Clearly, she anticipated spending time with the man. She liked Haylee and was interested in her physical condition. But to be placed in a position of opposition between father and daughter was decidedly uncomfortable. The die has already been cast, she thought with resolution. *We'll ride it out and see where it goes.*

She arrived at the Garrett house an hour before date time. Gene welcomed her with a friendly hug and another, "Thank you." Haylee, though more reserved than her father, was friendly and polite. After a few moments of chitchat, they all paused to regard the medical bag that Glori had brought in with her. Taking her cue, she inquired if it would be alright to evaluate Haylee in private. Clearly relieved, Gene agreed.

Alone in Haylee's room, Glori asked routine questions while taking blood pressure and vital signs. Finding nothing out of the ordinary, Glori could see no reason to keep the young woman from her plans. Looking for another way to be helpful she asked, "What form of birth control do you use?"

"What?" Haylee croaked. "No! I've never…"

Realizing her mistake, Glori quickly chastised herself for making assumptions. She sat next to Haylee and gently asked, "Do you have plans to become sexually active?"

When the girl regarded her with eyes as large a saucers, Glori again retraced her steps.

"Haylee, do you see my bag there?" Glori pointed. At the girl's nod, she continued. "Since I brought that, I am here in an official capacity. That means that anything you share with me stays between us."

"Oh…" Haylee responded. Her gaze traveled back and forth as she digested this information. Her eyes came to rest on Glori; her cheeks began to turn red. "I think I might be the only girl in my class who hasn't 'done it,'" she admitted.

Glori smiled a small smile. "That would be hard to know for certain. Besides, what other people do doesn't matter."

Haylee was quiet for a few minutes. "I have been in love with Curtis since fifth grade. I can't tell you how happy I am that he asked me to this dance!"

"Does he feel the same way about you?"

Haylee's expression faltered. "He barely knew I existed until a little while ago." Her eyes fell to her feet.

"So what's changed?" Glori had a feeling that she already

knew the answer to the question.

"He broke up with his latest girlfriend and I think he just…he likes me now."

"His latest girlfriend? Haylee, has Curtis been with a lot of girls?"

She nodded. "He's really popular!"

A frown line appeared between Glori's brows. "Do you know if he has been sexually active?"

Haylee's eyes were wide. "He's been with lots of girls. I've overheard them talking about it in the locker room. Glori, I am pretty sure that he will want to…"

"I have no doubt about that."

"I don't want him to think I am a virgin."

Growing decidedly uncomfortable with where the conversation was going, Glori said the only thing she could think of. "When it was my first time, I had been dating my boyfriend for almost a year. Our relationship was solid; we were both in love with each other. I think it's a good thing to have built a level of trust with your partner before you get to the point of taking your clothes off."

It was Haylee's turn to frown. "That sounds good and everything, but I think he might be expecting it. If I don't do it with him, he probably won't want to take me out again." Once the words were out in the open, Haylee realized how bad they sounded.

"Do you want your first experience to come from a sense of expectation?"

"No," she shook her head.

"It is perfectly alright to state what you want or don't want. If a boy is worthy, you should have no doubt at all that he'll respect your wishes."

Once Glori felt certain that Haylee had sorted out her feelings, she went over to her medical bag. Placing a bundle of small square packets in Haylee's hand she stated, "Whether it's Curtis or someone else, you should keep some of these in your purse."

Haylee sucked in her breath when she saw what Glori had put there.

"Nothing, besides abstinence, is 100% safe from preventing sexually transmitted diseases or pregnancy but condoms are a lot better than nothing."

Glori thought that Haylee looked more confident armed with knowledge...and a barrier method.

~ ~ ~ ~

Glori left Haylee alone to put on her finishing touches. Glori joined Gene and let him know that his daughter had been officially pronounced fit.

˙19˙

THE DATE BEGINS

Curtis was due to pick Haylee up in fifteen minutes. Her stomach felt fluttery. She'd styled her hair so it fell in a mass of curls around her shoulders. Leaning back a bit so it was out of the way, she pulled a piece of black velvet ribbon behind her neck, brought it up behind her ears, and tied a bow at the top of her head.

The final thing she needed was to find her pendant. As she pushed items in her drawer aside in search of it, she remembered the day that her mom had removed it from her own neck and placed it around hers.

"Remember, honey, if you plan to go more than an hour from home, take this with you."

"Why, Mama?"

"If you and the necklace are too far apart, you'll feel sick."

Fearful, Haylee asked, "Why would it make me sick?"

"It's nothing to worry about, sweetheart…it can also make you better if you need it too. When I was a girl, I walked too close behind a horse and it kicked me. I was having trouble breathing when my mom brought the pendant and put it in my hand. Once it came in contact with me, the pain went away and I could breathe again." Stroking her hair, Doris smiled at her daughter. "Just keep it close and you'll always be just fine."

Finding it, Haylee reached behind her neck to fasten the clasp. She was ready!

She took a few steps back from the mirror to get a full length view. Her mother's gray cashmere dress looked great. It clung to her body, showing off her new curves and lines. She wore black silk stockings and spiked heels. Silver dangle earrings swayed when she moved. She walked over to the bed to pick up a matching gray shawl threaded with silver strands. Draping it over her shoulders and flinging one corner across her neck and behind her, she regarded her reflection in the mirror. The outfit was perfect!

With a confident smile, Haylee walked into the front room where her father and Glori were waiting.

When Gene saw her, his eyes grew wide and misty. He was speechless.

Haylee could tell by the look on his face that he thought she looked too good. She was worried that he would change his mind at the last minute about letting her go.

He motioned her to a chair. "Haylee, sit down for a minute."

Haylee gripped her hands together tightly in her lap. She bit down on her tongue to keep herself from blurting out something she'd regret.

Gene was quiet for a moment as he searched for the right words. "I realize that I should have talked to you a long time ago about this and that this is not the best time to bring it up, but…"

Relief flooded through her as she realized where he was going with the conversation. Haylee's eyes flew to Glori.

"Dad! You're not going to talk to me about sex are you?"

He stopped, looking confused.

"They covered Sex Ed and birth control in Junior High. Plus, I just asked Glori about a few things," she offered.

Gene massaged his eyebrows. "Haylee, girls who look..."

He made another attempt. "All this guy is going to be thinking about..."

Glori looked like she was enjoying watching Gene dig holes and then try to back himself out of them.

"Boys make certain assumptions based on..." he tried again.

Finally, Glori came to the rescue. "Haylee, you look very beautiful. If Curtis starts anything that makes you feel uncomfortable, tell him 'No' and be firm about it."

When the doorbell rang, Haylee went to greet Curtis. As she stood in the doorway, the light from inside softly illuminated her shapely form. Curtis's eyes opened wide and he smiled. "Hey, Haylee, you look great!"

"Thanks. You look nice too." Nervously, she stepped back so he could enter. "Please come in; my Dad wants to meet you." She saw Curtis wipe his hands on his pants as he stepped in and felt relieved to know he was nervous too.

Gene looked Curtis up and down. Haylee tried to see Curtis the way an apprehensive father might. His sandy blond hair was neatly combed and he was dressed nicely in dark slacks, a white shirt, and tie. He was muscular, but she probably noticed that more than he would. He did have a slightly cocky look on his face that she worried her father wouldn't like. Curtis extended his hand. "Nice to meet you, Mr. Garrett."

Gene regarded the outstretched hand for a moment, then grasped it in a firm grip that looked almost painful, not letting it go. "Curtis."

A brief look of surprise crossed Curtis's face before he

hid it.

"I expect you to have Haylee home no later than 11:30. Is that clear?"

"Yes, sir," Curtis responded stiffly as the grip on his hand tightened.

Releasing him, Gene said, "Good!" He stepped into Curtis's space and looked down at him. "I expect you to treat my daughter with respect. If you don't, you'll have to answer to me. Is that clear?"

Stepping back, Curtis replied with a hint of sarcasm, "Yes, sir."

When Gene raised an eyebrow, Curtis looked away.

Haylee, wishing to extinguish the charged atmosphere, touched Curtis's elbow. "Are you ready to go?"

"Yeah," he replied with relief.

Haylee walked to her father to plant a kiss on his cheek. "Don't wait up for me."

Gene responded quietly, "I will."

Walking out into the crisp night air, Haylee and Curtis were silent until they were in the truck and driving down the road.

Haylee glanced at his stony profile. She had the distinct sensation that he was mad. Trying to lighten his mood, she said, "I think he liked you."

Still frowning, he looked at her in surprise. Seeing the broad smile on her face, he smiled in return. "Haylee, you're nuts." They laughed.

The school auditorium was decorated in a love and hearts theme. Pink and white confetti scattered the floor in drifts. Festive lights twinkled overhead. There was a large fountain in the center of the dance floor. The live band on the stage was playing "I Want to Know What Love Is."

A bunch of Curtis's friends surrounded them almost as

soon as they walked in. They made it no secret that they thought that Curtis had the best looking date.

Curtis was attentive and wooed her with compliments.

After one slow dance ended, Curtis held Haylee's hand as he led her from the floor. She noticed his former girlfriend striding purposefully in their direction. Curtis saw her too. Haylee felt him stiffen. The girl stopped in front of them with an angry look. She crossed her arms over her chest and said snidely, "Curtis."

He responded casually, slipping his arm around Haylee's waist and pulling her next to him, "Lauren."

The girl considered Haylee maliciously with blazing green eyes. Then they filled with tears. She looked at Curtis and whispered brokenly, "How could you do this?" Her tears spilled over, trickling down her cheeks. She tried to brush them away, but they kept flowing.

"Do what?" he replied.

Haylee squirmed uncomfortably. Curtis held her in place.

Lauren spoke with a hard edge as she squinted her eyes at Haylee. "If you knew what he did to me, I bet you wouldn't—"

Curtis's arm snaked out like lightening. He grabbed Lauren and propelled her away before she could get another word out.

Haylee was left standing there watching them walk in the opposite direction. She wondered what was going on. Curtis's friends jumped in to entertain her. They explained that all of Curtis's girlfriends have a hard time letting go when he breaks up with them.

Curtis returned shortly, looking tense and explaining away Lauren's tears by saying that she hadn't expected him to date again so soon after they'd split up. He told the group that he hadn't planned on dating for a while either, but when someone like Haylee came along, you couldn't pass her up.

Taking her hand again, Curtis said, "Hey guys, that piece of work bummed me out. Me and Haylee are going to take off."

Keeping a firm hold, Curtis tugged Haylee along behind him. Disappointed over their evening being cut short, Haylee tried to make the best of it.

"I'm sorry, Curtis. Maybe we shouldn't have come."

Not speaking, he continued walking quickly toward the parking lot. Once they were inside his truck, he sat there stony-faced, staring at his hands, which gripped the steering wheel. At a loss, she tried again. "You must have loved her very much."

"Fuck it, Haylee!" he exploded, slamming his hand on the wheel. "I am furious with that little bitch for ruining our evening!"

She reached out. "But it's not ruined. We can go back in."

"No we can't. The way she is, she'll just continue to mess with us. I think I should just take you home."

Haylee's heart sank.

"Unless…"

"What?" she asked.

"I have something fun I can show you."

"What is it?" she wanted to know.

"You'll just have to wait and be surprised."

⚡20⚡

GET AWAY

The night was clear and the stars twinkled brightly as Curtis drove. Haylee sat close to him on the bench seat. She willed herself to relax. When he turned the truck onto a deserted levee and parked about a quarter mile off of the main road, Haylee's heart began to beat quickly. She could feel herself starting to perspire.

She started thinking about all the news reports about young girls being kidnapped and worse. As she silently berated herself for her stupidity, Curtis interrupted her thoughts.

"Haylee," he chided, "you do know some of the girls I've dated, right?"

She looked at him confused, but nodded.

"Even after we broke up, they always came back to school. There hasn't been one disappearance by a girl who dated Curtis Carter yet."

Caught, she laughed nervously.

"Plus, your dad is an intimidating guy. I really wouldn't want to have to watch my back if he was after me."

Haylee smiled.

"This is my surprise is my 'get away' place. I have never

brought a girl here before. You're different, so I wanted to share this with you." He said as he stepped out of his door.

"Oh," she responded, feeling pleased.

Holding hands, they walked a little way. The uneven ground caused Haylee to totter on her heels. Curtis put his arm around her to steady her while he led the way. Turning a corner, they came upon a train track that went out over a trestle with the river flowing below. Helping her onto the railroad ties, they sat down on a rail. Curtis fished a couple of pennies out of his pocket showing her that the two coins had the current year on them. "I thought we could put them on the tracks to have the train fuse them together so we could remember our first official date," he explained as he placed them on the rail.

Haylee was touched. "Oh, how nice!"

Smiling, he looked into her eyes. "I am nice, and you are nice too. I hope that tonight is the start of something great between us, Haylee."

He leaned toward her to plant a soft kiss on her lips. It was over with before she realized what he had done. Haylee was surprised at how natural it felt.

"We'll have that coin memento before too long," he whispered before returning to kiss her again. This time he lingered, gently coaxing a response from her.

The small rumbles began then, both the ones in Haylee's core and the ones on the tracks.

Haylee was so absorbed in their kiss, it was a few moments before she realized that Curtis's hand was on her breast. Shocked, she moved her body so she could push him away. Tearing his mouth from hers, Curtis whispered, "Don't pull away."

Wedging her arms between them and pushing, Haylee complained, "Curtis, I don't want to do this. Let me go!"

Holding her tightly, he refused to let her increase the space between them. "Just relax. I won't hurt you," he replied, but

Haley could hear the annoyance and frustration in his voice.

"I said stop!" she yelled. The tone of her voice had gone up several octaves as fear set in. On its heels, another wave of quivering radiated through her, more strongly this time.

The train lights appeared a few miles out, and Curtis jumped to his feet, pulling Haylee along with him as he started walking quickly toward the river.

"What are you doing?" Haylee asked, starting to feel alarmed.

"Kick off your shoes," he directed as he kept tugging her onward. The ground beneath them dropped away as they started across the trestle.

Bending over to grab a shoe in each hand, Haylee could feel herself trembling. Glints of moonlight undulating along the surface of the water far below caught her eye.

Jumping from railroad tie to tie as they jogged along the tracks, Curtis urged her to increase her speed. Looking behind them, she saw the train fast approaching.

"Curtis!" she screamed.

"Run, Haylee!" He squeezed her wrist and smiled a wicked smile.

Haylee's heart hammered wildly as the tracks shook under their feet. She pulled her arm away, so she could focus on running. Curtis kept pace with her.

The sound of the whistle blasted through them as the engineer spotted the two figures running in the middle of the bridge.

Curtis laughed, but Haylee could not hear it over the high-pitched horn and the thundering roar.

They were about twenty yards from the far edge of the bridge when the train rolled onto the trestle. Running for her life, Haylee screamed. Fear of stumbling entered her mind. Adrenalin effectively masked the tremors that ripped through her. The sound and vibration from the massive amount of iron and steel breathing down their necks was overwhelming. She hated herself as she gave a moment's thought to how her dad would feel when he found out how she had been killed. Haylee was sure that she would be hit from behind at any second and was about to kick in her powerful running overdrive when she was roughly yanked at a right angle. She went flying through the air before tumbling down a grassy embankment.

It took a few moments to realize that she was still alive, that she had stopped moving, and that she could hear the engine and its cars rolling past her. She was relieved that nothing appeared to be broken, but then a white-hot anger flared up. Locating Curtis, she crawled toward him. He was laying on the hillside, laughing and shouting about how great that was!

Cursing, Haylee began to hit him with balled fists.

Easily holding her hands, Curtis drug her over onto him and began kissing her. She squirmed and cursed. He rolled on top of her to try to subdue her movements. Between wet kisses, he kept repeating, "You are so awesome!" Curtis held her in place while grinding his hips into her pelvis. She could feel his erection.

The vibrating within Haylee intensified. Her entire body felt as if it were pulsating. Something shifted in her mind.

Haylee ceased to feel afraid. A foreign desire had taken over. It was something that didn't care about boys with busy hands and dangerous senses of humor. It didn't care about the physical act of intimacy. It wanted something much deeper than that.

That something odd was going on finally seemed to penetrate Curtis's consciousness and he looked at Haylee uncertainly. She lay beneath him, unnaturally still.

A look of alarm crossed his face and he rolled off her.

Haylee sat up suddenly, regarding him with a steely gaze as if for the very first time.

Looking unnerved, Curtis began backing away—all desire drained from his face and his nether region.

She rose up to stand before him, still holding his eyes with hers.

She unfastened her belt, letting it drop to the ground and removed her dress in one simple movement. She stood before him, not shy or embarrassed but bold and sure. He inhaled deeply as he surveyed her; his cock, stiff once again, pressed against his pants. Her eyes glittered in the moonlight. "Is this what you wanted?" she asked in a slow, sultry tone.

Nodding as his breath caught in his throat, he reached out, bringing her to a kneeling position in front of him. Deftly, his hands reached behind her and released the hook on her bra. He buried his face in her breasts. She did not resist. Curtis ran his tongue over an erect nipple then moved hungrily to the next one. The rest of her garments fell away under his hasty fingers. Haylee made encouraging sounds. She did not want to frighten him again.

In a frantic rush, the boy hastily removed his clothing. Greedily he pulled the pliant beauty back into his arms. Vaguely, Haylee registered that the heat of their nude bodies pressed together was not unpleasant.

Curtis groaned and pushed Haylee onto the grass, edging his knees between her legs. At the moment that his manhood made the slightest pressure against her body, Haylee violently flipped him over. An 'oof' escaped him as he slammed against the ground with a thud. She watched as he tried to suck in air and saw the fear on his face when he realized that this was impossible.

With a detached point of view, like she was watching someone else, Haylee looked on as her fingers, the webbing in particular, molded themselves perfectly around the contours of his face. Struggling furiously, Curtis tried to remove it. The more he thrashed the more the webs adhered.

His struggles were in vain. It didn't take long for them to cease. At the moment that Curtis accepted his fate, Haylee closed her eyes.

The webbed hand that had been bonded to Curtis's mouth and nose released its hold. Slowly and delicately, she lifted it away. Her body quivered as if it were infused with a jolt of energy. The vibrations were replaced with a feeling of indescribable euphoria.

She took a deep breath and stood—stretching languidly. In a daze, she walked around to get used to this new sensation. There wasn't a bit of pain or soreness in her body. Her lungs filled and expanded with breaths that drew in more air than she ever thought possible. Her mind cleared as if a fog lifted and her thoughts felt ultra-alert and as swift as lightning.

After a while, Haylee wandered back to where Curtis lay, pale and trembling, taking shallow breaths. He was curled into a fetal position and looked to be suffering. Her eyes grew wide as she realized that she now knew a lot of things about him.

A surprise—since he always seemed so cool and confident on the surface—were the many nights he'd spent alone and afraid in an empty house when he was too young to fend for himself. His parents drank too much and fought too viciously. A distasteful look crossed her face when she learned about the pregnancy scare with Lauren and his harsh handling of the tender situation. She also knew that his main goal tonight had been to have sex with her. A tiny bit of guilt lurked inside when she noted that Curtis truly did have some feelings for her. She shrugged. *They weren't very strong*, she thought.

She dressed slowly. When she finished, she stood over him, watching. She picked up his clothes and threw them in a heap near his feet. "Get up and get dressed!" she yelled. When there was no response, she squatted next to him, shaking his shoulder. "Hey! Put your clothes on!"

As he turned toward her, Haylee was startled to see the

look on his face—or rather, the lack of a look on his face. His expression was totally blank. It was as if he were asleep with his eyes open. She called his name. "Curtis!"

She breathed a sigh of relief to see him moving at last. It was with irritation that she realized he was not capable of putting his clothes on without help. Once he was dressed, she tugged on his hand. His mechanical actions smoothed out and began to look almost normal once they got going. She led him back across the trestle.

On the other side, Haylee relived those awful moments running across the bridge and the shock of what she'd done to Curtis with her webs. She had to forcibly calm herself to keep the bile from rising up at those thoughts.

Reaching the spot where he'd placed the pennies, her eyes scanned for them. Not far away, they lay on the track, blended together into one. She picked up the fused metal. Her first thought was to put it in his pocket, but then she changed her mind.

Haylee drove him home. This time, there was no conversation. He stared straight ahead; so did she. Now that the adrenaline had dissipated, she was seriously creeped out. *What, exactly, have I done to him?* She glanced in his direction, wearing a worried frown as she tried asking him a question or two. He seemed capable of only answering with a grunt or a single word. By the time she parked his vehicle in front of his house, put the keys in his pocket, and nudged him toward his front door, she was feeling the acid burn of worry in her gut.

21

REKINDLING

It was only 10:00 p.m. when she stood at the edges of the pools of light cast by her own windows. With great stealth, she climbed into her bedroom. Taking off her dirty, snagged and ripped pantyhose, Haylee threw a fresh pair out the window followed by a clean pair of pumps. She covered the grass stains and holes in her dress as best she could with her shawl. While Haylee carefully climbed back outside, she thought through how she would explain her solo arrival.

She found Gene and Glori sitting next to each other on the couch. The TV was on, but the volume was so low, it was barely audible. Gene's arm rested on the back of the couch; Glori leaned her head on his shoulder. One of her hands rested possessively on his thigh.

Haylee was glad that they seemed preoccupied.

With a start, Gene noticed Haylee standing in his peripheral vision. "How did you get in without me hearing the door?" he commented, sounding flustered. Putting a little distance between himself and Glori, Gene motioned to Haylee to sit down to tell them how her evening went.

Noting Gene's demeanor, Glori smiled. Her thoughts wandered back to the last few hours. He had take-out food ready for dinner. Once they finished, they grabbed a couple of beers and wandered outside for a tour. Glori, having visited a few times, was always impressed with the size of his farming operation and the fact that he and Haylee handled most everything between them. She and Gene continued the process of sharing their history with each other as a new phase of their own began to take shape. Arriving back at his front door some time later, Gene gazed at her tenderly. He cupped her face in his hands and leaned down to make gentle contact. He moved his mouth slowly over hers.

Overwhelmed with the powerful emotions surging through her, Glori reached up to cover Gene's hands with her own. She returned his kiss freely.

Suddenly, Gene froze. He gently moved her away from him. "Glori, this was a mistake."

Her breath caught in her throat. "Gene, I…"

"Shhh…" he replied, placing a finger on her lips. "I didn't mean that we are a mistake, I mean that having you here is a mistake." He cursed and tried again. "Damn it! I feel like a bumbling fool! What I mean is that I can't have you in my house, because all I want to do is take you straight to my bed." He stammered, "I mean it's been a so long since I've been with a woman…"

"Gene, it's OK. I know perfectly well how to handle myself."

He laughed. "You might, but I sure as hell don't think I do! Glori, I like you…a lot. I think it's obvious that I am attracted to you. But I'd like us to get to know each other better before we hop into the sack."

Laughing in return, she said, "Agreed. I could have gone for just being bed buddies. I didn't think I was interested in having a relationship. But you might have changed my mind."

Gene looked surprised, but grinned from ear to ear. He stared at her with what Glori could only describe as amazement.

Their laughter filled the house with an energy that had been missing for too long. "Sweetheart, if you aren't just a wonder that walked into my life at the most unexpected moment."

"It's mutual, Garrett," she commented. "Since we are committed to hanging around your house this evening, I propose...a game."

Gene looked concerned.

"Sorry, Glori, but I don't think that we have any board games."

She took his hand and led him toward the furniture. "That's quite alright. For this game we don't need anything other than what we have."

"Huh?" he replied.

"You'll see!" she responded mysteriously.

Leading him to his couch, she motioned for him to sit. Doing so, he looked at her inquiringly.

"There are only two rules to this game."

He raised his eyebrows.

"Your hands can't move and you can't make a sound." She reached down to place his hands on his thighs.

"What is the name of this game?" he wanted to know.

Ignoring his question, she continued, "Lay your head back and close your eyes." Nodding, he complied.

A smile lingered on her face as she walked around to the back of the couch. Her breath was warm against his ear. The touch of her tongue there made him jump. He did the best he could to remain still as Glori explored the smell and taste of his skin, taking her time to move slowly and savor each new sensation. She was happy to see that Gene had to struggle to keep his composure.

The game came to a conclusion after Glori had taken a turn in the hot seat. Gene, too, lingered at his task, having caught on quickly to the subtleties of their interaction. He made sure that she had 'suffered' as much, if not more, than he had.

Afterward, feeling peaceful and content, they snuggled on the couch while speaking softly of their attraction for each other since their first meeting.

"The game is called Anticipation," Glori giggled.

He kissed her cheek, "Did you just make that up?"

"What do you think?"

~ ~ ~ ~

Glori's attention returned to hear Haylee describe the dance and what a wonderful date Curtis was.

If Gene and Glori had not been so inattentive, they might have commented on Curtis not walking her to the door.

Gene was relieved that the evening had gone well, according to his daughter.

Haylee said she was tired and that she wanted to turn in. She wished them goodnight.

Glori had an early shift the next day and got up to leave as well. Gene walked Glori to her car; already they were wishing that they didn't have to be separated.

.22.

REGRET

Haylee had a break from school for a couple of weeks for the spring holiday. During that time, she tried to keep as busy as possible. She decided that the chicken coop needed a thorough cleaning. It felt right to be covered in chicken poo when she was feeling like crap.

Spending time with the chickens helped to soothe her turbulent emotions. A chicken, when not frightened or hungry, was a content creature. They made soft sounds so that the other members of the flock knew that they were not alone—safety in numbers. Their methodic scratching, hunting, and pecking was absorbing in its simple, single-minded focus. They never failed to make her smile at their feelings of satisfaction when one of them discovered a beetle to eat. With a sigh, Haylee thought that living a chicken life might not be so bad.

One thing was a relief; her monthly cycle come and went without fanfare or hospital visits.

If she wasn't busy, she was haunted by the blank look on Curtis's face. She was confused about what she had done. She couldn't exactly explain it in words, but she knew that she had consumed some essential part of him. After she had stolen it, she was privy to all of his innermost thoughts.

Curtis wasn't the boy she'd thought he was at all. He was vain and self-centered. He didn't care for any of the girls he'd had sex with. He was very proud of his ability to "play the game" and planned to make Haylee just another notch on his belt.

Haylee did not want to think about the part of Curtis that liked her. He had begun to think of her as a friend, and he'd never had a girl as a friend before.

The conflicting emotions wore on her. She wasn't sleeping well. She was consumed with remorse for her actions—she was no better than he was. She had used Curtis to serve her own purpose then tossed him aside. Her compassionate side was appalled by the inexcusable theft she had committed, but her predatory side was elated with her first acquisition and eagerly anticipated the next.

Searching for a respite from her inner turmoil, Haylee tried spending time on the old tractor at the end of the day. This time, it did no good. She walked into the house feeling blue.

She had time to herself as her dad had gone to spend the evening with Glori. She was relieved not to have to put on a show of normalcy for him. And she was glad to see him happy these days. Haylee was even growing to like the redheaded nurse.

❦23❦

GENE AND GLORI

They'd agreed. Tonight would be the night. Gene noticed his nerves edging up on him as he showered and shaved with extra care. He did not want to disappoint her. They planned to go to an exclusive dinner club downtown and then would spend the rest of the weekend at her place.

Falling for Glori was exciting and thrilling. He couldn't remember smiling as much since before Doris had gotten sick. However, for every degree of emotional depth that he experienced for Glori, his feelings of disloyalty toward his dead wife increased. He was also plagued with worry about letting himself become too attached to someone again. *What if something happens to Glori?*

This type of thinking had been causing endless hours of tossing and turning during the nights.

He drove to her place with butterflies dancing in his belly. The large bouquet of red roses laying on the passenger seat sent perfume through the pristine interior of the town car he'd rented for the occasion.

"Just a minute!" he heard her call through the door at his

knock. The sound of her voice never failed to bring a smile to his face.

The door swung inward. Seeing her so beautifully dressed, he could not speak a word, but gathered her into his arms and kissed her with such thoroughness that his heart and respiration rate increased almost to a level where he thought their plans would have to change. He was pleased to see that Glori seemed to be struggling as much as he was. In spite of his obvious arousal, Gene maintained a clear head. He gently pulled back to allow them some space to regain their self-control.

Her flushed cheeks and slightly rumpled appearance were almost his undoing, but he wanted their first time making love to be special and memorable so he kept himself contained.

Glori straightened her dress and began the task of finding a vase for the flowers. She asked where he had parked his truck.

Laughing, Gene replied that it was at the car rental lot.

"Whatever for?" she wanted to know.

"Sweetheart, for our weekend in the city, I thought we'd have more fun in a town car rather than bumping around in an old farm truck."

"That doesn't matter to me," she replied.

"I know," he said with a wink.

Their date was all Gene could have hoped for—excellent food, great company, and easy conversation. A fragrant, gentle breeze drifted off of the river, lifting tendrils of their hair as they strolled hand in hand along the boardwalk later that evening. The wine they'd consumed with dinner had them feeling very relaxed. Gene steered them toward a bench where they could sit and watch the twinkling lights reflecting on the water. As they sat, he draped his arm around her, snuggling her in close. She leaned her head on his shoulder. After a while of companionable silence, Gene turned toward her, nuzzling her ear. She giggled softly. His breath tickled as he whispered, "I'm in love with you, Glori Ridgeway."

She closed her eyes to savor the moment, then responded simply, "I love you too." Their lips met and like warm drops of wax accepting the mark of an official seal, an invisible contract between their hearts was set.

Back at her apartment, soft strains of "Bette Davis Eyes" played on the stereo while Glori and Gene slow danced in her living room. Gene was in exquisite pain, trying to hold himself back. When their clothes started coming off, he had to concentrate fully to keep himself from groaning and racing forward. He could feel Glori's heart racing and saw the sheen of sweat break out on her face. Her body was flushed and he knew she was more than ready.

She looked at him with eyes that were a dusky purple hue that reflected her deep state of arousal. Wrapping her hand around the back of his neck, she pulled him toward her saying, "Please give in to it and let go..."

"Oh God, thank you!" he exclaimed as he kissed her deeply.

~ ~ ~ ~

Later, relaxed and content, they snuggled. With her head on his shoulder, Glori asked Gene why he was having trouble sleeping.

"How did you know that?" he asked. She pulled her head back and just looked at him.

"Ah, silly me," he said. He took his time organizing his thoughts as she settled her head back onto his shoulder. Taking a deep breath, he answered as honestly as he could. "Every day that I feel happy and fall deeper in love with you makes me feel guilty about being unfaithful to Haylee's mother."

Glori nodded. "I thought it might be something like that." She felt him move to brush a tear from his face. She waited quietly for a while until she felt his breathing return to a normal rate.

"I haven't told you about Brad," she began. "And you haven't met my sister-in-law Torie yet. Brad was my brother. He and Torie were childhood sweethearts. I can't even remember a time in my childhood when Torie wasn't there. She taught me how to shoot BB guns, ice skate, build forts, and play poker. They got married when they were eighteen. Neither my parents nor Torie's complained about that because everyone just knew they belonged together. They used to take me camping and hiking with them over summer breaks." She paused for a while, and when she continued, her voice was strained. "Have you ever heard of myocarditis?" she asked.

"No."

"Brad was only twenty-two when a fever came on. I remember Torie telling me that she planned to make him go to the doctor the following day. She wasn't especially worried about it. I woke up the next morning to hear my mother's shrill voice screaming, 'No! No! That can't be!' Torie had called my mom in a panic because Brad hadn't woken up."

Gene squeezed her closer. "Glori, I am so sorry."

"Myocarditis is a virus of the heart." Her voice cracked on the next words. "Torie was completely destroyed…we all were." She wiped away tears of her own.

"Brad is the reason I chose to work in medicine. When I started out, I planned to become a doctor. Anyway, I do have a point to this narrative."

Gene placed a lingering kiss upon her temple.

"There will never be another Brad. Torie and the rest of us will always love him. Even though we still think about him, miss him, and talk about him, we also want Torie to be happy. So when she met Simon and he helped bring her back to us… you know…like someone excited about life rather than a piece of drift wood…we loved him too. We love them both." She paused then continued. "Gene, I just needed you to know that I don't feel threatened by Doris. I know that she will always be an important part of your and Haylee's lives. I know that you still love her. I don't ever expect that to change…but I would like both of you guys to feel comfortable talking about her. In a roundabout way, I'd like to get better acquainted with the woman who made you both who you are today."

Rubbing his eyes with his free hand, Gene sighed. When he looked at Glori next, she was gazing at him. A sweet smile of relief and understanding broke out on his face and a gentle growl emanated from his throat. They came together in a long, slow, passionate kiss. They were in no hurry this time.

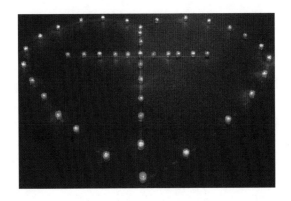

.24.

MOM IN THE ATTIC

The house was empty and dark. Haylee was at a loss for what to do. Normally she would have watched TV or read a book, but she knew that neither of these activities would take her mind off of her worries. Suddenly, she remembered that her dad had told her that she could rummage through her mom's things in the attic.

Being surrounded by her mother's possessions helped a little. She slipped on one of her sweaters and could smell a very faint waft of the gardenia perfume that her mom had always worn. In the bottom of one of the trunks, Haylee found a family photograph that must have been taken when she was about five. It was a black and white. Her dad had his hair cut in a flat top and stood in the background with his hands on her mom's shoulders. Her mom sat on a chair, holding Haylee on her lap. Doris's hair hung down to her shoulders and scooped up in a curl. The sweet smiles on all their faces brought an ache to Haylee's heart. She felt guilty that she couldn't remember what her mother looked like without help from photographs.

Haylee held the image to her chest. Even though she now

had many admirers, she felt more alone than ever before. If only her mother were still here…

On her continued search, Haylee discovered more old photographs from before her mom's time. Unfortunately, there were no dates or notes written on the backs. Many of the people in the pictures resembled Haylee and her mother, and more than a few of them were wearing a necklace just like hers.

Another photo caught her eye. In it was a woman, a child, a man, and an effeminate teenage boy. The little girl and her mother were off to one side with a wide gap between them and the two men. What startled Haylee was that the boy could have been her twin. Turning the picture over, she found some writing: "Polly (age 7), and Mother, 1849." Polly was wearing Haylee's necklace. She reached up to rub a finger on the pendant where it rested at her own neck.

Looking back at her mother's trunk, an ornate little box caught Haylee's eye. She pulled it out to inspect it. Writing in a language she could not understand filled the tiny surface. Finding a small button on the side, she pressed it. The lid popped open. Inside was a satin liner shaped around a wooden cradle. She recognized the shape instantly. It was made to hold her pendant, the one that she had to take with her whenever she traveled. *Did any of those people have to keep it with them all the time too?*

The box looked deeper than the pendant and its holder. Try as she would, she could not find any other compartments.

❧25❧

BUG WHEELS

In early spring, Haylee received a letter from UC Berkeley. She nervously read the first line. "Dear Ms. Garrett, we are pleased to inform you…" Letting out a whoop, Haylee clutched the letter and danced around the road. She was bursting with the news and had to tell someone right away. She couldn't find her father, so she called Glori.

Glori seemed extremely touched that Haylee wanted to share this with her. She was almost as excited as Haylee.

Gene was happy and proud when he heard the news, but looked sad at the thought of her leaving home. That weekend, the three of them drove to an amusement park in San Jose to celebrate. They rode on roller coasters and log rides. Haylee couldn't remember when she had had so much fun. They ate dinner at a restaurant near the airport where they could watch planes take off and land.

On the way home the next day, they stopped at the Berkeley campus to have a look around. They loved the majestic old buildings with red tiled roofs, combined with the manicured lawns, large eucalyptus trees, and the salty ocean breezes.

Haylee couldn't believe that in a few months she'd be living in this beautiful place.

All through the weekend, she noticed her dad and Glori exchanging sly glances. At first she thought that they were just flirting with each other, as was their habit, but when they kept it up, she began to get suspicious. When she asked them what they were up to, they would just smile and tell her that she would find out soon enough.

They drove to Glori's apartment that afternoon to drop her off. On their way through the parking lot, Glori stopped next to a little powder blue VW Beetle. The other two stopped behind her. Putting her arms on her hips, Glori whirled around with a stern look on her face. "Haylee! I thought I told you not to park your car in my parking space!"

Taken aback by her tone, Haylee's eyes grew wide. It took her a few moments before the words sunk in. Gene came up behind his daughter and dropped a set of keys into her hand. His huge grin made the comers of his eyes crinkle.

"Oh, my gosh!" she squealed. Looking at their smiling faces, she said, "Really?! This is really my car?"

"It sure is. I can't have my girl going off to college without a way to come home whenever she wants."

"Thank you, Daddy! Thank you!"

⚘26⚘

NEEDS

One Month Later

With each passing day, Haylee had a harder time going through her routine activities. She was consumed with a need that grew stronger every day. Her first warning was the small vibrations that started in the pit of her stomach and worked their way up through her arms. In the beginning, they happened only once a week. Then they started increasing in frequency and intensity.

Now she felt the vibrations riot through her body almost all the time. She was frustrated because she couldn't hold her hands still. This made dressing, eating, and anything else almost impossible. The effort to hide it from everyone was a tremendous strain. When her ears started ringing too, she thought she would lose her mind.

Instinctively, Haylee knew what would end her torment. She needed to feed, but she refused to give in to the urge. The memory of how awful she had felt after what she'd done to Curtis strengthened her resolve.

She put up a valiant fight for a few more days. She tried running for miles at top speed to try to release the tension. Nothing worked. Finally, when she couldn't stand it any longer, she quit trying.

Making sure that her father was asleep, Haylee moved around her room without turning on the light. She put on a black T-shirt, stretch pants, and running shoes. She deftly braided her hair and wound a rubber band around the end to hold it in place. Stooping down, she hoisted the backpack that she had packed ahead of time onto her back. As quietly as possible, Haylee opened her bedroom window and leapt out in one fluid motion.

She held her position as she listened for sounds. There were none. Breathing a sigh of relief, Haylee set off at lightning speed toward her destination.

Even while she had been rebelling against her overwhelming need, Haylee had thought about the best way to go about acquiring prey. She realized that she should not feed off of people that she knew—eventually someone would make the connection between her and her victims. She'd heard that even after all these months, Curtis's parents continued to take him to doctors to try to figure out what was wrong.

In some ways, it felt good to give herself over to the hunt. Her mind was clear and her thoughts moved very fast. Her body felt tight and extremely powerful. She decided that she would use her newly found sex appeal to draw a victim out to a deserted place.

After covering about twenty-five miles in an hour, Haylee's destination came into view. It was a sleazy bar located on a deserted road. There were about five pickup trucks parked outside. She stopped in a grassy, vacant lot about one hundred feet from The Spigot. She squatted low so the grass would offer some cover while she surveyed the lay of the land. Her keen eyes and ears missed nothing. The building was old and in disrepair. It was made out of pressed board and the corrugated tin roof looked in need of a good paint job. In each window, neon signs blinked on and off. The tunes of a country song playing on the jukebox floated through the air. She was satisfied.

With quick, purposeful movements, Haylee pulled the rubber band from her hair and loosened the braid. *Apparently, the tremors can be stopped with the knowledge that I am close to appeasing their cause,* she thought with irony. She shook her head to send the silken strands floating around her shoulders. Adroitly, she removed her clothing and knelt down to open her pack. She took a damp washcloth out of a plastic bag and wiped the sheen of perspiration from her body. The cool breeze on her moist skin was invigorating. The light from the moon lovingly caressed each line and plane of her body, making her look like she was crafted from marble. She pulled out a short, black leather jacket and skirt. With a rather wicked smile, she wriggled into the skirt. The jacket was next. She looked down as she pulled the zipper up, smashing her bare breasts to form ample cleavage.

Her last touch was a pair of black heels. *Thank you, Thrifty Shifts Store,* she thought.

She stuffed her discarded clothing into her pack, zipped it up, and made her way toward the building.

With one hand, she pushed the door open. With legs spread in a wide stance, Haylee stood on the threshold for a moment, letting her eyes adjust to the dark interior.

A row of men swiveled on barstools to gawk at the shapely young woman.

Haylee strode confidently into the smoky room. She assessed every man, disregarding most of them. They'd give up too easily. The stronger they clung to life, the more she would get out of them. Within seconds, Haylee spotted the one she wanted. She walked over to the bar and stood next to him. He eyed her boldly. His gaze lingered on her legs. Haylee thought that if she were a horse, he'd be running his hands over them to test out the firmness of her muscles. Haylee confidently returned the assessment.

He looked to be about twenty-eight or twenty-nine. Haylee thought that he might be a construction worker because he wore work boots and his arms were bulky under the rolled up sleeves of his shirt. He had short dark hair and a dark mustache.

The bartender asked Haylee what she wanted. She gave her companion a long, meaningful look before she answered the question. "I'll have a beer."

Without taking his eyes off the enchantress, the man next to her told the bartender to put her drink on his tab. "What's your name, darling?"

"S—Sandra. What's yours?"

"John." He regarded her for a moment, then smiled. "Nice to meet you S—Sandra."

She broke the look as her drink was placed in front of her. Haylee raised the beer in John's direction. "Thanks."

"My pleasure," he responded meaningfully.

You might think so, but the pleasure will be all mine. "What do you do?"

"Oh, I pound a few nails here and there."

She nodded. "Thought so." Haylee was growing tired of the chatter and her calm facade was beginning to crack as the tremors started to make their presence felt. She carefully set her beer on the bar, making a gargantuan effort to keep her hand from trembling. She turned to John, placing her arm across his shoulders and pressing her breasts against him. "John, I need a ride. Can you give me one?"

"How far you goin', darling?"

"Just down the road a bit." She moistened her lips and lowered her eyes. "I'll make it worth your while."

John stood up quickly, finishing his beer with one last swig and fishing money from his pocket. He placed his hand on the small of her back while escorting her out of the bar. A grin appeared on his face as his buddies made obnoxious catcalls behind them.

The sound of the gravel crunching under their shoes sounded loud to Haylee. Her back felt stiff with suppressed tension. She easily could have flattened him in the middle of the parking lot and been on her way before anyone could raise a rescue attempt...but she held herself in check. They climbed in his vehicle. As he got in, he said, "Which way are we headed?"

She wanted to scream and had to swallow hard to keep her voice calm. He noticed her trembling at that moment, and a small frown of worry appeared on his face. Though she was loathe to touch him in any romantic kind of way, she moved across the seat and planted a soft, quick kiss on his lips. He eagerly responded by running his hand up her bare thigh.

She broke the contact. "Just find a dark place to park in that direction," she said breathlessly as she nodded in a direction. "Make it fast."

"Damn! You're making my day, Sunshine." He grinned. She smiled.

John drove down the road at breakneck speed. Haylee rolled her window down to let the wind whip through her hair. She tilted her head back and closed her eyes. *It won't be long now...Just a few more minutes.*

~ ~ ~ ~

John glanced over to look at the woman with her neck exposed and hair flying. He couldn't believe his good fortune.

Lust pumped through his veins as he thought about having that naked body squirming underneath him. He pressed his foot down harder on the accelerator. He found a dirt road and a secluded place to park. He slammed on the brakes. Without even opening her eyes, the woman grabbed her pack, opened the door, and jumped out. A dust cloud plumed around them.

John would have preferred to take her in the truck, but... *Hey, if she wants it outside, who am I to complain?* he questioned as he followed.

She walked a little further into the cover of the trees. John ran up behind her, picked her up, and swung her around in a circle before setting her down. She laughed nervously as she turned around in his arms and raised her face. He grabbed the zipper of her jacket at the same time he bent down to meet her lips.

Haylee ducked away from his kiss and his hands and pulled him down with her to the ground. He followed without complaint and started fumbling with his pants. Before he knew what was happening, his body was slammed into the ground. Something terrifying clamped over his nose and mouth, cutting off his air supply. Surprise made his eyes open wide. He saw the beautiful woman crouched above him. Her face looked like it was carved from stone. Her expression was one of grim determination.

In a split second, he forgot about the pleasurable, all-consuming need that had been driving him. The thought, *I'm going to die!* flashed into his brain. With his heart making painful thunderous leaps inside his chest and the blood roaring in his ears, John attempted to take a breath and found that the hot, moist, leathery thing clamped to his face affixed itself tighter, if that was possible, successfully blocked even the slightest intake of air. In a herculean effort, he swung out, but the woman deftly avoided his powerful blow. Rage burst through him; he redoubled his efforts. His body bolted and twisted. Haylee's eyes glinted with a deadly sparkle as her extraordinary strength kicked in to subdue him. The expression on her face turned into one of wicked satisfaction.

John saw this change as she continued to press more forcefully down upon him. *I can't stop her! I can't stop the bitch!* he thought, terrified.

Many people speculate what one's last thought would be. John Mason's last thought was, *Shit! This is really it!* Almost as quickly as the struggle against his fate began, it ceased, as acceptance washed over him.

~ ~ ~ ~

Haylee felt her body pulsing with energy. With each surge, she grew stronger while she watched her victim grow weaker. Near the end, her body quivered with intense pleasure. At the moment that John accepted his death, Haylee became perfectly still.

~ ~ ~ ~

John could feel his consciousness fading as if it was a picture tube reducing to a tiny point.

For a few moments, or it could have been hours, John was nothing. He didn't have a name or a gender or a personality. He merged into a vast serene ocean of blankness—the place where those with no form reside.

Dimly at first, he was aware of a nauseating, dizzy sensation, as if he had been seized from a great distance. The feeling increased as he came rushing back into his ruined human abode. It was cold and clammy. He opened his eyes. Instantly, he was assaulted by a skull-crushing headache, and doubled up into a fetal position as vomit erupted from his mouth.

For a while, he lay there shivering; the only warm spot

on his body was the side of his face where it lay in a pool of stinking liquid. Slowly, the nausea and pain ebbed. Disoriented, he raised into a sitting position.

It was dark. He could see his truck parked nearby. He knew how to get home, but he couldn't remember how he came to be there in the first place. Reaching out, he found the nearest tree trunk and braced himself as he rose onto wobbly legs. Momentarily, an overwhelming wave of grief overcame him. It was so strong that he almost lost his balance. As quickly as it came, it was gone. For what he grieved, he knew not.

~ ~ ~ ~

From a distance Haylee watched as John Mason gingerly climbed into the driver's seat of his truck. After a few false starts—grinding the ignition, jumping forward and slamming on the breaks–he inched the vehicle around and drove slowly away. Haylee briefly wondered if he'd find his way home or if he would still have the ability to pound nails.

When Haylee could no longer see the headlights, she breathed a sigh of contented relief. She stepped into the moonlight while she lazily stretched her arms up toward the heavens, then lightly ran her hands down her sensuous breasts, waist, and hips. A contented smile spread across her beautiful face. A purr almost emanated from her. She was sated and relaxed at long last.

She took a few more minutes to come down from her high before retrieving her pack. As she removed the leather clothing and used the damp cloth to scrub the smell of smoke and sweat from her body, Haylee thought about what she had done. Her mission had been successful. John had not known what to think about the woman he met in The Spigot. He'd thought that she was a call girl. Shameful feelings surfaced before being replaced by necessity and logic. She was sure that her sleek female disguise could in no way be connected to Haylee Garrett.

She allowed herself a few moments to reflect on the details she now knew about John Mason. He came from a big family back east. Most of his siblings were in trouble either with the law or social services. He was basically a loner who roamed the western states getting odd jobs here and there. She had chosen him well. He didn't have anyone close to him who would push for answers about what had happened to him.

She stood up to put on her running clothes and looked down at herself. A little sadly, she remembered how excited she'd been when she'd first realized that her body was beautiful. Now she was beginning to think of it as a curse. She had just used that body to drain life from John Mason. Her desire to feed was strong. She sensed that if she resisted it she would die.

Silent tears trickled down her face, catching glints of the moonlight as she dressed and prepared for her run home.

27

WORK EXPERIENCE

More than ever, Haylee was driven to get out of her small town and disappear. She could not keep up her 'normal' life and her nighttime hunting activities. As high school drew to a close, she spent time in the city looking for a job and an apartment.

Stumbling upon a veterinary assistant job in the paper, Haylee pounced on it right away. The Solano Animal Clinic was on the outskirts of Berkeley. She was relieved when they called and asked her to come in for an interview. In the middle of the interview with Dr. Jamison, a ruckus erupted from one of the back examination rooms. Excusing himself, the doctor hurried out. Haylee wasn't sure what to do. A frantic chatter echoed down the hallway, as did expletives from the people trying to get control of the hysterical animal. Haylee peeked into the room where a desperate squirrel was attempting to take chunks out of a fellow wearing gloves.

Immediately understanding the problem, Haylee went to the young man and whispered in his ear. He paused to look at her strangely, then left the room, calling the others to go with him. Dr. Jamison asked Haylee what she thought she was doing. With a pleading look she said, "I know what's wrong. I will explain after we get this poor girl taken care of. Would you please move to where she can't see you?"

Mystified, but intrigued, Dr. Jamison stepped out in the hallway where he could observe.

Haylee relaxed her mind and communicated with the emotional creature. After a few moments, the squirrel's breathing slowed. Still rocking back and forth, the animal eyed Haylee. Slowly, the squirrel relaxed its stance and let the fur that had been standing on end, smooth down. Seeming to understand that the girl meant to help, the squirrel hesitantly stepped toward Haylee and climbed onto her hand. Haylee crooned to the creature as she lifted her gently, carrying her over to her cage.

When the transformed creature had been contained, Dr. Jamison asked, "How did you do that?"

"If you listen carefully, you can tell the difference between the scream of an animal that was raised in captivity and one that was caught in the wild," she improvised. Then she related what the squirrel had told her. "That squirrel was born and raised as a pet. But she escaped and has been living with wild squirrels. She just had her first litter of kittens and is desperate to get back to them. Her former owner, the man who brought her in, doesn't understand. He thinks she is just acting wild and crazy...but her babies will die if she isn't there to care for them. She promises to behave as long as he will let her get back to them right away." Haylee responded.

Dr. Jamison did a visual exam on the female squirrel, confirming that she had given birth recently. He offered Haylee the job on the spot. After that, finding an apartment had been easy.

After she went through her high school graduation ceremony and they'd properly celebrated it, Haylee pretended to be excited about the new life that was waiting for her.

Beneath her happy facade, Haylee was plagued. In the months since she had stolen John Mason's spirit, she'd made two other forays into the night. Four victims...and she carried the memory of each of their lives within her.

Haylee was eager to be on her way to the city. She needed space to think about what to do next. Plus the vibrations were starting again. Haylee wanted to be as far away from the small town of Elverta as she could before she started hunting again. People around these parts were beginning to comment on the strange, unexplainable occurrence of young men behaving like cyborgs.

28

MOVING

Gene and Glori helped Haylee load her car for the move to Berkeley. With each item, Gene grew more heavy-hearted. His child was leaving home. In a way, he wanted to hold on to her and never let her go. In another way, he was extremely proud of her accomplishments and goals. In the very core of his being, Gene had a feeling that something wasn't right with his daughter, but she covered her tracks so well that he couldn't put his finger on what it was that was bothering him.

Haylee looked sad too. Gene knew she would miss him. Once she left home, things would never be the same again for either of them. Haley swallowed hard and looked as if she would break down into tears as she prepared to go.

Glori attempted to keep the atmosphere light. She promised Haylee that they would do something fun together the next time she came home and that she and Gene would enjoy coming to Berkeley to see things that Haylee would discover. She gently teased her about all of the young men who were sure to fall head-over-heels in love with her at school.

When the packing was nearly complete, Glori gave Haylee

a quick hug and wished her luck. Discretely, she left Gene and Haylee alone to say their final good-byes. Gene's voice was thick with emotion. He smiled, but it didn't reach his eyes.

"Well, it looks like you are all set." He still couldn't shake the persistent feeling that something was wrong.

Swallowing with difficulty, she whispered, "I'll miss you, Dad."

"Me too, sweetheart." He held out his arms. She walked into them. For a moment they just hugged each other quietly, each lost in their own thoughts. Gene rubbed her back, clearing his throat. "Hay Hay, you know you can always come to me if you need anything, right?"

She looked at him, surprised. "Dad you haven't called me that since…"

He nodded as he watched her blink rapidly to keep her emotions in check.

"I am all grown up," she croaked as she reached up to grasp her crystal pendant.

To lighten the mood, he said, "Yes, you are. And I know that once you start your job and meet some new people, you will be so busy, I'll have to beg you to come and visit your old dad."

Not answering immediately, she pressed her face into his chest, inhaling deeply as if to memorize his smell. She squeezed him a little tighter then pulled back again and with a mischievous twinkle said, "Yea, you're probably right,"

They laughed together for a moment. He placed his hands on her shoulders, saying tenderly, "Drive carefully."

She rolled her eyes. "I will." She got into her car and waved out the window as she started down the long road that would lead her to her future.

Gene stood there watching her car grow smaller. He was feeling empty and a little lost. Memories of Haylee flooded his mind. He could clearly picture how she'd looked the day that he and Doris had brought her home from the hospital, her first steps, and her chubby, smiling face surrounded by curly chestnut locks. Regret filled his heart as he thought about how much time he'd wasted lost in his own misery. He also realized that, for the first time, he could think about Doris without hurting.

Glori slipped up beside him, putting her arms around his waist. When Haylee's car was no longer visible, Glori wordlessly took his hand. Together they walked quietly through the walnut orchards.

Mighty blossom with sorrows so vast.

A monitoring device blinks in its mounting. For millennia, its messages have displayed an expected looping pattern: Protect, Awake, Activated, Engaged and Recovery.

There are those who interact with the device periodically; Tethalana, the elder wise-woman who embodies grace, charity, and compassion, Elin and Nile, the youthful components who provide precision and drive, and the male, Darion, who watches and monitors with a disdainful eye.

Burden of the Powerful

Part Three

29

SAYING HELLO

Haylee parked her car near the curb of an old but well-kept two-story house about two blocks from the Berkeley campus. It had been built in the 1930s, and had salmon-colored trim surrounding light purple walls.

Haylee felt a little nervous as she went in search of Mrs. Murphy, the boarding house owner. The woman was a plump widow who'd never had children. Her gray hair was kept in short curls. She had an annoying habit of constantly patting them when she spoke. She was friendly and tried to mother her boarders.

Within moments of Haylee's arrival, Mrs. Murphy had her sitting at the kitchen table with a chicken salad sandwich and a glass of fruit juice. It didn't take Haylee long to get over her anxiety. After eating the sandwich and writing her first check for rent, she set about unloading her car.

Her upstairs room was furnished simply with a double bed and a bureau. The curtains and the bedspread both had a spring flower design that gave the room a cheery feel. It suited her. It was simple and functional.

When she had everything arranged the way she wanted it, Haylee took a few minutes to gaze out the window. Just over the rooftops, she could see the huge eucalyptus trees on campus. Directly under her window was a tiny backyard. It was overflowing with plants. Some of them looked like herbs. Woven through the hodgepodge of vegetation was a brick path. Haylee thought that it was utterly charming; she looked forward to spending sunny afternoons there, reading and soaking up the ambience of the place. With a satisfied nod, she also acknowledged that it would offer many hiding places in the dark.

A tremor traveled through her. She closed her eyes while it completed its cycle. It was insistent but not overwhelming… yet. Haylee had some time left before she must venture out to hunt.

Taking a deep breath, she headed for the door. She wanted to orient herself to her surroundings and to her hunting grounds.

Haylee drove to the campus and walked around. She was glad that she had several months before classes started. It would give her time to get to know the area before she had to bury her head in the books.

She stopped at an outdoor cafe and ordered a yogurt smoothie. She liked the organic feel of the place. The waiter was tall and slim. He had thick, curly, light brown hair, big blue eyes, and glasses. After taking her order, he waited the other tables but she noticed that his gaze kept returning to her. He sat down at her table when he returned with her drink. At her look of surprise, he said, "You don't mind, do you?" His grin was disarming. "I can always tell when someone first moves to town. They look lost until they've been immersed in the culture for a while."

Haylee smiled indulgently. She leaned back in her chair

crossing her arms over her chest. "And what exactly might that culture be?"

"One of brotherly love and peace, baby." His voice was soft; he looked sincere and friendly.

Haylee laughed. "What decade did you come from?"

"This one—but I sure miss the 60s."

"You're not old enough to remember the 60s!"

"OK. So the 60s thing isn't going to work with you. What does a guy have to do to get acquainted?" he wanted to know.

"Saying 'hello' might be a good start."

With a wide grin, he leaned over the table and held out his hand. "Hello, my name is Josh. What's yours?"

She regarded him for a few moments. Reaching out, she firmly shook his hand, saying, "Haylee. Nice to meet you, Josh. What makes you think that I just moved here? Maybe I'm a tourist just passing through."

"Ah ha. The woman questions my deductive abilities. I like that." He winked. "Observations: many tourists travel in groups and speak with accents. A lot of them wear clothing with San Francisco scrolled across it because they always go there first. And they love it when I talk like a hippy." He shrugged his shoulders. "Since you exhibit none of the above, I deduce that you must be a student. I guessed that you just moved here—you are here earlier than most newbies, but that probably means that you are an over-achiever....am I right?"

She liked his outspokenness. Giving him a sly look, she nodded, "So the hippy talk was a 'tourist vs. student' test?"

He laughed. "You're a quick one!"

"What's your major and what year are you?"

He laughed again. "So she has deductive powers of her own!" He leaned his elbows on the table. "Philosophy and grad student." He was about to ask what her major was when one of the servers passing by told him that his other customers were starting to get annoyed. Giving Haylee an apologetic look, he got up. "I'll be back." He winked before leaving.

The smile she'd worn at the cafe was still on her face as she drove back to her place. Her dad was right. It wasn't going to take long to meet new people. She'd only been here a few hours and already she knew one person! Another tremor hit then, wiping her smile away.

~ ~ ~ ~

By the time Haylee made it back to her room, she was angry and frustrated. She had to stop stealing souls! Whenever she relaxed, she could clearly remember each and every victim, their thoughts and feelings. She paced around her room. At home, she had a lot of space to work out her frustrations. Here she was beginning to feel cramped. Although running didn't make the tremors stop, it usually helped to get rid of some of her aggravation. It was almost dark, but she decided to go out anyway.

Sitting on the edge of her bed to tie her shoes, she smiled sadly as she remembered her father and Glori giving her dire warnings about staying inside at night. *They're worried that something will happen to me. What they don't know is that I'm someone people should be afraid of.*

With her mind focused on gaining some kind of release, Haylee trotted down the staircase. Mrs. Murphy saw her. "My dear, you can't possibly be thinking about going out now?"

Haylee whirled around to face the woman, practically growling at her. "I pay my rent here. That gives you the right to talk to me about how I treat your property." She slowly enunciated the next few words. "It does not give you the right to butt into my life!"

Wide-eyed, Mrs. Murphy put one hand to hand to her throat and patted her hair with the other replying, "Quite."

Haylee hadn't meant to snap at the woman. She softened her tone. "Thank you, Mrs. Murphy." Without another word, she made a hasty exit.

The ocean breeze felt cold at first, but as Haylee worked up a sweat, it was exhilarating. She berated herself for being cross with the landlady. Then, after a little more thought, she realized that it was probably good to make sure that the woman didn't get too snoopy about her comings and goings. By the time Haylee was ready for a break, she wasn't sure how far she had gone. Spotting a park, she jogged over to a bench, flopping down onto it. Immediately a violent tremor shook her body. Through chattering teeth, Haylee uttered, "Shhiiitt!"

When it was over, she slumped down, laying her arms out across the back of the bench and letting her head hang back so she could look up at the night sky. Closing her eyes, she realized that she must feed, and soon. She couldn't afford to have the tremors hit her while she was trying to do her job.

Her keen ears picked up the sound of someone shuffling through the park. The sound stopped. She sensed that she had been spotted. The footsteps began scuffling in her direction. Haylee sat up straight, moving her head so she could see her visitor coming toward her.

Not saying a word, the man walked over and stood looking down at her. He appeared to be in his thirties. His only clothing was sweatpants and sandals. Dirty-blond hair hung limply around his shoulders. He had a long, frizzy beard. He had a slender build with a slight paunch around the waistline. Light-colored hair covered his chest, stomach, and shoulders; he reeked of body odor.

Nodding his head, he sat down next to Haylee. She watched his eyes dart back and forth as if he were afraid some- one would see them together. She smiled seductively, turning toward him, ready to play his game. She couldn't believe her good luck.

After gazing into her eyes for a long time, the nameless man reached out, putting his hand on her shoulder in an attempt to draw her toward him. She complied until her face was just inches from his, then she swiftly stood up, grabbing a hold of his hand as she did so. He seemed startled by her movement, possibly even a little angry. "Come on," she coaxed quietly, "I have something special for you."

Haylee led him to a clump of bushes nearby. He seemed pleased with her actions. She ducked low, pulled the branches aside, and went in. He followed.

If there had been any passersby, they would have heard a faint —*thwap* followed by a rustling of the branches before all of the sounds of the night returned to normal.

Haylee came out a few minutes later wearing a pleased smile and brushing dirt off her clothes. She stretched, feeling relaxed and satisfied. She sniffed the air and frowned. Bringing her hands to her face, she wrinkled her nose. Glancing around, she spotted a drinking fountain. After washing her hands and wiping them on her socks, she started her run back home.

Haylee now knew that his name was Frank Wheaton. Mr. Wheaton had made a habit of taking advantage of vulnerable people—in unusual and cruel ways. A look of revulsion passed over Haylee's face as she saw more of his twisted thoughts and deeds.

⚜30⚜

WORKING GIRL

During the next week, Haylee started her summer job. The woman who usually worked in the front office was out sick. That left only the Doctor and his assistant, Deanna. After a few cursory instructions from Dr. Jamison, Haylee was given the front office.

The first hour had gone well. Patients came in slowly. Haylee was able to find their files and put them in exam rooms in an orderly fashion. But all of a sudden, it seemed like the little waiting room was swamped with animals and people. A maine coon cat got loose from its owner at the same time as a fox terrier. Pandemonium broke loose. The terrier went after the cat, and all of the other dogs in the waiting room and in the holding pens started barking. Everyone who had carried in their cats had to struggle to keep a hold on them.

She knew that Doctor Jamison and Deanna were in the middle of an operation and couldn't help. Throwing her files down, Haylee rushed out from behind the counter only to slip and fall in a puddle on the floor. A man with a boa constrictor wrapped around his neck rushed over to help her up. Laughing, he yelled to be heard over the din. "The nice thing about owning a snake is that they didn't bark or scratch."

Mortified with her predicament, Haylee got up, determined to bring some order to the waiting room. She yelled at everyone still in possession of their pets to wait outside. She stood guard at the door to make sure that the loose animals didn't get out. Once the room was cleared, she asked the hysterical cat owner to go outside too. The only ones left in the room were the snarling cat on top of a file cabinet, the barking dog, and the dog's owner. Haylee ran to get a pet carrier. When she tried to retrieve the cat, the furious animal snarled and raked its claws across her arm, drawing blood.

Unmindful of her injuries and upset with herself, Haylee grabbed a blanket, threw it over the cat, bundled it up, and stuffed the hissing, spitting creature into the empty pet carrier. With that done, she told the shocked terrier owner to grab her dog. Haylee picked up the cat in the box and took it to its owner. The woman accepting the cat looked at Haylee's scratch marks. "Oh my goodness! Did my Charley do that?"

Haylee scowled at the woman. "Next time Charley comes in, make sure he is in a carrier."

Meanwhile the terrier owner had collected his animal and joined the others outside.

Haylee then addressed the group of gawking pet owners. "Everyone has to stay outside for a few more minutes until I get the waiting room cleaned up. I'll bring out more boxes. Uncontained pets will not be allowed back inside the building." No one said a word.

Haylee walked back into the office, closed the door behind her, and surveyed the waiting room. Chairs were toppled, magazines were strewn all about, the files on her desk were hopelessly messed up, and there were several puddles on the floor. Haylee looked at her arm as she started to feel the pain from her injuries. Calmly, she grabbed some of the doctor's clean operating clothes and some alcohol and went in the bathroom.

She regarded the haggard look on her face in the mirror. As she started to remove her soiled clothing, she began to cry. She was sure that she would get fired; her whole career would be ruined! She sniffed loudly as she got into the clean clothes. When she dabbed the alcohol onto her wounds, she cried harder because it stung so bad. Finishing up, she wadded up a bunch of toilet paper so she could blow her nose, then started to laugh as she pictured herself slipping and falling in the puppy puddle in front of all the patients.

Feeling much better, she set about cleaning up the waiting room, taking pet carrier boxes outside, and sifting through the mess of files. One by one, the patients came back inside. The atmosphere was subdued, almost quiet. By the time the doctor was ready to see more patients, Haylee had everything back under control.

Once the day was done, he took Haylee into his office so he could look at her scratches. "You did a fine job cleaning and dressing your wounds, Haylee. I must apologize for throwing you to the wolves this afternoon. I didn't expect to be quite so short staffed."

She breathed a sigh of relief. "I thought for sure that you would ask me not to come back tomorrow."

"On the contrary, I am impressed with how you handled yourself and our waiting room fiasco. I would be disappointed if you decided not to come back."

They smiled their understanding to each other.

Haylee was exhausted, but after her talk with the doctor, she was looking forward to giving it another try.

In the next few weeks, Haylee grew comfortable with her job and her surroundings. She made the acquaintance of several of her fellow boarders; they were students like her.

Although she enjoyed even the limited contact that she allowed herself, she kept everyone at arm's length. She couldn't risk anyone finding out about her secret, nor did she want to grow close to someone whom she might hurt. It was sad because Haylee finally had people around her who weren't intimidated by her intelligence and genuinely wanted to get to know her. She desperately wished she had someone to talk to and confide in, but it wasn't possible.

Every now and then, she went back to visit Josh at the smoothie cafe, but she refused to engage with him beyond his place of work.

Haylee liked Josh. He told funny stories about his customers. She thought that he would be safe from her if she didn't give him any information about herself. They would talk about school and childhood experiences, but Haylee wouldn't tell him where she'd grown up or even her last name. Because she was a mystery, he seemed to want to pursue her even more. He tried to guess things about her, but she would neither acknowledge nor deny them. Her only response was a beguiling smile. Haylee knew Josh intended to find out more about her once classes started.

By the end of summer, she almost trusted Josh. If there was anyone in the world whom she thought she might be able to talk to, it was him.

Lately, she started worrying about stealing the souls of those closest to her. She would wake up at night, drenched with sweat and terrified.

About two weeks before classes were due to commence, Haylee's dreams started to have a different feel to them. One dream in particular began repeating.

It always began with Haylee watching her dad kneeling on the floor, crying. Haylee could feel the pain radiating from him. She would go to comfort him. He would pull away from her, as if she had burned him.

Suddenly, Haylee realized that she was the cause of his misery. Turning to escape, she ran down a dark passageway. Her heart beat furiously.

Haylee then found herself in an old town with wooden walkways. She didn't recognize her surroundings. A great roar could be heard in the distance. Smoke filled the air. Animals and people screamed in terror as red, orange flames filled the skyline. She cried out for someone—someone she loved.

Her pillow was always soaked with tears; she felt desolate and empty. It took a long, long time to get back to sleep afterwards.

31

UNIVERSITY

September, 1985

Haylee talked Dr. Jamison into keeping her on at the office part-time while she was in school. She had progressed from working in the front office handling incoming patients and filing to assisting with examinations and first aid. She felt a great sense of accomplishment when she sent pets home well and happy.

The doctor was appreciative of her ability to calm frightened animals and to relay unusual information about them that almost always led to better treatments. When he questioned her about it, Haylee would look at him, smile, and then shrug her shoulders.

There was a chill in the fall air as Haylee made her way to her Introduction to Philosophy class. She was excited about most of her courses. They would be interesting and challenging.

As she walked, she watched other students joking and chatting.

Haylee yearned for friends and people she could fit in

with. She wished for the freedom to laugh, relax, and have fun, to be just a normal college student with nothing to worry about other than getting good grades.

At times like this, a deep sadness would seep its inky way into her consciousness. *Why am I even bothering with school? I could easily disappear and practically no one would notice that I was missing. I could live on the fringes of society, targeting victims with fat wallets, and have no personal connection with another living soul. It would be easier than what I am doing now. What would become of me if I gave into that? Would I become an animal taking down prey when the need arises?*

When she reached low points in her mental gyrations, Haylee's inner strength and resolve would rise up to keep her focused. *No! I have to stop thinking that way. My mom had her heart set on my attending her alma mater. If I can find a way to fix this thing, I still have to have a life I can resume. It's best to be in a big city so that I can keep my family safe and still get what I need…when I have to… until I can figure out how to stop it.*

Haylee's eyes followed the group of students laughing and giving each other playful nudges. She also noticed the appreciative glances she received from assessing males. To those, her only response was to watch her feet as she trod resolutely toward her next destination.

Haylee sat through class, anticipating the return of her first quiz. She was sure she'd done well on it. The professor announced that his teaching assistant would be conducting the bulk of the lessons and coursework during the semester. When the assistant walked through the side door to join the professor, Haylee's heart stopped; she dropped her pencil. "Class, this is Joshua Herkowitz," announced the professor. "He will be grading all of the papers and class assignments. At the end of the semester, he and I will go over your scores and I will assign your final grades." He nodded to the class and promptly left the room.

Smiling, Josh searched the room until he found Haylee. He directed his comment to the class, but his eyes never left her. "When I call your name, come up and get your paper. If you are happy with your grade, you can leave. Otherwise, you can talk to me after class. I do need to tell you, however, that if you argue with me and I find no validity to your argument, I will be deducting points."

With this last sentence, he scanned the faces before him, satisfied that his message had gotten across.

Haylee squirmed in her seat. Until this moment, she had been fairly confident that she would never run into Josh on campus. After all, he was a graduate student and she was a freshman. She realized that as a teacher's aide, he had access to information about her that she preferred he not know. She smiled at her own naivety. She remembered how Josh had casually advised her to take Introduction to Philosophy. If she knew anything about him, it was that he always had a point to make or a goal in mind. By purposefully evading his questions about her, she had given him a challenge that he couldn't resist. Most of the students were gone by the time she reconciled herself to the circumstance. *So now he knows my last name and where I live. Big deal! That doesn't mean anything. I'll still be able to keep him at arm's length.*

The room was virtually empty when Josh held up the last paper and said very slowly, "Haylee Louise Garrett."

She continued to sit in her chair with an elbow propped up on the desk. Her chin rested in her upturned palm. The name she'd written on the paper was H. Garrett. She raised an eyebrow, "Touché, Josh."

He returned her smile. "I had to work so hard just to learn your last name. I wonder how difficult it will be to find out your other secrets?"

Haylee's body froze. A hard, almost cruel look transformed her face, but passed quickly. Haylee stood up stiffly and
walked toward him. "If you know what's good for you, you'll
cut the curiosity," she stated harshly. "There are reasons that I
do what I do. It's not a game!" She snatched the paper from his
hand. Trying to ignore the confused and wounded look on his
face, she stomped out of the auditorium without looking back.

❧32❧

HUNTING

November 1985

The room she always thought seemed so cozy now appeared brash. To Haylee, the colors looked out of proportion and ran together. A low growl emanated from her. Her pupils were dilated; she kept her eyelids half closed to reduce the painful glare from the light. It was dusk, but as far as Haylee was concerned, dark would be too long in coming.

She wiggled into her short, black leather skirt and slipped on the matching jacket, zipping it up only three quarters of the way to display cleavage. She viciously raked a brush through her hair until it was voluminous and bouncy. She looked in the mirror, satisfied with her appearance. Haylee then applied glossy, red lipstick to her full lips. The last touch was to put on spiked heels.

They clicked across the floor as she paced. She was wound up so tight, she kept flexing her hands to keep them from cramping. A sheen of cold sweat covered her body as the violent tremors struck her every few minutes.

She had always been so concerned about not being seen in these provocative clothes. Today, none of it mattered. Her hunger was voracious; it was the only thought in her mind. Her only desire was to sate it.

Haylee stood by her window, pulling back the curtains so she could scan the street. She let out a long sigh. "At last!" she muttered triumphantly. Her window opened outward easily. With fluid movements, she leaped out onto the roof. Her sense of balance and strength didn't even register in her mind...it just was.

~ ~ ~ ~

As the day gave way to night, Josh walked on the sidewalk heading toward Haylee's house, looking at the address numbers as he went. He'd memorized it weeks ago. Something just didn't add up with her. He was determined to figure out what it was.

When he was a couple of houses away from Haylee's, Josh happened to glance up and catch a movement on a nearby rooftop. His hair stood on end as he watched the spot where he thought he'd seen something. As a rabbit freezes in place when it's in the sights of a predator, a survival instinct warned him that if he stayed out in the open, he would be in mortal danger. As quickly and quietly as he could, he stepped behind a nearby hedge and held his breath.

~ ~ ~ ~

Haylee stood on the roof for a moment, completely still. Her eyes scrutinized the surroundings. Almost as if she were sniffing the air, her head turned in the direction of the street. In an effortless movement, she jumped from the roof to the ground.

~ ~ ~ ~

Josh's eyes grew wide as he watched her approach his position. His breath caught in his throat as he surveyed the clothes she was wearing…and the gorgeous body they revealed. His sweet Haylee looked anything but sweet at the moment. *I didn't know it was possible to feel sexually aroused and scared shitless simultaneously,* he thought. He knew that his very life depended on being as quiet and still as humanly possible. His heart thudded so hard that he was sure it could be heard from across the street.

Click, click, click, click. The sound of her heels echoed down the street. As she neared Josh's position, Haylee's pace faltered. Suddenly, she stopped and became perfectly still.

He could see her clearly now, a lethal and beautiful animal poised in the moonlight ready to strike. He couldn't breathe as he gazed at her. *Oh my God! What's happened to her?*

Her head turned in his direction, as if she'd heard his thoughts. Her movements were quick and mechanical.

Fear like he'd never known coursed like ice through his veins. He held himself rigid, not daring to breathe. It seemed like he stayed that way for an eternity, when in reality it was only a few seconds.

As suddenly as she stopped, Haylee continued down the walkway. Click, click, click, click.

The sound echoed in his mind long after it was gone. Sick inside, Josh slowly came out from behind the bush. He was having trouble taking a full breath. For the first time in his life, his mind was a total blank. As some semblance of normalcy returned, Josh realized that his pants were warm and wet.

~ ~ ~ ~

The November night was clear and crisp. About four blocks from her home, Haylee stopped under a street light. She should have been cold dressed the way she was, but her body was covered with perspiration. She looked so hot that steam practically exuded from the pores of her skin. She stood in the light for a moment with hands propped on her hips, tapping one of her toes. The look in her eyes was hard and calculating. No trace of the compassionate, empathetic Haylee could be found there.

~ ~ ~ ~

Josh wasn't sure why he was following Haylee. Every fiber in his body told him to get as far away from her as possible. But once he got his wits about him, he was too curious to just let her go. He sensed that this was why she always kept to herself. He was amazed at her ability to move so swiftly and fluidly. He had to watch closely to see which direction she headed because once she was on the move, he couldn't keep track of her. He observed from afar, then when she moved, he would run as fast as he could to where he last saw her and hope to gain another glimpse. He was frightened to lose her because then he'd really be in trouble.

The way she was dressed would make any man ache with desire. Josh had found her incredibly attractive before, but now she was… He was at a loss for words, which was a new experience.

~ ~ ~ ~

Haylee knew that if she headed for the main drag, she would be able to satisfy her hunger. But it was too risky. Although she was starving and practically radiating with tension, a sense of self-preservation prevented her from going into a well-lit and populated area. She had to keep to the side streets. With a flash, she was off.

Like a piece of cloth being blown by the wind, Haylee rounded the corner of a brick building, flattening herself against its wall. Spotting potential prey, she quivered with anticipation. Haylee watched a young man standing at a bus stop. He looked strong. He wore coveralls like an auto mechanic would wear and shuffled his feet. He kept bringing his hands up to his face to warm them with his breath.

When he felt a hand on his shoulder, he whirled around to see who had the audacity to invade his personal space. Surprise, as he beheld the beauty, left him speechless.

The name tag on his coveralls read "Stan." Haylee stood with one finely molded leg out before her. Stan's eyes were drawn to it before working their way up to her chest where it lingered at her exposed breasts. Hands at her hips, she slid them down toward the hem of her skirt. Stan's obedient gaze followed where she led. Haylee began to slowly inch it upwards. His eyes widened in wonder. Then he smiled in a knowing way. "Fer sure, you're bitchin', bimbette." Stan nodded vigorously. "My joystick would love nothing better than to take you for a nice long ride...but I got no cash on hand." He pulled out his empty pockets to show her.

Haylee smiled. "I might be willing to trade..." she whispered. Her hand lightly caressed a breast then dipped her thumb down between them. Appearing to be lost in thought, Haylee flicked a fingernail repeatedly over her jacket zipper.

Stan gulped audibly. His eyes zeroed in on her finger and breasts. He bit on his lower lip as if that pinch would remind him to keep from grabbing what he wanted.

Haylee's eyes lowered to the bulge in his pants.

"What do you want?" he croaked.

Haylee smiled triumphantly. "I'll tell you after...."

He lunged forward, closing his eyes as he clutched the firm roundness. In a flash, there was a soft —*thwap*! Stan's eyes flew open in time to see a webbed hand with fingers spread wide rushing at his face. It was clamped tightly over his mouth and nose before he could react. He struggled, but Haylee was too strong and she dragged him into a deserted corner of the bus stop shelter. He held fast to her arm and resisted with all of his might, but it was not enough. Stan's spirit was lost even before his fighting ceased.

Haylee stood up and tugged down her skirt. She dusted her hands off against each other. With a contented smile, she regarded his vacant eyes. "Thanks, Stan." She turned to walk away.

~ ~ ~ ~

Josh arrived just in time to hear the sounds of a struggle followed by a feminine sigh a few minutes later. He ducked farther into his hiding place as Haylee emerged from the shelter, adjusting her skirt. Something about her seemed different. She was more relaxed now, less frantic. Even though she seemed more like her usual self, Josh knew he should stay hidden. Once she was out of sight, he quietly slipped over to where she had been.

It was so quiet, he was surprised to find anyone inside. Josh was shocked by the sight before him. Like a forgotten doll, a young man lay unmoving, propped up on the interior bench, staring lifelessly at nothing. Upon closer inspection, Josh realized that the boy was still alive. His eyes were open, but there was no consciousness in them. Josh read the man's name patch as he patted his face in an attempt to bring him around.

Realizing that it was no use, and with Haylee getting further away with every passing moment, he raced over to a nearby pay phone to call an ambulance. He hung up and went back to Stan. That vacant look in his eyes was deeply disturbing. Josh removed his coat and placed it over him. "Haylee, what have you done?" he whispered. Knowing that the ambulance would arrive shortly, Josh turned in the direction Haylee had taken and left to pursue his frightening, sexy, and bewildering surveillance subject.

Haylee strolled down the street at a leisurely pace. Stan had been satisfying. He was young and healthy and had put up a decent fight. The struggle heightened the experience for her. The harder they fought, the better it was. Laughing softly at her train of thought, she reached up to run her fingers through her hair. After feeding, she usually felt overwhelmingly sated, but this time her satisfaction wasn't as intense as it usually was. As a matter of fact, she was still hungry! As this realization came to her, a small tremor traveled down the length of her spine. In her current mood, the idea of continuing to hunt did not bother her at all.

She flexed her hands, then flicked them—*thwap*! Holding them up, she thought her webs looked beautiful in the moon-light. The soft glow from the streetlights brought out their iridescence.

She heard what she thought was the sound of footsteps behind her in the distance. Her body became tense and still. All of her senses were on alert. She was ready to find her second course. She waited. Maybe it was just wishful thinking. Off to her left, another sound caught her attention. Her head turned in that direction as she listened intently. Someone was whistling. She broke into a grin and licked her lips. With a burst of energy, she was off in a flash.

~ ~ ~ ~

Haylee moved swiftly down the street of old houses. It was late; lights were on in windows here and there, but mostly the city slept. To keep her heels quiet, she ran across the front lawns. She was so sure-footed and lithe that she hardly noticed her shoes. Around her, she registered many sounds: those of the night creatures, people moving around inside the houses, and someone attempting to follow her. At this moment, her focus was on the whistling she was traveling toward. Another sound accompanied the whistle—a guitar playing softly.

Reaching her destination, Haylee crouched in the shrub-bery across the street to assess the situation. It looked like a frat house. Two men were sitting on an old couch on the front porch. The one on the left had black, shoulder-length hair. He was solidly built and muscular. The man on the right had a medium build with straight red hair and a beard. Their medley stopped briefly. She saw the flame of a lighter and a small cherry red glow as the smoker inhaled. The guy who first lit up passed it to his companion. Haylee caught the unusual scent. They were smoking pot. *Good! Their defenses will be down!* Realizing that she would have to deal with both of them, she almost changed her mind; she usually liked to take her victims one-on-one. Smil-ing, a thrill ran through her at this new challenge and test of her skills—*two at once!*

They resumed their mini concert, one playing the guitar and the other whistling. Neither one of them were prepared to see the woman spring up out of nowhere to land on the porch in front of them. Startled, they jumped; their mouths hung open at the sight. She stood there, legs spread wide, hands resting on her hips, cleavage clearly visible and pressing tightly against the zipper of her leather jacket. She smiled seductively, raised one eyebrow, and shook her head so her dark locks swished around her shoulders. In a low whispery voice she spoke, "I am a spirit of the night; half woman, half animal. You've conjured me up with your music. If you play for me, I'll make your wildest dreams come true."

It took them a moment to respond. Haylee was somewhat relieved to see their dilated pupils and delayed reactions. She hoped they weren't so out of it that they wouldn't fight for their lives when it was time.

The guitar guy finally blurted out, "No shit?"

She merely looked at him and nodded. With a raised

eyebrow, she made eye contact with the silent whistler. He was built like a football player. Mentally she rubbed her hands together in glee.

"Bob, I don't know if I can whistle," he muttered under his breath, glancing at his partner. "This chick is so frickin hot, my mouth has gone dry."

"You do it, or I promise you, Tom, I'll beat the crap out of you!" Bob repositioned his guitar and began playing "Stairway to Heaven." When Tom didn't pick up the tune, Bob elbowed him in the ribs. Focusing on Haylee's shoes, Tom started to whistle.

Her right foot tapped to the rhythm, then her other one joined in. Her hips swayed and soon her whole body swayed in time with the music.

The men's eyes locked on her. Haylee kicked off her shoes and inched in close. She danced facing them, then turned around to let their eyes feast on the rest of her charms. She moved her arms fluidly until they were above her head. In one quick movement, she swung her arms down—*thwap!*—and turned to face them.

The music stopped as they stared in shock at her hands.

Displaying them, she spread her fingers wide, "Pretty, aren't they?" In one swift movement, she fell on one knee between them. Simultaneously, she clamped her hands over their faces.

Eyes bulging, it took them a moment to register what was happening. Then the struggle began. Her victims' first response was usually to try to rip the suffocating object from their faces; these two were no exception.

A surge of elation traveled through Haylee; power pulsated though her body as she pushed her captives deeper into the couch. Arching her back, her eyes glittered dangerously. "Yessss, that's it. Fight me!" she hissed.

The one who looked like a football player, Tom, must have taken her words to heart, for as soon as she uttered them, his hands left his face, balled up into fists, and began pounding her body with painful blows. He hit her in the ribs and on the back. Once he almost struck her in the face, but she saw it coming and jerked out of the way.

The surprise almost caused her to lose the upper hand, but almost doesn't count in a battle for life and death. With fire in her eyes and expletives on her lips, she clamped down harder. She tensed her body to take his blows. On the other side, Bob was almost done for, but Tom fought on. Haylee realized that the next few moments would be tricky; she had to make sure that the moment Bob accepted death she could pull him back so that their final surrender would happen at the same time.

Making a quick decision, she eased up on Bob, giving his burning lungs a small sip of air. As she did this, she pushed down harder on Tom. Finally, his body went limp under her. Equalizing the pressure on both of them, she brought them to the brink of death together. Ruthlessly, Haylee led them into the void, the dark place where they would spend the rest of their lives.

The skin on her entire body radiated with a molten heat. A deep sigh escaped her. "Aaahhhhh, that was so gooood!" After a moment, she slid her hands down their faces to their chests. Pushing herself back, she looked at their blank expressions. Drawing in a deep breath, she spoke as she exhaled, "I can honestly say you were the best I've ever had." She reached over to turn Tom's face toward her. "Thank you." She leaned down to press a light kiss onto his unresponsive lips. The webs on her hand caught the light as she moved.

~ ~ ~ ~

Still in the bushes across the street, Josh couldn't believe what he was seeing. In his wildest dreams, he never imagined that anything as bizarre as this could exist in the world. He had read all of the classic novels—Frankenstein and Dracula—and had even taken a few classes in mythology. He always thought that ignorance and fear were the primary reasons that people throughout history believed in monsters. *This is the stuff of fiction, right?* his mind screamed.

Haylee sat down between the two men on the couch, shoving the limp bodies around until she had them situated the way she wanted. Then she leaned her head on one man's chest and tucked her feet under the other man's leg, looking like she was preparing to take a nap. *How could she do what she just did to those two guys, then curl up and sleep on them?* He would have laughed hysterically if he hadn't known that it would mean a death sentence. Josh hunkered down. He knew he was trapped there until she was on the move again.

While he waited, his overloaded brain attempted to sort things out. He had a hard time reconciling the Haylee he'd known all summer to the fiendish creature he'd been following all the night.

He remembered the day she had acted so defensively when he'd teased her about figuring out her last name and wondering what other secrets she kept. Her reactions had been more than just defensive; they'd been primitive. He remembered his fleeting feelings of fear. He hadn't known then just what she was capable of.

Most perplexing of all had been the fact that she kept coming by the cafe even though she had told him to stay away from her. Whenever they'd begin debating any subject, she would liven up and become animated. She told him once that he was the closest thing to a friend that she had.

A shudder passed through him when he thought about what could have happened if he had been able to convince her to go out with him. Of course, he would have wanted to take her to a dark secluded spot somewhere. *Ahh, but what a way to go,* he thought with morbid humor.

He came out of his thoughts as he saw Haylee stir from her brief nap. She straightened out one arm and then the next. A shapely leg stretched out, followed by the other. Gingerly she stood up.

She glanced down at the two men with a blank, unemotional expression. Feeling sick, Josh watched Haylee disappear inside the large house. He knew she was looking for more victims. Making no move to leave his hiding place, he waited. He wondered how many more would fall before she was finished. About twenty minutes later, he saw her come around from the back of the house. She walked up the front steps to collect her shoes. Carrying one in each hand, she stopped at the edge of the sidewalk. It was lighter now and he could see her clearly. When she was directly across from him, she stopped and appeared to sniff the air. The hair all over his body stood on end. After a moment, she put one shoe under her arm while raising a hand to cover her mouth while she yawned. She zipped her jacket up all the way. Casually, she slipped on her shoes.

Josh heard her moving down the street. Click, click, click, click.

❧33❧

DISCOVERED

When Haylee arrived back at her boarding house, the morning light was still dim and the shadows were long. Haylee kept to the shadows just in case anyone was out and about. Although tired, she cleared the back fence easily. She lingered, crouching in the waist-high bushes as she studied the house while listening for movements within. Someone was up, but they were in the kitchen downstairs. Staying low, she crept over to a side wall where she grabbed a drainpipe and effortlessly scaled the wall to her second-story window.

It was a relief to finally be home. Stripping off her leathers, she wrinkled her nose at the smell that emanated from them. Leather was not the best material to wear when you did a lot of physical activity. She decided that this outfit had been on its last outing. Haylee crawled in bed. She was too tired to even think about showering. With a sigh, she shook her head from side to side, as she thought, *Josh, you are the smartest idiot that I know... what am I going to do about you now?* A single tear rolled down the side of her face and soaked into the pillow that cradled her head.

When Haylee woke after a few hours, she didn't feel rested at all. The dream of her father had come to her again; this time it was more vivid than it had ever been. Fear coursed through her veins. "I'll kill myself before I do anything that will hurt my father!"

Her mouth tasted terrible and she felt groggy. Even after a shower, Haylee didn't feel refreshed. One look in the mirror confirmed that her outward appearance matched how she felt. She was extremely pale, and she had dark rings under her eyes. While she brushed her teeth, she thought about the night before. Five! She'd consumed five souls in one night! That was more than she had consumed all last year. She was revolted by her own actions. Closing her eyes for any length of time made the jumble of thoughts and feelings from her victims seem louder inside her head. *What happened last night? I can't go on this way! Somehow, I have to stop this!*

She froze as the memory of Josh came up. He'd dogged her all night. *Now somebody knows.* The idea of taking him out caused her to dry heave over her sink.

Haylee pulled her hair back into a single ponytail and dressed in dark, baggy clothes. She only had one class this afternoon, then she was supposed to head home for Thanksgiving break. She was worried about that because she had crossed a boundary last night. Her victims, in the past, had been menaces; there had seemed to be some morality in ending their lecherous pursuits. She had been confident that when she felt the tremors increasing in frequency, she'd have enough time to plan a hunting excursion. Now she was afraid that she didn't have control anymore. Everyone she'd taken last night had been a good person. There was not one speck of morality in what she'd done.

Haylee sat in her statistics class only half listening to the lecture. All of a sudden, she sat up straighter. In that moment, it dawned on her that she needed to get back into her mother's things to retrieve something she'd seen in there.

For weeks, she'd been laboriously thinking through every aspect of her life and those of her parents in an attempt to figure out what this thing was, and more importantly, how to stop it. She'd concluded that her mother had to be connected because of some of the unusual things she'd said.

Haylee rushed across campus, weaving between the people in the crowd. From out of nowhere, a hand reached out and grabbed her elbow. Spinning around, she came face to face with Josh. "Haylee, I've got to talk to you," he said gravely.

~ ~ ~ ~

Josh observed that she wore no makeup, and her skin was pale and drawn. In her severity, Haylee still didn't look plain; even her forlorn, exotic beauty held an allure for him. He forcefully squelched those disturbing perceptions.

For a moment, they stood facing each other in tense silence. Both of them attempted to quiet tumultuous thoughts. They had been acquaintances, almost friends, and Josh had wanted much more than that...but now they regarded one another as adversaries.

He was well aware that he could easily end up like any one of her victims. He wasn't sure how to handle the situation. He only knew that he had to try to stop her.

He looked at Haylee now and wondered why he had remained safe. The realization dawned on him that maybe she kept him at a distance to protect him. "I don't know what you've done..."

"Not now, Josh! I've got something that I have to do."

An eerie stillness came over her; her nostrils flared. Under her statue-like scrutiny, all of the color drained from Josh's face. His mouth went dry. He watched the primitive, elemental side of her focus in on him and prepare to wipe out the danger he represented. His heart raced. Every hair on his body stood at attention. He shivered as he felt, more than saw, every fiber of her body lean closer to him. He hoped like hell that there really was safety in numbers!

His legs began to tremble and when every instinct screamed at him to run, he held his ground.

Clearly, he witnessed the torment in her eyes and sensed her inner struggle to hold herself in check. This is what kept his feet rooted in place. "You have to stop it," he stated simply and quietly.

With tear-filled eyes that looked huge in her face, Haylee croaked hoarsely, "I wish I could, Josh, but I don't know how!" Her body began to shake with sobs. She brought her hands up to cover her face.

He wasn't sure what kind of reaction he'd expected, but it sure wasn't this. Instinctively he wanted to comfort her, but his logical side warned him to keep his distance. Pushing up his glasses, he waited for what would come next.

Gaining some self-control, Haylee rubbed her eyes. In a low voice, she whispered, "You are the only one who knows. You can't possibly hate me more than I hate myself. I don't understand it, but I have been trying to figure out how to stop it."

She looked so distraught and remorseful that he felt sympathy for her. "You know what I always say, Haylee: two minds are greater than one."

"Huh," she muttered under her breath. "What about ten?"

"What?" he asked.

"Never mind."

"Haylee, I want to help. Will you trust me enough to see if that's possible?"

She nodded. "OK, but not here." She started to leave, then

turned back when he didn't budge. He could see the hurt that his indecision caused her on her face and thought, *If she's willing to trust me with the truth, I have to trust her in return.* He followed.

~ ~ ~ ~

They went to his apartment above the cafe. As they walked in, Haylee surveyed his sparse, utilitarian decor. A few beanbags and pillows were the only pieces of furniture in the living room. Indicating the kitchen table, Josh invited her to sit. Setting her pack down, she took a seat but continued to fidget nervously.

Noting her agitation, Josh raised an eyebrow. For a moment, they regarded each other in silence. Both were uncertain how this would go. Finally, Josh broke the tension by joining her at the table. "OK, spill it."

She stood and began to pace quickly back and forth across his small living room space. "Josh, I know what I do is a terrible thing—"

"What do you mean, 'What I do?' Are you saying that you do that on a regular basis?!" He stood up too. Crossing his arms over his chest, he kept his eyes on her…and maintained a healthy distance.

"No!" she yelled. Taking a deep breath, she continued. "I mean, yes, but before it was only one every couple of months. Last night I couldn't stop myself after the first one."

Josh blinked rapidly as he thought, again, about the picture of her curling up to take a nap on those frat boys. Taking a few calming breaths of his own, he tried to tone down the charged atmosphere. "OK, Haylee, one step at a time. How long have you been doing this?"

Suddenly it was like a dam broke open; her story came gushing out. "It started a year ago yesterday…on my birthday."

Josh normally would have offered birthday salutations

upon hearing this news. However; in this case he held his tongue.

"I'd been having this problem of not developing normally...I mean physically." She stopped suddenly, turning a bright shade of red.

"Then everything happened all at once." She glanced down at herself waving her fingers from her neck down to her toes. She looked up at him and he nodded to let her know he understood her meaning. Haylee continued, "My appetite for food was humongous. The more I ate, the stronger I got."

"This guy I had a crush on all through high school took me out on a date...to my first dance." She paused to close her eyes. "His name was Curtis. I always thought that he was a good guy, you know? But he wasn't good. He was a shit. I know that doesn't excuse it, but he was the first one."

Josh would have spoken, but Haylee held up her hand so she could finish. "I don't know how or why I got to be this way. I think my mother may have been connected to it somehow." She grabbed a pendant she wore around her neck. Holding it in her hand, she zipped it from side to side on its chain. "I have to get home to find out if my guess is right."

"Time out, Haylee." He made a 'T' shape with his hands. "Before we go chasing down 'maybes,' let's back up again. Tell me what you do know. What is it that you are doing?" he asked.

She walked over to stand directly in front of him. His heart began beating faster. She flicked her hands out away from her body. Josh heard a soft, muffled —*thwap*!

Sweat broke out on his upper lip as he gazed at the webs between her fingers. He couldn't tear his eyes away. They were gossamer and iridescent. At this close range—which made him extremely nervous—he could see tiny veins running through them. They were pulsating. His mind was fascinated by the sight, but his blood ran cold. He stumbled back a few steps.

Josh's voice quavered when he next spoke. "Alright, you made your point." He stepped even further away. He couldn't think. The webbing was a shocking sight; to have them so close to his face had shaken him to the core.

Seeing him go pale, Haylee flicked the webs away. "I don't want to hurt you Josh. I don't want to hurt anyone. As best as I can describe, what you saw last night was a partial stealing of a soul...or a life force...or energy. Leading up to it, I have fits that build in frequency and intensity over time. I try to resist it for as long as possible, but the longer I do, the harder it is to have any control over the stealing."

Finally finding his voice, Josh asked, "What happens after?"

"After...the shakes go away. I don't feel the need to feed any more. My body feels stronger than normal; I have so much energy. My mind is extremely clear. It feels great, actually." She met his eyes. "I know I've stolen their spirit...or their minds... because after it's over, I have their thoughts inside my head..."

At that, Josh ran into his bathroom to be sick.

~ ~ ~ ~

With certainty, Haylee knew there was nothing Josh could do or say that would change anything. The longer she stayed here the more danger he would be in. In a quick, silent motion, she grabbed her bag and took off.

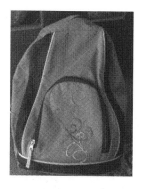

⚜34⚜

DANGEROUS ALLIANCE

He knew it, of course, even though he hadn't even heard the slightest sound as she left. *The question is, do I go after her?*

It took Josh less than two minutes to shove a few clean clothes in his own pack and race down the steps. The fact that it was holiday weekend with traffic snarls would work in his favor.

He caught up to her just as she finished loading her car. Spying him coming toward her, Haylee sighed. "Josh what are you doing here? I appreciate your willingness to try to help, but there isn't anything you can do."

"I'm going with you," he said simply.

"You can't, you'd be too vulnerable."

"The way I see it is this; you already did what you needed to do last night, so you should be good for a while, right?"

Shaking her head from side to side, she said, "I really don't know," she replied. "Maybe."

"We can hash through things on the drive; once we get there, I'll help you look for whatever it is you are searching for."

Haylee stood there gazing at him, tears filling her eyes.

This time, Josh did not hesitate. He closed the gap between them to enfold her in his arms. It felt right to hold her next to him...out in the open.

Later, as they sped down the freeway, Haylee confessed, "I can't guarantee that I can keep my hands off you, Josh." They laughed uneasily at her bad joke. "Seriously, I'll cut you lose at the first hint that things might go wrong. I won't take the chance of hurting my family...or someone I care about."

He digested that quietly, then said, "Well Haylee, if you do it to me, at least you'll know for sure that I'm not a shmuck."

She responded softly, "Oh Josh, I've always known that you are not a schmuck."

~ ~ ~ ~

Gene and Glori were looking forward to Haylee's visit. So much had happened that they wanted to share. They still had their own places but they had decided to change that since they spent most of their time together anyway.

A long weekend trip to Arizona to introduce Eugene to Glori's family had gained him a hearty stamp of approval. Everyone was looking forward to meeting Haylee too, sometime soon.

Glori looked down at the ring finger on her left hand, noticing the sparkles that reflected back in the light. She was so happy she had to pinch herself every once in a while to believe it was all real.

Two weeks ago, Eugene had mysteriously disappeared for a day. Not one to worry or dwell on actions she didn't yet understand, Glori had continued with her routine. At the end of her shift, she'd tiredly walked out of the building. It was then that she'd noticed a limousine parked where she thought she'd left her car. Just as she had started to feel alarmed, Gene had stepped out of the door.

"Your chariot awaits my dear." He had bowed formally and invited her to enter the plush interior.

They had driven for several hours to Calistoga while sipping chilled Champagne and snacking on fruit and chocolate.

Shortly before arriving at their destination, Glori had asked Gene why he'd arranged such a treat. He had kissed her soundly, then casually stated, "Well…I thought I'd wine you and dine you and make love to you all weekend after I ask you this question: Glori Ridgeway, will you do me the great honor of becoming my wife?"

She had screamed, jumped into his arms, and answered that question all weekend long.

~ ~ ~ ~

The tires of Haylee's car crunched on the drive as they parked in front of her house. It was expansive and cluttered with farm equipment. Not far off were the barn and the animal pens. She wondered how it looked to Josh.

Her dad and Glori came out hand in hand. Glori had frosting in her hair and Haylee smiled, knowing she had baked a cake for her nineteenth birthday. Haylee was touched. She was really glad for both her dad and herself that they had Glori in their lives now. Her father saw Josh getting out of the passenger side of Haylee's car and his steps faltered. Glori waved to urge him forward.

Haylee jumped from the car and made a beeline for her father. They exchanged a big hug. He lifted her up off her feet. As Glori stepped in to hug her as well, Haylee said, "You guys, I'd like you to meet Josh. He's a really good friend. He's the graduate student teacher in my philosophy class." Her eyes met Josh's in dismay as she realized that she needed to explain why he was here.

Stepping toward Eugene with hand extended, Josh commented, "It's a pleasure to meet you, Mr. Garrett. When Haylee found out that I was planning to stay on campus during the break, she insisted that I join her. She's been telling me about your walnut operation this last year. I was curious to see it as I have family members in Los Angeles County who work in citrus."

Haylee eyed Josh in amazement. The smug look he returned said, *I have surprises up my sleeve, too.*

Gene barely let Glori say hello before whisking Josh away for a tour. The girls giggled as they commented on Gene's reaction.

Alone for a while, they caught up as they settled in and prepared a place for Josh to sleep. Haylee was thrilled to see Glori's ring and to hear about their plans.

"Is there anything romantic between you and Josh?" Glori asked.

Haylee looked down. "I think he would like there to be…" She hesitated.

"But?"

"I care about him an awful lot, but…I can't let myself think about him that way," Haylee replied.

"Why ever not? He seems like a nice young man and he's clearly gone for you."

"What makes you say that?" Haylee wanted to know.

"Oh honey, it's written all over his face."

Haylee blinked rapidly and suddenly turned pale.

Glori reached out to take her hand. "What's the matter Haylee?"

Haylee had to forcibly stop herself from pulling away. "It's nothing." She stepped back, removing her hand, and fluffed the pillows. "It's complicated."

Glori's brows drew together as she watched Haylee. "You are an intelligent, resourceful young woman. I have faith that whatever it is, you'll solve it."

When the fellas arrived back at the house, they both looked relaxed and at ease in each other's company.

The birthday celebration was a quiet dinner out at Haylee's favorite restaurant followed by cake and ice cream back at the Garrett house.

Gene and Glori placed two small packages in front of Haylee to open. Wearing a smile, Haylee opened the first one. "Oh!" she gasped as she saw the topaz gemstone earrings. Immediately pulling them from the box, she put them on, letting everyone comment on how beautiful they looked.

Josh leaned in to whisper that he was sorry that he didn't have a gift.

"Oh my gosh, Josh, the fact that you are here is a terrific gift! I can't tell you how much it means to have your support... and friendship." They shared a smile.

Opening the next box, Haylee discovered a necklace with a stone that matched the earrings. Feeling quite pleased, she lifted her hair as Glori moved behind her to fasten the clasp.

Suddenly, Haylee was struck with a clear memory of her mom doing exactly the same thing.

They had been about to say goodnight on the eve of her seventh birthday when her mom surprised her with the pendant. As she clasped it onto her daughter's neck, she said, "This necklace is a very old family heirloom, Haylee. It is a tradition in our family to pass it on to our daughters before they turn seven. When you have a daughter of your own, you must remember to give it to her when its time."

"Ewww. I don't want any kids, Mama! What happens if I never have any?" Haylee had asked.

Laughing, her mom replied, "You have a long way to go before you have to worry about that, honey. You can decide what the right thing to do is when you get there."

Josh tagged along with Haylee as she did the animal feeding chores. He was amused to see them so excited by her presence. He listened to her speaking to each of them as if they could understand her. "I can see why Dr. Jamison likes having you around! You're a regular Dr. Doolittle," Josh commented.

As they approached the pigpen, the big mother pig squealed and made a ruckus. At first, Josh thought it was more of the same, but when he saw that the swine was keeping her eyes on him, he was startled.

"She must sense what a good guy I am," Josh joked.

Laughing, Haylee said, "That's not it! You gave her a bite of apple when you met her yesterday. She wants to see if you have another."

All humor died in his Josh's eyes as he stared at her in amazement. The realization of what she had just disclosed wiped the smile off Haylee's face.

"How did you know that?" he asked. "Is this another ability that developed after you turned eighteen?"

"No…I've had this one my entire life."

~ ~ ~ ~

They had the place to themselves. Glori was at work at the hospital and Gene had a meeting at the produce packing plant, so Haylee and Josh decided that the time had come to search the attic.

Haylee had explained about the pendant box and some of the photos that she thought could hold clues.

On their way up the narrow stairs, Josh inquired, "Are you feeling alright?"

Not speaking, she merely nodded in the affirmative.

At first, it was uncomfortable revealing pieces of her history to Josh. Once they got into a rhythm, Haylee realized how much she appreciated having someone to bounce ideas off of.

They knelt together side by side, as she pulled up one photo after another. "All of these people are wearing the pendant that my mother gave me. That has to mean something! I wish she were still here so I could ask her!" she said in frustration.

"Would your dad know anything?" he asked.

"No. All of these people are from my mom's side of the family. She told me that my special abilities came from them and not to talk to my dad about it because he wouldn't understand."

The pendant box was the same as before. It was made out of a beautiful green, blue, and gold material that seemed to be part glass and part stone. After opening it to show him the interior, Haylee handed it to him. Josh ran a finger over the foreign writing on the outside surface. "Do you know what it says?"

"No clue."

"It's too thick for just your necklace." He turned it over to inspect it.

"I know."

"Is there anything in the bottom portion of it? "

"I don't know, I haven't found a way to open it."

Josh asked if she'd tried to break it open. She told him that she had. As far as she could tell, it was unbreakable. They decided to take it with them to try figuring it out later. Haylee put it in her pocket.

"How old were you when your mom died?"

Blinking rapidly, "Seven." Her voice faltered.

Reaching up, Josh rubbed her back. Haylee grew still under his touch. She turned to look at him. Josh ran his hand up behind her neck and applied gentle pressure to bring her closer. Their lips met softly as their eyes closed. The contact sent a wave of warmth through Haylee. When Josh began to open his mouth, she stiffened and pulled away. Josh let his hand drop.

"I'm sorry but I can't…" Haylee apologized with a frown.

Coughing and turning his head away, Josh replied, "I don't know what came over me. That was stupid."

Looking down, Haylee whispered, "Yes."

Josh made a show of straightening his clothes as he stood up. "I think a good use of my time may be doing genealogy research of your mother's side of the family at the library."

Looking sad, Haylee agreed, thanking him again for his efforts.

Listening to Josh trundle down the attic steps, Haylee noticed how the atmosphere had drastically changed. One minute she was feeling hopeful and comfortable and the next she was on the verge of tears and wondering if there were things in the dark corners of the attic that were watching her.

Haylee noticed that the pendant box, resting in her pocket, had started to feel warm. An irritating tingling at the base of her neck made Haylee reach up to scratch at it.

❧35❧

NOO!!

Hours of searching had passed. Tired and frustrated, Haylee was losing patience. She found it especially annoying that the pendant box kept feeling warmer. The itchy feeling on her neck had moved up to her scalp. Reaching up to scratch again, Haylee let out a aggravated, "Arrgh!"

She was about to remove the box from her pocket to see if her body heat had been affecting it, when she was suddenly struck with the idea to locate her pendant.

Racing down to her room, Haylee was dismayed to hear sounds of someone else arriving at the house.

Digging through her drawer, she fished around until she located it. As soon as her fingers touched the necklace, she knew that something was going on. It was as warm as the box!

~ ~ ~ ~

Only 90 miles away, but in the year 1849, another woman paused in her movements. Her voluminous skirt pooled around her as she knelt before the wardrobe to place clean linens in the bottom drawer. As her hand reached inside to shift the contents, an unexpected warmth radiated from within. Her eyes grew wide as cold fear instantly filled her veins. Her breath came in short gasps. She dropped the sheets to the floor then rushed to remove everything from the drawer. With a trembling hand, she clawed at a secret compartment. Inside the small dark space, her fingers groped for a hard object. It fit in the palm of her hand. It was normally cool to the touch, but now it was warm. Blue lights pulsated at regular intervals from within.

Emis reached up to scratch her neck and ears. She remembered when the crystal's call had been hers, how the traveling itself had made her feel like the skin would be burnt from body.

Another wave of fear crashed over her hard, like a giant swell that rose up from a tsunami. "Merde!" she cried. "The Traveler, she comes."

Shaking, she rose to her feet. Clutching the crystal, she began to pace. A different kind of tingle settled over her shoulder blades as images and scenes began to pass in front of her mind's eye. Sometimes the visions were sweet and beautiful; at others, they were disturbing and confusing.

These occurrences were familiar to Emis, as she had had them throughout her life. The one that most called her attention now was of the first variety. It was of a family. The father pushed a small boy on a swing while the redheaded mother stood at the front, grabbing the child's toes. The mother chuckled every time the boy squealed with delight. The woman turned to her husband, and said, "We should go in for lunch, Eugene."

Emis did not know these people. Their clothing and surroundings were strange. As one who has lived a bitter life playing the role of pawn to royals and nobility, Emis forcefully ejected the visions. She would never use her seeing powers ever again!

Her eyes continually strayed to the bottle of gin on her nightstand. I *won't do it. I won't be a part of the Upholders Redemp-*

tion! She'd been making a mighty effort to stop drinking. *I can't let this happen! I refuse!*

Walking with purpose toward the bed, she tossed the offending rock next to the bottle. "Would that I could be finished with you once and for all!" she snarled as she brought the container to her lips, finishing its contents with several large gulps.

~ ~ ~ ~

"Haylee! Are you home?" called Glori.

Cringing because she needed time to process her discovery, Haylee decided to sneak out of the house before Glori discovered her presence. She shoved the necklace into her pocket and felt waves of current reverberate out from her middle. *Not now!* Haylee screamed in her head.

A low oscillating hum started to be noticeable in her ears. Haylee scratched at them in distraction.

Taking a few deep breaths, Haylee attempted to calm herself so she could assess the urgency level of her hunger. She thought she could hold out for a while, but could not risk staying close to her family. Quickly, she grabbed her bag and began to shove things into it.

Glori appeared in her open doorway at the precise moment when another tremor hit. "Hi, Haylee!"

Haylee had sunk to her knees as it rolled through and instantly, Glori was at her side, reaching out to feel Haylee's forehead.

"No!" Haylee swung her arm back to keep Glori away. *Thwap!*

A fierce instinct made Haylee throw Glori to the floor, her webbed hand clamped to Glori's face. Their eyes met.

"Nooo," Haylee cried out again as she attempted to pull her hand back. *This is Glori! I can't do this!* Haylee's arm did not respond to her mental cues.

A muffled cry escaped from Glori as she kicked and clawed at the suffocating appendage blocking her breath. Fear and confusion blazed through her dying gaze.

*I can't...*Haylee thought even as she pressed her hand down more forcefully. I...Haylee closed her eyes; she had to block out the sight.

It was over quickly after that.

Glori's voice exploded in her mind, *Haylee! Stop! Stop! What are you doing? I can't brea—*

Haylee's body tensed as if she'd been physically punched. For self-preservation, she closed her mind so she could no longer hear the voice that she had come to love.

She trembled and stretched. Haylee moved away from her latest victim. Then a deep, unimaginable darkness settled over her as the first icy touches of sorrow made contact with her heart. Grief slid around the smooth contours of that strong, yet tender muscle like cold fingers, clenching and crushing. *Oh my God! Oh my God! I can't have! Glori! Not Glori! No...no...noooooo!*

A constant stream of tears coursed down Haylee's face as she led Glori, moving as if wooden, to her father's bed.

The rhythmic vibrations in her ears grew louder. So much so that Haylee pressed her hands over them to try to block it out. *I can't face him. I can't look in his eyes,* Haylee thought as she imagined the look on her dad's face.

~ ~ ~ ~

Elated with the information he'd collected, Josh was eager to show it to Haylee. He gathered his backpack and the stack of printouts he'd made as he headed toward her front door with lightness in his step.

Finding the Garrett house silent, the hairs at the back of his neck stood on end. He located Haylee in her father's room.

When he saw her sitting next to the bed crying, he sucked in his breath. Glori staring vacantly up at the ceiling could only mean one thing.

Hearing the movement, Haylee turned in his direction. "Josh! I couldn't stop it!" she cried.

The papers he'd been holding floated to the floor. Blazing anger shot through him. "You said that you'd leave if you started to feel anything!"

"I was getting ready to when she surprised me!"

Josh continued to stare at Glori in shock. Out of the corner of his eye, he saw Haylee's body go rigid and begin to shake. "Fuck!" he shrieked.

Haylee jumped up to run past him.

Startled by the force and speed of her movement, Josh lunged in her direction. His only thought was to keep her from escaping.

Everything happened as if in slow motion.

Haylee turned her head toward Josh. She swung one hand out to her side. A sound like an empty sail suddenly catching air filled the room. Her webbed hand came up toward his face just as his body slammed into hers.

They hit the floor together, knocking the breath from their lungs. Josh's glasses slid across the floor. Only one of them could fulfill their need for air.

When Josh attempted to inhale, he found his nose and mouth blocked. Instantly, his mind registered what was happening. He grabbed her arm, trying to pull her hand away. They rolled and struggled. Josh tried to get his feet between them so he could kick her off.

Almost effortlessly, Haylee rolled on top of him while pinning his head to the floor. She jammed her legs on top of his, effectively immobilizing him.

Still struggling, Josh was amazed at how tightly the webs clung to his face. It was similar to plastic wrap on a hot dish. They felt warm and slightly moist, and he could even feel them throbbing.

Holy crap! I blatantly asked for this!

The Haylee that Josh loved was gone.

How could I have let my emotions overrule logic?

In her place was this ruthless animal.

I deserve this.

While his body writhed under her, Haylee remained still and poised. Her eyes took on a hardened, faraway look.

The frantic beating of his heart sounded loud in his ears. *Every overly self-confident hero is, in reality, an idiot.* He knew he was done for. A moment before all light from his world began to disappear, he ceased his struggles. In a last act of rebellion, Josh stared directly into the cold eyes above him.

Fearless, he met his fate.

His last sight was the anguish that returned to her gaze. Blackness surrounded him. He felt himself fading. It wasn't altogether unpleasant. As soon as an overwhelming peacefulness surrounded him, it was gone. In its place was dizziness and nausea. Then nothing.

Haylee's unnaturally still body lay on top of Josh. Her hand stayed tightly clamped to his face. A shiver traveled through her as she consumed the last remnants of his energy. Suddenly his voice was in her brain.

Haylee...

Her heart constricted. Like a pincushion, millions of pointed stabs amassed into a massive ball of agony that lodged in the center of her chest. She threw her head back. "NOOO!!!" reverberated through the room.

⚜36⚜

VOICES IN MIND

Haylee slowly lifted her webbed hand from Josh's face. Gently she crawled off him and knelt at his side. She tried to inhale deeply, but the constriction in her chest prevented that. As she looked down into his vacant eyes, great tears of grief cascaded down her face. "Josh," she moaned.

Hearing his name out loud broke the dam. Laying her head down on his chest, she sobbed. By stealing the soul of her friend, the one who knew her secret yet still wanted to help, she had, indeed, shattered the rest of her fragile world.

Feeling like wood herself, Haylee guided and nudged what was left of Josh into her own bed. She bent over to press a kiss onto his unresponsive lips. Her tears plopped onto his face as she stroked his temples and forehead. "I am so sorry," Haylee whispered. Grieving for the look that should have been there and the caustic comment that he should have uttered, Haylee stumbled into the living room. Hunkering down into a chair, she rocked miserably in a dark corner.

The full impact of what she had done settled over her like a gloomy cloud. Her throat constricted as she sat in the silent house. Those internal repetitive waves of sound grew so loud that Haylee curled up into a ball, her hands clenched into fists rammed up against her ears. The prickling, squeezing sensation in her scalp now traveled down her spine. Her physical distress did not compare to the mental and emotional.

Haylee miserably let Glori and Josh's thoughts fill her mind.

Glori adored her father. In the deepest part of her soul, Glori understood what it had cost him when he lost Doris. Now Haylee understood this too in a grown-up way that she never had before. Glori was so thrilled and happy to have found Gene and Haylee that she had been bursting with vitality and with life…a life that was now over.

Haylee's thoughts descended further into darkness when she envisioned how her dad would react to his most recent loss.

Josh. His favorite color was red. He'd won the State Championship for freestyle swimming three years in a row. He and his younger brother had backpacked and hiked through Copper Canyon in Mexico last summer. He and his dad had a running chess game going on four months now. He never told anyone about filling in for his mom's dance partner in waltz competitions.

He hadn't told his parents yet that he'd decided on a subject to pursue for postgraduate work.

Haylee smiled sadly as his thoughts and memories filled her head. With each one, her heart ached more. Josh was truly afraid of what she had done. His logically trained mind had difficulty grasping what his eyes had seen. Yet he'd still had hope. He'd had faith that solutions could be found and that there was goodness in her.

For a brief moment, there was a glimmer of something profoundly positive, something Josh had discovered. But the haze of self-hate sent her thoughts down other paths. She could not comprehend the depth of feeling that he'd had for her. *He's in love with me! Before he knew what I really was, he was fantasizing about us making a life together!*

She allowed herself to imagine what things might have been like if she had met Josh as a normal person. *He's the kind of person my parents would have wished for me to find.*

Haylee felt totally alone in the world. Even the loss of her mother and the years of rejection from her father could not compare to being the person directly responsible for ending the lives of the people she loved most.

Haylee realized that her worst nightmare had come true.

❧37❧

GONE

Mystified by the dark, quiet house, Eugene turned the doorknob while muttering, "Where is everyone?"

Haylee's hysterical voice coming out of the blackness startled him. "Daddy, I am so, so sorry! I'm sorry! I'm so, so sorry!"

"Haylee? What's wrong!?" He fumbled for the light switch.

Finding it, he laid eyes on his daughter. Her red rimmed, tear stained eyes looked huge in her head. The lack of color in her face was alarming. Grasping the backpack on her lap with one arm and a fisted hand pressed to the side of her head, Haylee was rocking back and forth in a way that looked crazed.

Instantly worried that she was having another spell, Gene took a step in her direction.

"No! Don't come near me!" Haylee croaked. She held up a hand to stop him—her webs were clearly visible.

"Haylee!" he cried.

She pulled something from her pocket then dropped it as if it burned.

"Ahhh!" she screamed looking down into her lap. Haylee swiped at her legs as if it they were on fire.

~ ~ ~ ~

The pulse beats coming from inside her head spread outside of her body. Haylee barely noticed her dad reaching for her. A furious globe of power roiled around her drowning out all sound. It was as if she were the nucleus of a churning ball of energy. Haylee felt like her skin was on fire; that she was being torn apart. Somewhere in her mind, it registered that her hands were hotter than any other part of her.

Haylee had no way of knowing if she moved or if she stayed in place. All she knew was that she was being consumed by a red-hot inferno. Her head was thrown back, her spine was arched, and her arms and legs were thrown out away from her body. She blacked out.

~ ~ ~ ~

Gene lunged toward Haylee. In a blink of a second, she was gone. Eugene slammed into an empty chair. In shock, he got up to repeatedly press his hands around the material of the seat searching for something that by all rights should have been there!

What he had yet to discover waited quietly under the covers, staring at nothing…

Welcome the Traveler and wish her Godspeed.

The Observers, as they thought of themselves, were present, as they had been for millions of years, to witness each traveling event. Two slender members of their group stood before the panel that displayed numerical equations in pictographs as data occurred in real time.

The blazing sphere, driven by the crystals, powered by energy fragments from bipedal land dwellers, shot up out of the earth's atmosphere. Its trajectory into deep space was completely controlled. When it returned to the planet, its speed slowed. Slight smiles appeared on the faces of the Observers. Once again, Upholder technology had proven itself. Customarily spoken by Nile and Elin, their statement was verbalized. "The contamination and mutation of the genetics has been mitigated with the temporal shift. This Traveler is prepared to serve her function."

The occupant inside the sphere remained unharmed.

❧38❧

SHIFTED TIME

Unconscious, in her charged cocoon, Haylee floated gently toward the earth. Silently, it held her for a few moments, rocking gently, suspended about six inches above the ground. Iridescent hints of rainbow colors skittered across its surface in every direction. Still unaware of her surroundings, the sting of charred flesh receded. Once the process was complete, the sphere lowered its occupant gently upon the terrain. It transformed itself from an orb into an egg shape in order to accommodate her body positioning. Four voices whispered from within, "We honor your service to the Upholders" before the sphere winked out of existence. By the time Haylee awoke, scratching her arms and face, no one would have been able to tell what she'd been through.

"Dad?" Haylee called out. The sound of her voice in the inky vastness threw her. An inhaled breath smelled of trees and fresh air. Reaching down to feel the solidness beneath her, Haylee felt dirt. With a hammering heart, her panic grew. *What just happened?*

Remembering the searing heat and pain, she stretched out

her arms to see if she was covered in burns. They looked alright. Haylee put her hands to her face to see if she still had one. *How is this possible?* She wondered. Miraculously, everything else checked out.

Where am I?

She felt something hot near her hips and worried that whatever had happened was happening again! Springing to her feet, her pendant dropped to the ground. Haylee stared at it thinking that in some way, it was responsible for all of her troubles. Blazing anger and vivid frustration caused her to act without thinking. She picked it up and threw it as far away as she could.

Relieved and exhausted, Haylee bent forward with her hands on her knees, letting her breathing return to a normal rhythm. Her eyes adjusted to the darkness.

A full moon rising in the distance radiated enough light to see by. The stars looked clearer than she'd ever seen them. *No light pollution,* she thought, remembering comments on the subject that an Astronomy teacher frequently made.

A dirt trail stretched out in either direction. The only other things in view were oak trees and grasses that swayed gently in the crisp night breeze…nothing but open expanses as far as she could see…and silence.

Haylee walked down the trail then turned around and walked the other way. *I have no idea where I am, and I have no idea how I got here.* She wanted nothing more than to crawl into her bed and pull the covers over her head; tears of frustrated self-pity gathered in her eyes. Heading over to a rock outcropping, she plopped down. "Is there anybody here?" she called out.

An owl, disturbed by the sound, voiced its displeasure.

Haylee shivered. Hugging her arms around herself, she realized she had no idea where her bed—or any bed—was.

The tears released; she let them. She wailed; she didn't care if anyone heard. As she sobbed out her fury, she let thoughts linger that fed her troubled emotions.

At least I can't hurt my dad if he's nowhere nearby. What is he going to do when he goes upstairs? It took him so long to recover after mom died that this'll probably push him over the edge. It would have been better for him if I'd have stolen his soul.

What could have I been thinking to jump on Josh? How are his parents going to feel when they find out? What are they going to think when they see him? Is my dad going to have to call them and say, 'Hey, guess what? My daughter destroyed your smart, handsome son.'

Once her rant stopped, her mind rested, thankfully blank. Another shiver reminded her of how cold it was. A formidable desire to lie down and close her eyes had her swaying in place. Taking a few wobbly steps, she located a hole between two rocks. She gathered leaves and brush, piled them on top of herself as she curled into a ball, and let sleep claim her once again.

~ ~ ~ ~

"Blasted mule! Will you get a move on?"

Haylee squinted as she woke up. Disoriented, she put a hand up to shield her eyes from the late afternoon light.

"Sophie, if you don't get a move on, I swear I'll sell you to the next man I meet!" the male voice bristled with irritation.

Frowning, Haylee crawled up on the rocks she'd hidden behind the night before. She saw a man riding a mule across the grassy field. His sweat stained, wide brimmed hat was pulled low over his brow. He was hitting the mule on its rump with a stick and nudging its flanks with his heels, urging the reluctant animal into a faster gait. *If he wants to go faster, why doesn't he just drive?* she thought. Frowning, she looked around again. The fellow looked homeless. He had long dirty hair and a beard that was the same. His clothes were dusty and crusty. Digging tools clanked on top of the mule's pack as the animal moved. Noticing that there were no roads in sight, Haylee apprehensively glanced up into the sky. This place seemed unnaturally quiet.

After leaving her rocky haven, Haylee ran in the opposite direction. She wanted to stay out of sight until she could figure out where she was. Haylee began trotting along the trail. *I am a freak…pure and simple.* The physical exercise helped to loosen the constant ache in her heart. *Why did I think I could do anything about this? I tried to be so careful and I still ruined my family and my best friend.* The trot turned into a jog, which then opened up into a full high-speed run. *I hate myself!* When she moved quickly, Haylee was able to focus her cluttered emotions. *Why is this happening?*

She'd covered miles before she came upon a crude wooden structure that looked like it might be inhabited. Concealing herself in the brush on the outskirts of the cleared land, she could see a laundry line with clothes waving in the breeze. Keeping alert for any sounds from within, she crept closer. It was a one-room building with several windows on each wall. On the low porch that spanned the front sat a rocking chair and a spittoon.

All was quiet. Summoning up her courage, she stole along the back wall and dared a peek in the window. It looked like a museum display. A simple wooden table with a couple of chairs sat in the center of the room. An uncomfortable-looking cot hugged the opposite wall.

Looking around to make sure she was alone, she trod lightly over the porch to lift the door latch. Stepping inside, she waited a moment for her eyes to adjust to the dim interior. There wasn't much more to see except for a few pelts hanging from the rafters and bags of flour and potatoes on a low shelf. She walked over to lift the lid on a cooking pot that sat on top of a wood stove. Wrinkling her nose, she smelled the burned beans inside.

Her gaze wandered around the room. The only other space left inside was filled with iron tools: hoes, shovels, picks, and a pile of pie tins.

There were a couple of hand-drawn maps in a gunnysack stored near the tools. Growing impatient, she looked around again. Her eyes landed on a coat hanging on a hook by the front door. Haylee was across the room in three strides. As soon as she lifted it, she could tell there was paper in it somewhere.

Excitedly, she reached into the breast pocket and pulled out a letter. Haylee ran her thumb over a pretty wax seal. The date, written boldly across the top of the page, read August 21, 1849. They year seemed to jump off the page while sending shivers down her spine. *1849! It can't possibly be!*

She stood there, blinking slowly. Finally, gathering her wits, she read on.

My Dearest Husband,

The children are asking if you will have found enough gold to return by Christmastime?

You have written that California is no place for a woman. That adventurers and criminals labor side by side in the gold fields. That gunfire and fighting are daily occurrences and that a God-fearing woman in that place would be looked upon as an oddity and as a distraction.

If the Alta California is as lawless and filled with evil as you say, then I believe that it is my duty to join you.

My sister has agreed to keep Jason and Jack and has loaned us the money for my passage on the wagon train that leaves next month.

Your ever-faithful wife, Patricia

Carefully refolding the letter, Haylee put it back where she'd found it.

Feeling the rise of panic, she looked around again with

fresh eyes. She scrambled to open every door, drawer, and trunk in the house. Running outside, she raced through the crude barn and root cellar.

Chickens in a nearby coop flapped and cackled at her quick movements. Walking over to them, she spoke softly while focusing her thoughts so they could hear. This helped to calm the birds and herself.

A line from the letter kept repeating in her head, *No place for a woman.*

Haylee pulled in deep breaths of fresh air. Still disoriented from finding herself in a strange place and deeply grieving over what had happened at home, she felt on the verge of losing it at every turn. The deep breathing exercises helped to keep the crack in her composure from breaking wide open—temporarily.

Far off in the distance, her acute sense of hearing picked up the sound of horse hooves and chains jangling.

Still not totally believing what her ears told her, and not wanting to face anyone, she turned to run away from the sounds.

The movements of her body once again helped to focus and clear her thinking. Not long after she'd gotten going, she began to notice a sense of nausea that increased with every footfall. She stopped to rest then started out again walking.

Five more paces and she was forced to stop dead in her tracks. Salivating and sweating profusely, Haylee leaned over her knees as dry heaves pulsated through her mid-section. Catching her breath, she backed up a few steps. The nausea noticeably abated.

Turning to face the direction she'd come from, she walked in a straight line feeling better every moment. She realized what was going on.

A memory surfaced along with her mother's words: *Once the pendant becomes yours, you have to keep it close to you. If you get too far away from it, you'll feel sick until you are back together again.*

Haylee could hear her childish response, "So it's like we are friends? We have to stick together?"

Smiling, Doris had said, "Yes, my sweet girl, that's exactly what it's like!"

It did not take Haylee long to retrace her steps back to the place where she'd first made her debut in this unfamiliar place. Searching for the pendant in the grassy field turned out to be extremely discouraging, as she did not remember which direction she'd thrown it.

Every now and then, Haylee heard trekkers coming along the path. Hiding behind the rocks, she listened to their conversations as they passed by. Most of them were on their way to town to sell gold, get cleaned up, and to pay visits to the gambling halls.

Haylee overheard snatches of a conversation.

"Mary never makes no mention if I bathe before I get on her…it saves me a few ounces to buy more whiskey."

"Ah ha ha ha," they hooted and laughed.

"Thanks for telling me that, Sam. I will have to follow you over there," replied another man, this one with a long unkempt beard. He wore a brown shirt that must have been white once; large sweat stains under his armpits were clearly visible. His hands constantly made gyrating motions in his beard, in the straggly hair under his hat, and in other places Haylee didn't want to see.

Another one chimed in, "Cynthia's a skinny one, but she does things none of the other ones do!"

Their laughter made the skin across Haylee's forehead and arms feel too tight. A shiver of revulsion jumped its way up her spine.

Haylee was glad to see their forms disappear around a bend. She still could not entirely grasp the ramifications of the information that she'd gathered. She continued her search while wondering why she was the way she was...and why she was here. It was not long before another matter that needed attention came up. She was famished!

Still unable to find her pendant, Haylee could not stop thinking about the burned beans in the cabin. Knowing that it was right on the boundary of her distance limit from the bothersome pendant, she headed back...this time with a plan.

ॐ39ॐ

FEMALE MALE

The return trip to the cabin had been useful. Fortunately, she'd found it as it was before—empty. She assuaged her hunger by finishing off what was left of the beans and she borrowed a set of clothes.

She paused to peer at herself in a tiny mirror that hung on a wall. She saw herself the way Josh must have seen her. All signs of the beautiful woman she had become disgusted her.

Her eyes dropped to a straight razor laying open on a dresser top below the mirror. The sharpness of the edge called all of her attention to it, the moment seemed frozen in time.

Can I do it? she asked.

Her gaze flew back to the mirror where she met her own eyes.

"What is wrong with me?" she said out loud, as she blinked rapidly.

The comment from Patricia's letter to her husband returned to her mind, *California is no place for a woman.*

Straight razor and tiny mirror in hand, Haylee sought a tree outside where she could work. Balancing the mirror on

a branch, she gazed at her reflection. Holding up the first sacrifi-
cial hunk of hair, she paused.

"Ow!" she yelped as the not-so-sharp razor sliced its way
through. She squeezed her eyes shut against the burning tugs
on her scalp. Wispy brown clumps gathered in ever-increasing
piles around her feet. They moved with the breeze. Every now
and then, small assemblages of them lifted off to drift across the
landscape. Nesting animals preparing for winter would treasure
those locks.

Putting down her cutting tools, Haylee rubbed her hands
over the spikey surface on her head. Bobbing around so that
she could verify that it was mostly all cut to the same length,
she gulped. The part of her that wanted punishment and
retribution nodded with grim satisfaction. *It's a small start.*
Already her head felt considerably lighter. *At least I don't have
to look at myself,* she thought.

Next was a venture back inside to attack the sleeping cot.
She removed the rough wool blanket and turned her face away
as a noxious cloud of body order assaulted her senses.

You'll thank me for this Patricia! Haylee thought.

Steeling herself for what lay ahead, she began to rip the
cloth into six-inch wide strips.

Within the hour, Haylee had the smelly strips neatly tied,
mummy style, across her chest. She was pleased with how the
bulky shirt fell from her shoulders. Several layers of under
shirts sufficiently increased the mass of her shoulders and upper
body. She completed the ensemble with baggy jeans cinched
at her waist with left over cloth strips, ankle boots, and a wide
leather hat. Haylee searched through her own clothes to find
something she could leave behind in trade for all that she was
taking.

After another full day of searching near the rocks, the
pendant finally turned up. She wondered what had gotten into

her, tossing away something precious her mother had given her. *I always thought of it as a gift, but that was before I started to realize that 'gift' might not be the right word…'curse' might be a better word.*

She understood now that it used heat to control her direction…and the threat of sickness to force her to stay near. Sighing with resignation, she reached down to pick it up. "I guess I couldn't get away from you if I tried," she spoke to it. "Apparently I don't have much choice about following the path you've laid out."

Her first sighting of a wagon train lumbering in her direction was astonishing. It was preceded by the sounds of whistles, barking dogs, and a cloud of dust. Haylee felt apprehensive as the mass of people and equipment approached. She was still having a hard time believing that any of this was real. Thinking that now would be a good time to see if she could pass as a man, she held herself in a manly stance and tried to make her outward appearance calm.

Fifteen covered wagons filled with road weary travelers halted behind the train leader. A few people in the back hopped off their rigs to stretch their legs and run into the bushes. The leader let out a shrill, complicated whistle, then sent the man sitting next to him to run down the line spreading the word that they were only a few miles from town. They only had a short time to take care of business or check gear before they set out again.

The driver leaned over to ask Haylee about the conditions ahead.

"Don't know," she replied in her deepest voice. "I am going that way myself."

"Where's your gear son?" the driver wanted to know.

"Lost everything in the river."

He inquired if she wanted a ride. Nodding, Haylee replied, "Thanks!" He motioned her up to the seat next to him, introduc-

ing himself as Nathaniel "Nate" Johnsen. Haylee took his outstretched hand while telling him that her own was Hal.

They resumed their trek. The hard wooden bench and
the screech of the vehicle as it lurched forward was an exciting
experience for Haylee. The horses puffed as they labored to pull
their burden.

She was pleased at how easily Nate accepted her as a man.
Haylee learned that they had set out from Saint Louis and were
heading to Yerba Buena after dropping off a few rigs at New
Helvetia. "The place where all this gold foolishness started," he
said. Nate declared that the real money was in transporting all
the hopefuls. At this, the road-dirty, unshaven man laughed and
struck his knee, sending up a small plume of dust.

Quietness settled over her as she realized that, though she
felt like she was a million miles away from home, she hadn't
really left. It was still the same valley she was used to—a giant
bowl surrounded by the Sierra Nevada Mountains to the east
and the Coastal Range to the west. She enjoyed seeing it this
way—open, free, and wild. No highways, cars, and housing
tracts that behaved like a spreading cancer on the land. The valley floor, where her dad and so many other farmers grew their
famous California crops, was just scrub brush with a few gnarly
oaks trees here and there. That she could see both mountain
ranges suddenly delighted her. She'd grown accustomed to the
accumulating smog that obliterated the long-range views. Only
at certain times, when the storms blew through and cleared out
the valley, could those views be seen.

As they traveled closer to town, large farmsteads began
to appear. Mostly Spanish in style, the low, flat, tile roofs stood
out in her line of sight. Haylee's eyes grew wide and she tried
to hide the intake of breath at her first view of New Helvetia—
a place she would know as Sutter's Fort in her own time. Rows
and rows of tents stretched out as far as the eye could see.

Bearded men wearing high wasted pants and suspenders loitered in the streets, yelling and cursing. Horses and carts were everywhere, making the scene chaotic. *I can't believe I'm actually seeing this!* Haylee thought.

Nate glanced over, noting her anxious expression. She commented, "There are so many tents!" He shook his head from side to side. "As I said…hopefuls."

Nate called out and whistled, signaling that they were about to come to a halt.

Jumping down with a rushed, 'Thank You,' to Nate, Haylee quickly made her exit. She didn't want to talk any more.

⚜40⚜

WESTERN WORK

Finding a relatively quiet corner, Haylee took some time to observe her surroundings. The carousing, shooting, and all around wildness of the men in the streets made the place feel like a gathering of wild dogs let loose to snarl and fight at will. Once she began to acclimate to the commotion and mayhem, she began to pay attention to other elements. Keeping her wits about her, she navigated her way inward, toward the heart of town. She quickly realized that most of the loud activity was focused around tents that housed gaming, music, and alcohol.

As she was beginning to question if she should have kept herself hidden in the countryside, Haylee spotted a burly man placing a 'Stable Hand Wanted' sign outside of the livery tent. Without taking time to think it over, she ran across the street, grabbed the sign, and followed the man inside.

Haylee entered, pausing for a moment to let her eyes adjust. The familiar smell and the presence of animals eased her frayed nerves. "Help you?" The big man asked.

"I am here to help you," Haylee responded as she held out the sign he'd just put out.

He folded beefy arms across his barrel chest, eyeing her up and down. "Don't think so," he replied with a shake of his head. He turned to walk back out to replace his sign.

Accurately guessing what was going through his mind, Haylee trotted behind him. "Wait! I know I look small, but I'm a hard worker and I know horses better than anyone you've ever met."

"Right," he said, not breaking his stride.

Reaching out to grab his arm, Haylee stopped him at the entrance, making him meet her eyes. "I'll prove it," she said. "I'll work for free for the rest of the day."

Raising an eyebrow, the weathered stable owner considered Haylee's offer. Holding out her hand, she said, "The name is Hal, and if you give me a chance, you won't be sorry."

He paused so long that Haylee was about to pull back her hand and admit defeat, when he reached out to take it, saying, "William MacDermott. If you don't do as you say, your outta here first thing in the morning."

~ ~ ~ ~

Six days of mucking out horse and mule poo had been good for her. William wasn't much of a talker, which was a good thing as far as Haylee was concerned. He did confess that he'd had his doubts about her being strong enough to do the work, but that she did have "quite a manner with the ponies."

These horses worked much harder than the ones Haylee was used to, but their basic emotions and thought processes were the same.

She spent her time at the livery practicing her male behavior, absorbing the environment, and thinking.

On the fifth night, while in an exhausted sleep in the hay pile, Haylee awoke with a start. A tremor ripped through her. Rather than fight it, she cursed, and moved silently so as not to disturb the others who also slept in the livery lofts. She could have easily fulfilled her need with any of the strangers, but a deeply entrenched desire for secrecy sent her out into the tent city.

Even though it was late at night, shouting and gunshots persisted. Heading straight toward the drinking establishments, Haylee knew how to quickly solve her dilemma.

Abraham Miller, already passed out along the edge of a dark alleyway, became her first victim in the year 1849. Once the euphoria of the feed wore off, it was his experiences and memories washing through her mind that finally helped Haylee accept the fact that she had traveled to another time.

More guilt and shame heaped on top of the mountain of it that had formed within her chest, as Haylee patted him down for valuables. The pouch of gold that she lifted off of him was meant for his wife and son back in Boston. He'd had a lot more before the card game tonight. Losing what he thought was a sure hand was as good a reason as any to soothe his sorrows with whiskey. Shoving the pouch down into her pocket, she noticed its warm interior.

She weaved slightly and burped as she walked away from the still form. Haylee hoped that some kindhearted soul would take pity on the poor fellow and that his waiting family would be alright.

Removing her warm necklace from the handkerchief in which it was wrapped, Haylee acknowledged that her time at the stable had come to an end. She'd been expecting it, but was still reluctant to leave what had begun to feel like a safe haven in the midst of chaos.

⚶41⚶

RATTLER

The following morning, William MacDermott dropped coins totaling $1.50 into Haylee's palm. "If you pass by this way again, come see me." Shaking hands, the two went their separate ways.

As directed by William, Haylee walked three miles west of town to the Higgins's farm in order buy a mule "for a deal."

Haylee introduced herself to the toothless old man when she arrived at his place. He was pleased to know that MacDermott was sending business his way. He led her over to the corral where a lone mule stood.

When Haylee had asked why Mr. Higgins called the beast Rattler, the wizened codger threw back his head, cackling with glee. Haylee tried to hide her repulsion as the smelly man spewed spittle through the space in his mouth where his teeth would have been. Pushing the nugget she handed him into his pocket, he picked up a bridle and quickly slipped it into the nag's mouth. Giving it a hard yank, he pulled the resisting animal out of the enclosure and passed the reins to Haylee.

Rattler set her ears back while staring at the girl. When

Haylee made a move toward the animal, Rattler bared her teeth, and made a hissing sound.

Haylee backed off immediately, which sent Mr. Higgins into peals of laughter. "You ain't spent much time around mules. You gots ta show 'em whose boss right from the get-go." He walked over, jerked the reigns out of her hands, and wrenched the mule's head so that he could glare straight into the animal's eyes. He whispered something in Rattler's ear, then turned to Haylee, telling her to hop on. Giving him a skeptical look, she did as she was told. In one quick movement, Higgins tossed her the straps and gave the mule a hard whack on her hindquarters. The angry animal leapt forward, almost throwing Haylee off.

All the way down the drive, Haylee could hear Mr. Higgins hooting with merriment.

About a mile from the farm, Haylee came upon a fork in the road. Both directions looked the same and, having no idea where she was headed, she arbitrarily chose the road to the left. Almost as soon as she made the decision, she noticed that the crystal started to grow warmer. With a look of concern, Haylee reached down to feel the pocket that was getting hotter with every step that Rattler took. Within the moments that it took for Haylee to struggle with the animal to get her to stop, the crystal became burning hot.

Haylee yelled with aggravation as she hopped off the mule. With fumbling fingers, she hastily unbuttoned her jeans, then shoved them down around her ankles, only to realize that her boots kept her from removing the offending garment completely. Losing her balance in the haste, Haylee slipped, landing with a splash. Frigid water and slick mud molded to her backside, causing another, louder shout.

Swiftly, Haylee realized that the cold water had stopped the burning. Hearing a slight hissing sound, she looked down at her crinkled mud soaked pants. The area where her pocket was located was steaming! She slid around in the muck as she struggled to extricate herself. Scrunching her face with distaste, Haylee pulled up her pants until she could reach into her pocket to fish out the pendant. She located a small stick and, using it as a tool, she hooked it through the pendant chain and lifted it out of her clothing. Miffed, she raised the stick up, angling her wrist downward. The jewelry slid off the stick, plopping into the murky water. "See how you like that," she intoned in her best bratty voice. Haylee was not amused when the puddle began to bubble.

Sloshing her way to a drier spot, Haylee readjusted her clothing with a look of disgust. Thinking about a hot shower just made her more furious. First things first. Looking one way and then the other, Haylee attempted to locate Rattler.

She could make out the mule in the distance, near the fork in the road, nibbling grass.

Reaching back into the warm puddle, Haylee felt for the necklace. She paused, contemplating a re-entry into the mire.

Knowing she'd pay for it later, she stripped down and stepped back in. Warm goo oozed up between her toes. Sitting down the rest of the way, she sighed with pleasure as she intentionally covered herself with the slippery warm sludge. Reclining in it, Haylee reached toward the sky then began to laugh as she looked at her gray-coated hands and arms. Still smiling, she rubbed mud all over her face and hair. *What a totally ridiculous situation!* she thought. *Stuck in God-knows-where, doing who-knows-what after having wiped out practically everyone I care about.* The humor died. Haylee just lay in the warm mud staring up at the sky, working really hard not to feel sorry for herself...not to feel anything.

⚘42⚘

LOVEY

She must have fallen asleep because the next thing she knew, Haylee was awakened by a raspy tongue moving across her forehead. Eyes popping open, she was surprised to see Rattler looking down at her.

The two beings regarded one another. If Haylee even moved a finger, Rattler backed up. Rather than trying to pet and coax the animal into relaxing, Haylee closed her eyes, calming her own thoughts so she could listen. *She is named Rattler because she likes to scare people with that hissing sound. Her first caretaker hit her. She discovered that if she made that sound, he would leave her alone. She's lived with too many people and is used to not being liked.*

Haylee softened. She whispered in reassuring tones, gently floating her own thoughts toward Rattler.

Opening her eyes, Haylee mimicked Rattler's hissing sound almost identically. Rattler's ears popped straight up. Haylee almost burst out laughing at the look on the animal's face, but she knew that if she laughed now they would never become friends. She slowly moved into a sitting position as she spoke in a firm but gentle tone. "I mean you no harm. If you will trust me, I will care for you. To show you that I mean what I say, I want to call you by a different name. From now on, I will call you" — quirky smile lit upon Haylee's face —"Lovey!"

The mule formerly known as Rattler cocked her head to the side. "'Lovey' was a character in one of my favorite TV shows; she was very kind." Haylee chuckled again.

As Haylee got to her hands and knees to fish in the mud for her pendant, Lovey backed up, cocking her head again. She'd never seen a human do these things.

"Ah ha!" Haylee proclaimed as her fingers closed over its hard surface. The sludge made a slurping sound as it gave up its heat source.

Haylee held it out away from her body — letting it dangle by its chain. She imagined that she probably looked like the Creature from the Black Lagoon. Going through her pack, she pulled out her wool blanket, grimacing as she used the scratchy cloth to scrub off as much of the mud as possible.

She began to shiver and her teeth chattered. A thought occurred to her. Wrapping the crystal in the corner of her blanket, she wrapped the excess around herself and turned to walk in the opposite direction from where it directed. A glow of heat soon enveloped her. She remained in that position until she felt warm enough to start traveling again. She felt a small level of satisfaction at having figured out how to use the pendant to serve a purpose she wanted.

Turning to resume her journey, Haylee looked at Lovey and stopped. Just because she was ready to go, there was no guarantee that the animal would cooperate. The closer Haylee got to the mule, the more the mule backed away.

Sighing, Haylee picked a handful of grass. Once again, she floated gentle thoughts to the animal, asking as nicely as she could for her help.

The first sign that this tack would work was Lovey's

nostrils flaring as she sniffed the air. Lovey stepped forward. Haylee felt her warm breath and then her soft lips nuzzling her hand as the mule gently accepted Haylee's offering. For a moment, Haylee just stood there smiling. Slowly, she reached out her other hand, placing it on Lovey's forehead. Lovey slowed her eating to eye her. Still speaking softly, Haylee made her way around as she continued petting and scratching the animal. Haylee explained what she was doing as she picked up the reins and smoothly mounted.

Lovey tensed, setting her ears back. Haylee leaned down to hug her neck and spoke to her. After a moment, Lovey relaxed. Haylee coaxed the mule back onto the road. Keeping up a constant chatter, Haylee and Lovey headed toward their unknown, crystal guided destination.

As the day wore on, the mud dried, causing Haylee's entire body to itch. She alternately scratched and flicked dried mud off of her as she began telling Lovey her story. She could swear that the animal was paying attention.

~ ~ ~ ~

For two days, Haylee traveled west. She found out rather quickly that the crystal would let her travel about a half a mile from the road she was supposed to take. It stayed at an even temperature that she could stand, as long as she didn't veer too far off the path. She preferred to avoid other travelers. They tended to want to stop and talk. Right now, she wanted to keep as low a profile as she possibly could.

At dusk, Haylee would search out a secluded spot beneath some oak trees, set up a small camp, and start a fire. She told herself that the fire was so she could prepare dinner, even though her dinner consisted mostly of jerked meat. It really was more of a comfort than anything else. Somehow, it helped abate her feelings of loneliness. She'd grown to love the mule, but it was not the same as human companionship.

Haylee dreaded the darkness the most. When the night surrounded her, she thought about each and every one of her victims—as well as heard their memories.

She tried to create an imaginary companion there with her, sitting on a log, staring into the fire. At first she'd tried to imagine her dad, but that brought on a fresh flood of tears as she wondered about what he'd felt when he saw Glori. Next, she tried thinking about Josh, but then she remembered that she was responsible for replacing that wonderfully alive and intelligent face with a vacant visage. Finally, she realized that the only way she could ward off her loneliness was to imagine a stranger.

He believed that she could undo the damage she had done. Staring into the flames, Haylee imagined that this stranger was tall and muscular. He had thick, dark wavy hair and sensual lips. She heard herself telling him that he should keep his distance because everyone who got close to her got hurt. He moved closer to her on the log, wrapping his arm around her. She could feel the heat of his leg pressing against hers. She wouldn't look at him, so he reached over to turn her face. Haylee could see the reflection of the fire in his eyes. She could feel his warm breath as he spoke in low, husky tones. "I believe you could destroy me, but I know that you won't."

Haylee closed her eyes as their lips made contact. He held her close; Haylee leaned back into his arms.

The next thing she knew, she was sprawled out on the ground next to the log. Pressing her lips together in a straight line, she dusted herself off while shaking her head and chastising herself for letting her imagination get away with her. *Why am I even letting myself think this way? I know it's not possible. Just look at what I've already done!*

Haylee wrapped her arms around her chest and stared up

into the incredibly clear night sky, feeling cold and even more alone than before. A while later, she climbed under a small mountain of quilts and blankets and sighed at the warmth radiating outward from the covers. *At least I can enjoy some simple things that life has to offer.* She'd camped far enough away from her path so that the crystal heated up her sleeping area.

⚜43⚜

HUNGRY

On the morning of the third day of her trek, Haylee became aware that she had a headache and a slight ringing in her ears. She lay awake under her blankets but didn't open her eyes. Knowing what these symptoms would lead to made her feel sick. She didn't want to steal any more souls! Haylee made an angry swipe at the moisture that gathered at the rims of her eyes; her body quivered in an effort to hold back the powerful emotions that raged through her.

Suddenly Lovey, who had been some distance from camp, stepped forward, lowered her head, and nuzzled her friend. Haylee was touched by the animal's actions. She laid her head on Lovey's forehead; stroking her velvety, soft nose. Mentally, she thanked her for being so compassionate. For now, this attention helped Haylee get her mind off of what she knew was inevitable. Just the thought of taking yet another soul made her shudder. Knowing that her time was limited made her quickly give Lovey a hug and break camp.

~ ~ ~ ~

Kicking her heels lightly on Lovey's haunches sent her into a trot. Haylee and her baggage bounced up and down on

Lovey's back as they hurried on their way.

The scent of salt in the air and a drop in temperature stopped her in her tracks momentarily, as she lifted her head to savor the smell. Goosebumps prickled across her skin. It registered that she must be awfully close to where San Francisco ought to be.

In another instant, she was oblivious to the elements as her body reminded her of the need to hunt.

Haylee discovered an abandoned shack with a fairly intact corral. By this time, she was pale and stiff from keeping such a tight grip on herself. Well aware of the change in Haylee, Lovey was skittish and trying to jerk the reins from her hands.

Haylee rode her into the corral and was about to throw her leg over the side when another tremor hit. This time, instead of dancing around in place when Lovey felt her passenger hunker down and begin to vibrate, the mule panicked and started bucking. As she'd done all morning, Haylee crouched low over Lovey's neck and gripped her mane to keep from losing her seat. Luckily, her grip was like iron when she was in the throes of a tremor.

As soon as the vibration subsided, Haylee used her formidable strength to pull hard on the harness to cease Lovey's antics. Keeping a tight hold on the leather straps, she jumped down and reached over to begin unburdening the animal. Lovey was breathing hard and trying to pull away. Coming right to the edge of losing her patience, Haylee jerked Lovey's head around so she could look into the mule's eyes. In a very low voice, she ordered her to stay still. Lovey seemed to be paralyzed and stood there motionless.

As Haylee walked a short distance away, another tremor knocked her to the ground. Fighting it, Haylee clenched her teeth together so hard, she bit her lip. The salty taste of her own blood filled her mouth. Heart racing and sweating, she rode it out. Her hands ached; every fiber in her body urged her to get up and search out prey. It seemed like it lasted an eternity, but finally it passed. Haylee knew she couldn't withstand the urges much longer.

Still rooted to the same spot, Lovey started breathing hard again when Haylee approached. Her eyes widened in fear. Lovey trembled as Haylee got closer, her nostrils flared—but she still did not move.

As Haylee reached for the bridle, she met the gaze of the frightened mule. Tears gathered in her own eyes as she recognized the distress in them. As Haylee unbuckled the saddlebag straps and drew the lead over the Lovey's ears, Lovey rolled her eyes and pulled away violently. The belts dropped to the ground as Haylee turned west. Almost in slow motion, her body condensed, then exploded with force as she leapt forward. The last sound she heard before her humanity faded into animalistic instinct was the mournful echo of Lovey's bellow.

❧44❧

HOMER

On the salt air, Haylee caught a whiff of something that immediately put all of her senses on alert. It had a rank, musty smell and could only be human. Her keen hearing honed in on the sound of branches breaking. In a flash, she was off. She moved so swiftly, she would be a blur to the human eye. In no time at all, she saw the dark hair of a man in a brown leather jacket crouched behind a bush, spotting a deer. She took all this in and planned her attack without even breaking her stride. He pulled his rifle up and had his sights on his target when some instinct must have told him to look behind him.

Just as he turned around, Haylee flew through the air with webbed hands outstretched. She saw his surprise and fear. She hit him with all the force of a raging bull.

He went down immediately. His rifle went flying; the deer bounded away into the brush. Even though he looked to be a strong man, he was no match for Haylee's voracious appetite. She didn't bother to prolong his struggles. In the instant that she slammed into him, she pinned his arms and legs and slapped her webbing onto his face.

Her body arched as she absorbed his energy. She breathed in deeply, feeling the ecstasy of the moment and thankfully welcomed back her right mind. Her body stilled. She gazed down at the quiet man beneath her. In dire need of a good scrubbing, he was basically healthy. Homer Scott...another miner, this one from Liverpool, with dreams of making a better life.

Regret and sadness washed over her. *Is this the way the rest of my life is going to be?* She crawled off of Homer; stood up and remained planted to that spot as she regarded him. These poor fellows, she thought. Out loud, she said, "Even Curtis. He didn't deserve to have his life snuffed out. This can't continue...I won't let it...I will stop it...one way or another."

Haylee realized that she couldn't leave Homer out in the scrubland alone. He'd die of exposure. Telling him to stay put seemed ridiculous, but she needed him to so she could retrieve his horse who'd run off when all commotion started.

Sometime later, Haylee returned with a tall, chestnut colored equine in tow. She knew from Homer's memories that his name was Titan. Although excitable when surprised, Titan had a stoic, hard-working personality. She was relieved to find Homer right where she'd left him.

Like she coaxed timid animals, she calmly encouraged Homer to stand. Getting him to mount the horse behind her turned out to be a challenge. She solved it by finding a big rock for him to stand on. She brought Titan right up next to it. Guiding him to step over the horse's back had almost caused an accident where everyone got hurt. The stepping part had gone alright, but Homer had no control of his downward descent. He dropped all of his weight suddenly on Titan's back. Calming the dancing horse while holding onto Homer had taken all of Haylee's physical strength and will. Realizing that the heavy man would not balance or hold onto her to keep himself from slipping, Haylee lashed a rope around them both.

Finally underway, she breathed a sigh of thankfulness that at least they were moving. Homer's head fell on the back of her shoulder. He began to snore. Having him lean on her while the events of his life unfolded in her mind made her heart ache. She squeezed her eyes shut tight, realizing that resistance was futile.

Back home, he'd been struggling to find his way in his father's law firm. Homer couldn't count the number of times he'd been chastised for daydreaming while he should have been studying case law. It was expected that he'd take over for his father one day. His parents had neatly arranged his marriage to a pitiful woman with a knack for grating on every one of Homer's nerves. An heiress with a title, no less! And he'd gone along with it all until he felt like he was drowning in his own life.

On the fateful day of his escape, Homer had taken a courier errand upon himself just for a bit of air. While en route to deliver a sum of cash to one of their top clients, he heard barkers at the waterfront. "Riches to be plucked from the ground in California!" "Voyage fare only $400!" "Ship's a sailing in two hours' time!"

Homer had argued with himself about duty and honor, but ultimately he couldn't bear the thought of going back to his office, his wife…or any part of his life. Hastily ripping open the parcel, he had been relieved to find enough money for the fare, plus a little extra. He'd signed the passenger manifest Alfred Pool.

Haylee had a clear vision of his sketchbook, with its thick brown leather cover, hand tooled with embellishments. The book itself had been a treasured expense. In Homer's memories, beautiful, detailed illustrations that he'd done of birds, plants, and animals appeared. He felt such joy and satisfaction in the details of creating a body of botanical work in a new environment. Camaraderie with other gold seekers offered a level of social acceptance that he valued. Living in squalid, filthy conditions, but still managing to survive, to make a life of his own choosing, had been a very good thing as far as he was concerned. Though he'd felt bad about what his parents must be thinking regarding his disappearance, he knew that he'd made the right decision. "Oh Homer…" Haylee sighed.

His thoughts brought up memories of her night with Curtis. Her first that she'd spent time with 'after.' She thought about guiding Curtis—with his awkward gait— across the trestle bridge. At the time, she hadn't fully understood what she'd done. It had happened so fast.

~ ~ ~ ~

Lovey did not take kindly to the appearance of the strangers, either two-legged or four-legged. She reverted back to flattening her ears and hissing. Titan, feeling likewise, bared his teeth and began to stomp as Haylee urged them closer. "Lovey! Stop it!" Haylee yelled. "Titan! Settle!"

Not wishing for a repeat of the earlier mule fiasco while trying to get Homer to dismount, Haylee was prepared to turn around to get out of Lovey's sight, but Lovey seemed more curious than afraid.

Thankful for the turn of events, Haylee continued to lead her mount toward the corral fencing. Haylee found a secure foothold on the planking. Still keeping Homer strapped to her back, she hauled them both off over the side while grabbing onto the fence. Nudging Titan away sideways with her free foot, Haylee spoke and sent thoughts to him to move slowly so that her foot would not get caught or tangled in the gear.

It worked! She experienced a moment of elation a split second before realizing how heavy Homer was when his entire weight was upon her. The fence cracked under their combined weight. It went down with a crash. Haylee let out an "oomph!" as she took the full force of the impact. Again tasting the salty brine of blood in her mouth, she wiggled out from under him while working to untie the lashes that joined them.

Lovey, having pranced away from the commotion, walked closer to inspect. Seemingly reassured that the woman was uninjured, she daintily stepped over the downed fence and sauntered over to make Titan's acquaintance.

~ ~ ~ ~

Later that night, Haylee stared across the fire to the form sprawled on the ground opposite her under a pile of blankets. Homer had packed well for his hunting trip. Haylee was grateful for the biscuits and canned beans that she'd discovered in his provisions. It had been easy enough to feed him as long as she put the spoon to his mouth. Shortly after dinner, they'd almost had an incident when he abruptly stood and began rocking back and forth. At first, she did not comprehend what he was doing. His rocking evolved into a sort of jig. "Oh!" Haylee exclaimed. She jumped up, grabbing his hand to drag him toward the bushes. Fumbling with the front of his pants, she barely got him situated before he let loose a steady stream. Deeply embarrassed, she turned away. She wondered what the heck they were going to do when he had to do more than pee!

Heating water from a nearby creek, Haylee did the best she could to give herself a sponge bath. She didn't stink nearly as bad as Homer did. Still, she was eager to scrub as much of the leftover mud off as she could. She couldn't bring herself to do the same for Homer, so she sufficed with wiping his face and hands.

Technically, she now had company around the campfire. Dropping her face into her hands she muttered, "Homer, what am I going to do with you?"

A dry laugh escaped her as she imagined having to take care of all of her victims…at the same time.

Wrapping her arms around her shins and resting her chin on her knees, Haylee let the quiet settle over her. More of Homer's drawings began to take shape before her inner eye. He'd begun experimenting with people. Scenes, rough at first then rapidly improving, of miners with gold pans and digging tools. A woman with a tolerant expression. The same woman laughing, thinking, and daydreaming. Across the bottom, Homer had written, Martina Mercede. Feelings of longing and protectiveness bubbled to the surface. Haylee could see his fingers gently shading her curves. Softy Haylee whispered, "Oh…Homer, you're in love."

⚘45⚘

YERBA BUENA

They trod through the outskirts of the sprawling tent city, taking their time so that Homer, draped over Titan's back and covered with blankets, would not slip off. The sights, sounds, and smells were not as shocking as the first time she'd seen them in New Helvetia. But San Francisco…or Yerba Buena as it was called in 1849…was still an impressive sight!

Haylee paused to survey what lay in the distance. Her interest was captured by the forest of perpendicular timbers that populated the water's surface. Sailing ships of all sizes jammed together to form a floating landmass. *What the heck?* she wondered.

As they got closer to the water and the wooden buildings, the streets grew increasingly gloppy and deep, sucking with ever-increasing strength against boots and hooves.

When they passed other travelers, Haylee made mental inquiries of the horses that went by. She asked how they were treated at the liveries in town. It quickly became clear that there was a favorite. Haylee had to search for the building by sight as none of the equines paid much attention to signs or writing on the buildings.

By midafternoon, she'd located the place and paid for Lovey and Titan's board. She made a point to let Lovey know that other horses she'd communicated with thought that this livery was good and the caretakers here were quite friendly. The stable master looked on in surprise as Homer slid out from under his blanket, landing in the hay under Titan's feet with a grunt. Haylee hurried over to help him muttering, "My brother...stewed."

Shoving Homer's hat on so that it covered his face, she led him out onto the street. Once again, they wandered in search of something, this time it was Homer's tent. Haylee kept to the boardwalks. Traversing through the mud with him would be difficult. On more than one occasion, they were rudely shoved out of the way by bands of unruly men as they erupted from the gambling parlors. Haylee kept her own hat low and did nothing more than grunt when they were yelled at or pushed.

Haylee was exhausted by the time they reached Portsmouth Square. She could tell that Homer was too by the way he dragged his feet. Piano notes, raucous laughter, and the smell of roasting meat drew Haylee toward a set of doors not far away. Two men sprang out into the air in front of them as they approached. Haylee held Homer in place in case more were about to follow. Looking out from the door was a buxom woman wearing a flowing dress. She turned her head to regard Haylee and Homer. "We just made room for two more. If you have money or gold, you can come in."

Haylee read the sign over the front door—Bella Union. "We just need food, we're not looking for a game...or anything else."

The two men who'd been thrown out, got on their feet, and began to wander away on a weaving, drunken path. The woman's eyes regarded them. She replied, "My cook has plenty." Her eyes snapped back to scrutinize Haylee. Feeling uncomfortable with the inspection, she offered, "My name is Hal."

"Maybel," the woman responded as her gaze traveled over Homer, lingering there. "You two don't look like the sort who'll break my glassware. I don't need any more of that today!" She nodded in Homer's direction. "What's wrong with your friend? He sick?"

"My brother hit his head when he fell off of his horse a while ago. He just needs to be quiet for a while."

Holding the door open, the woman stepped aside. "You come on in. I'll find you a quiet table, get you some food. If your brother needs to see the doc, he's inside." Glancing back over her shoulder, she said, "By the looks of it, he'll be here for a while."

Stepping into the dimly lit interior, Haylee was assaulted by the smell of cigar smoke and cheap perfume. Underneath those layers of smells was the cloying scent of unwashed bodies.

Maybel led them through the room, winding between gaming tables crowded with men. A few women served drinks, one woman led a man up a set of stairs, and several more leaned over the balustrade at the top, wearing…not much at all. Haylee's cheeks flamed.

Focusing her attention away from those disturbing sights, she watched the layers of clothing sway back and forth over Maybel's behind. Haylee thought that the dress must be hot, heavy, and uncomfortable. She was glad to be wearing men's clothes.

People glanced curiously at Homer as he clomped along in the rear. Moving through a set of curtains, they were led into a small room with only a few tables, one of which was occupied by a tall, thin man in formal attire and a woman dressed similarly to Maybel. The hostess's eyes met the other woman's. An imperceptible nod communicated across the space between the two. Maybel seated Haylee and Homer farthest from the couple.

A hearty Slumgullion Stew with biscuits arrived. It smelled wonderful! Haylee would have liked nothing more than to shovel it down. But she noticed that the woman at the other table, although chatting and interacting with her partner, kept sending quick glances in their direction. The woman looked familiar but Haylee could not place where she could have seen her before. It made her nervous.

Eating slowly, pausing to put spoons of thick broth to Homer's lips, Haylee surreptitiously studied the other woman as well. Dressed in a ruffled, deep purple gown, dark hair swept up on her head revealed clear olive skin. Tendrils that escaped confinement snaked their way along her graceful neck.

Her table partner leaned in close to whisper in her ear. She laughed, placing her hand on his cheek. He moved his head down to nuzzle her neck. Letting her head fall back, her eyes met Haylee's.

Haylee could feel the burn of embarrassment scorching her face.

The man stood, making a curt bow to the woman as he took his leave. "Until next time, Martina."

Haylee's eyes grew wide when she recognized that name and realized that she'd seen this woman in Homer's drawings. *Shit! Shit!* she thought. *Can I possibly have any luck that's not bad?*

As soon as her customer was out of sight, Martina made a beeline toward them. Grabbing Homer's shoulder, she turned him so she could reach for his chin with her free hand, "Al! Mi cariño, what has happened?"

Seeing his nonresponsive eyes, she turned to Haylee. "Who are you? And what is wrong with him? Why does he look as though he does not see me?"

Thinking fast, Haylee stood, crossing her arms over her chest. "My name is Hal. I'm family from England. I arrived in port today. Why are you calling him Al and who are you?"

The two women challenged each other until Martina lowered her eyes.

From the other room a drunken male voice bellowed, "Where's my Chileno?!" Martina's eyes widened. "I must go," she said hurriedly. Laying a possessive hand on Homer's arm, she said, "I love this man. Please tell me what has happened"

Haylee hesitated. "He fell from his horse and hit his head."

"I will get Doctor Carlyle." She turned to leave but Haylee reached for her sleeve. "Wait! Where is…Al's…tent?"

Martina's eyes dropped to the hand. Haylee quickly released her hold. "North. Near Coolie Town. Find Chen's place, he'll show you."

"Thank you," Haylee replied.

"Sí. Take care of him."

~ ~ ~ ~

It was dark by the time Haylee and Homer reached his shelter. After fumbling and cursing while attempting to light an oil lamp, Haylee got them settled in for the night, Homer on his cot and she on the floor. They both fell into an exhausted slumber.

~ ~ ~ ~

Mr. Chen seemed happy enough to take Homer over to his laundry tent to bathe him and change his clothes…for a fee. While he was gone, Haylee thought about her meeting with Dr. Carlyle while she searched through the contents of Homer's belongings. The doctor had been convinced that the fellow's symptoms—malaise and partial immobility—were clear indicators of scurvy.

She had carefully questioned him regarding care options for patients with no family. Carlyle told her about the sailor sanatorium. *I wonder if Martina would take care of him?*

Try as she would, Haylee could not mine the information she wanted out of Homer's thoughts. She spent considerable time searching his small space for his stash of gold. When she discovered the metal dynamite box buried below several inches of loose dirt under his cot, Haylee smiled in triumph.

She sat on the bed leafing through Homer's sketchbook. Viewing his drawings and paintings, she felt the sentiments he'd felt and heard his thoughts as he created each one. The experience was both beautiful and bittersweet. She lingered over the likeness of Martina. Having seen the woman in the flesh made their love more real.

"Once I have enough gold, will you marry me?" she heard Homer ask as he watched Martina brush her hair.

With a sad smile, Martina had looked up into her mirror to meet his eyes in the reflection. "I make very much money mi amour. The men break their backs in the fields. All I have to do is lie on mine and they give it to me. On my back, I can make more gold faster than you can dig it up."

Miserably, Homer had turned to leave, but Martina had stopped him, pressing herself into his arms as she kissed him in a way that made it impossible for him to think of anything but his want of her. Looking urgently into his eyes, she'd gripped his elbows and implored, "Querido, I will take the gold from any man, but there is only one man who holds my heart." Placing her hand on his chest, she'd said, "Once you think you have enough, I'll consider it."

Haylee glanced up at the heavy satchel sitting next to her on the bed. Homer's hard earned savings. Mr. Chen would claim a bit of it.

Feeling the need to move on, Haylee hastily turned the rest of the pages. She spotted a few of the faces of the women she'd seen at the Bella Union. Homer must have spent a lot of time in that place. It was amazing that more people hadn't recognized him when they'd been in there. Haylee closed the book and tucked it into the heavy bag.

~ ~ ~ ~

Free of Homer, Haylee wandered the city; she had no other ideas about what to do next. As she approached the wharf, the mud grew thicker and deeper. Where the boardwalks ended, "stepping stones" crossed the streets. The "stones" consisted of barrels, tables, crates, and other pieces of wood that temporarily remained at the surface of the mire.

At one intersection, she paused to watch a group of men sweating with exertion as they unloaded cartloads of sand and brush into a yawning hole. At another, she laughed to find herself balancing on top of a cooking stove that barely had any surface area left.

Finally making it to the docks, Haylee stared out at the floating city. She spent a long time just watching. She noticed planking that wove a crooked path spanning the distance between many of the vessels. Noisy activity conglomerated on more than a few of them, but there were still many more, farther out, that appeared void of life. She wasn't sure what lay ahead or how long this would take. *Maybe this is where I end up for the rest of my life. It doesn't look like today is the end, so I better figure out where I am going to make camp. There's no way that I am staying in Homer's tent, although it would be easy hunting. I can't*

afford a surprise. Making a decision, she clutched her satchel
tighter and steeled herself to enter the crush of males jamming
the outer perimeter of the floating city.

❧46❧

DICEY

It was pitch black when Haylee awoke. For a brief moment, she thought she was in her bed at the boarding house.

A rolling motion and the sound of creaking wood reminded her that she was living on an abandoned ship in Yerba Buena Cove. There was lots of confusion about this place. Some people still called it Yerba Buena; others called it Upper California, though its new official name was San Francisco. Although the state was no longer governed by Mexico, it had not yet been included in the United States of America. It was a lawless place where anything could happen. If she'd grown up during this time, she'd have chosen to remain back east with the women who waited for their men to return once they'd attained their piles.

Footsteps above made Haylee sit up straight. Hastily throwing on clothes, she grabbed the heavy stick that she kept by her bed. Silently, she crept to the upper deck while keeping to the shadows.

The intruder, like all of the others, believed that the ship was abandoned. He wasn't even making an effort to be quiet as he rummaged around. Making her voice as deep as possible, she asserted, "You won't be finding what you are looking for on my ship! My gun is pointed right at you."

Startled, the fellow turned toward the voice while raising his hands high in the air. A stream of words Haylee could not understand burst from him.

"Move on then!" she called. Immediately, the man jumped overboard. Haylee walked to the edge of the rail to watch him swim away.

Taking a few deep breaths to calm her racing heart, she made her way back to the captain's cabin.

Haylee had set up living quarters aboard the clipper ship Dicey. It hailed from New Zealand. She'd chosen this particular vessel because it was in a remote, mostly uninhabited sector of the Boneyard, as Haylee had heard the floating city called. This vessel had not been littered with decaying garbage or infested with rats.

The ships closest to shore, the ones that fit so tightly together, housed taverns, billiard parlors, and supply stores where captains sold cargo directly off their decks.

Unable to get back to sleep, Haylee lit an oil lamp. Practice had improved her lantern lighting abilities, but they were still fumbly. She wrapped herself up in a quilt and went to sit at the captain's desk. Pulling out the ship's log, she lazily turned the pages. She'd read the entire book from cover to cover when she first set up her living arrangements. The neat penmanship and detailed accounts of their travels and business dealings comforted Haylee. Now and then, Captain Knights included his own thoughts among the log entries. One that Haylee kept returning to was, "My motto has always been, never despair; persevere, and never give up hope."

She wondered where Knights was now. *Did he abandon this ship like his crew?* She didn't think such a meticulous person would do such a thing.

Picking up his quill and dipping it in the jar of ink, Haylee began to write.

November 1849

Dicey floats among hundreds of empty sailing ships that populate Yerba Buena Cove. Rail to rail, they bump against one another other.

In the Captain's quarters, Haylee Garrett has taken up residence. A young woman who masquerades as a man...

Haylee unwrapped the pendant and arranged it on the desk next to the journal. She stared at it quietly, watching the shifting flickers of light dance within its mysterious depths. It was neither hot nor cold— just warm. It had remained that way since she'd arrived in town. For the first time, she wondered how far back it had traveled through her family. *Who made it… and why? Did the pendant ever take my mother to a different time? Did Mom know about what was going to happen once I turned eighteen?*

Haylee was tired of running. Tired of hurting people and tired of not knowing what was coming next. And very, very tired of feeling alone.

Dragging Homer around had lessened those feelings some, mostly because she'd been so busy figuring out what to do with him. Without him, her loneliness wrapped itself around her like a cold, wet blanket.

Haylee crawled into bed. While she did so, she let Josh's thoughts bubble to the surface of her mind. It hurt to let them in, but she did it anyway.

The intrigue of Haylee occupies too much of my thoughts. How can I desire someone who preys on humans? There is something about her that keeps me coming back instead of running in the opposite direction. That, truly, would be the logical course of action. Therefore, I must be insane.

A dry, ironic laugh escaped her as she followed him to his conclusion. "Insane, you were not." She swiped at the tear on her face. Closing her eyes, she was unaware when the transition between weeping and sleep occurred.

~ ~ ~ ~

Days of torrential rain kept Haylee indoors. She was grateful for the supply of canned food that she'd found in the galley and a stash of books. She attempted to nap when she couldn't stand the boredom.

Deep in her sleep cycle, Haylee tossed and turned under the heavy quilts. Flinging out an arm, she dreamed that she was in pursuit of another frightened victim. "No!" she cried out, trying to stop herself from a behavior that was too powerful to control. "No…no…no…" she murmured as she watched herself bring a young woman down to the ground, cutting off her screams abruptly with a flick of her hand and a little pressure. A satisfied, "Ahhhh…" escaped Haylee when the girl's soul came to rest.

Haylee lay peacefully, unmoving for a time.

Visions of Josh came next; a gentle smile appeared on her lips. Then, she was Josh, seeing the world through his eyes, feeling his sense of confidence and anticipation. A blue eyed, blond girl skipped beside him laughing…Rita. Haylee felt his heart warm as Rita took his hand, squeezing it in a way that communicated her feelings. They hurried to "their" secluded corner. Arms wound around each other as their lips met. Josh breathed in deeply to catch the scent of the cinnamon gum she always chewed. He laughed to discover that it had migrated into his own mouth.

Bitter feelings arose when Josh realized that Rita had

manipulated him into having sex. Weeks afterward, he'd come to understand she'd lied about it being her first time. He would never admit it to anyone, but the experience left him feeling used.

Waking up an hour later, Haylee didn't retain the specifics of her dreams, only a nagging feeling of missing Josh and wishing for something she couldn't name.

⚘47⚘

SEARCHING

The weather cleared. Haylee dressed warmly, tying her boots extra tight to keep the mud from sucking them off. She headed out to walk the streets in search of what the pendant wanted of her. It was frustrating that it remained warm—not giving her any further clues.

Haylee had chosen Dicey for its seclusion from the other ships. Securing the daypack she'd fashioned out of sailcloth to her back, she climbed down the rigging to the dingy she'd pro-cured. A tremor nearly sent her into the water. With only a split second warning, she clamped onto the rigging with a lock-like hold. Over time, Haylee had learned that the outer edges of her vision blurred right before the vibrations hit.

Cursing and shaking her head, she quickly continued, knowing that the day's events would not unfold exactly as she'd planned.

A sense of haste permeated her movements as Haylee retraced her steps to the square. Morning was not very busy there. After a few hours, she wandered toward the Chinese encampment. Men dressed in utilitarian clothing with thin braids hanging down their backs worked at large vats filled with boiling water. Bedding, blankets, and all assortments of clothes filled laundry lines, drying in the midday sun. Other men pulled hot irons out from fires to press wrinkled cloth into smoothness. A few of the 'Chinamen' greeted her with a friendly wave, but mostly, they attended to their work at hand. At first, Haylee been shocked and appalled to hear the derogatory racist language that everyone seemed to use…even more appalled at how certain groups of people were treated based on their heritage. None of the history books she had ever read mentioned that. Practically everyone here came from somewhere else. *What gives any group the right to think they are better than any other?* Haylee wondered.

Approaching Powell Street, Haylee stopped to look at the building where Homer now resided. The calls of the milk and watermen drifted to her. At this early hour, Haylee didn't feel the tension she usually carried over having to be alert when spontaneous gunfights broke out. For a time she lost herself in the wonder of seeing, smelling and hearing the birth of a beautiful city.

At Brannon Street, newspapermen shouted, "Alta California, get your day's news." Rounding the next corner, Haylee broke out in surprised laugh. Inching its way up the middle of the street was a ship! A team of horses strained to pull a wide shallow wagon that held the craft. She joined a crowd of on-lookers, listening to their chatter about the fellow who made his business moving vessels and houses. This one, its destination three blocks north, would become a boarding house.

⚜48⚜

POLLY

Six and a half year old Polly Laurent was thoroughly enjoying her day outside. She especially liked it when Song Zhao made her laugh with magic tricks. He never made her feel like he wished she were somewhere else. Today she was going with him to pick up flour, sugar, and bolts of new cloth. She skipped beside him, bringing a smile to his face. She anticipated their stop at Keener Brothers Mercantile. *Young Mr. Keener will surely give me a taste of sweets today!*

The thought made her happy, but her contentment faded as she remembered the day she and her maman had first arrived in Yerba Buena.

~ ~ ~ ~

Maybel had been waiting on the docks. She shoved her way through the crowds as soon as she laid eyes on Maman. A hurried conversation between them had Maman near tears but nodding her head. "Now that that is settled…" Maybel led them to a quieter spot farther from all the people. She leaned down wearing a big smile that didn't look real to Polly, "You can call me Auntie May or Owl Arms. Everyone calls me that because of my big white arms!" Laughing, the woman sent a cloud of stinky breath straight into Polly's face. Her mother cut off her sassy reply by grabbing her elbow and moving them forward.

In the days and weeks that followed, Polly's Maman cried a lot during the day. By the time sundown arrived, she'd be all prettied up and smiling. Always sent to bed early, Polly'd snuck out of her room a few times to spy on Maman and the other women who lived at the Union. They took lots of different men into their rooms. The men were not always nice to them.

Polly and her mother used to go for walks in the early mornings. They visited the Keener Brothers store a lot, as Maman thought of new supplies she needed to make their rooms more like home. Older Mr. Keener, Reece, was the only one Polly had seen who could make her Maman smile. Both of the Keeners were polite and gentlemanly, a lot like the shop-keepers back home. *I think that Maman likes that because it reminds her of France.*

Younger Mr. Keener smiled and played games with her sometimes, saying that she reminded him of his sisters.

It was older Mr. Keener who told Maman about Song, "I know a family man with good references who may be able to help with domestic chores." His voice lowered. "And to keep Polly away from things you might not want her around."

Her mother's smile died then. Her eyes fell to floor as she replied, "That's decent of you, Mr. Keener. Thank you."

Song came into their lives after that. Then he was the one who took her to Keener's instead of her mother. *Maman doesn't go outside much anymore. The drinking makes her not as nice as she used to be.*

"I don't want to think about that now!" Polly yelled loudly before breaking out into a run.

"Polly!" Song called as he raced to catch up with her. "No!

No! Too dangerous to be on the streets far from Song." As the girl mumbled an apology, he held out his hand for her to take.

~ ~ ~ ~

Song Zhao had long ago stopped trying to correct the misunderstanding about his name. In China, the family name is stated first and the given name second. Most Americans mutilated the pronunciation of his first name anyway—Song was easier to say. It came as a mild revelation when he realized that he'd started to think of himself as 'Song.'

He had discovered a balm for his weary spirit at the Keener Brothers Mercantile. Men with his skills were well regarded back home. Here, he was valued for his ability to work hard, but as a person, he was considered nothing more than a "Chinaman"—lower than dirt. The Keener brothers treated him as a man and regarded him as an equal. For this attitude alone, the two young men had earned his respect. Whenever he had a supply need, Keener's is where he went. The day that Mr. Reece told him about the job with Ms. Emis had been a good one. Working for Emis and Owl-Arm Maybel, Song had gained a certain admiration for the women. In his own country, such women were looked down upon. Here they were prized and held in high esteem.

He would never understand why Ms. Emis had brought her daughter to this place. He shook his head. As much as he missed his own children, he was grateful that he'd left them at home in the Chinese Empire.

Everyone here was an adventurer. They had all left behind a troubled past in order to take advantage of the rewards to be found on a new frontier. Shaking his head with a bit of melancholy, Song realized that the price paid for adventure was a dear one.

The door to the Mercantile jingled a bell. Haylee saw a

Chinese man and a little girl enter. "Monsieur Edward!" the girl called.

"Miss Laurent, it's a pleasure to see you again." Edward Keener came out from behind the counter to squat down to greet her.

As the girl chatted amicably with Edward, Haylee looked down at her and her eyes grew wide. She couldn't take her eyes off of the blue sparkle that twinkled at the girl's neck. *She's wearing my pendant!* Haylee tried to remain calm. She reached down to trace the hard form of the identical pendant inside her pocket. It was then that Haylee noticed its temperature—or lack of. Understanding dawned. *It led me here...to this little girl.*

Haylee noticed the man who had come in with the girl watching her suspiciously. She moved her hand away from her pocket.

Edward, also apparently seeing the exchange, stood and said, "Song, Polly, I'd like you to meet Hal Garrett. I've just hired him to work in our storeroom and office."

Haylee shook herself while brushing off the front of her new shopkeeper's apron. She tried to act casual as she walked toward the little group of people.

Edward continued, "Hal will carry your purchases back to Bel's."

~ ~ ~ ~

Haylee focused all of her attention on following Song and Polly down the boardwalk. With the heavy sacks balanced precariously on her shoulders, she bit her tongue in order to keep from groaning or making any other straining noises.

Once out of sight of the Keener store, Song, noticing the beads of perspiration accumulating on Haylee's upper lip, offered to assist with the packages.

"No, sir!" Haylee responded, a bit breathlessly. "At Keener

Brothers, we work harder to keep our customers happy."
Haylee recited what Edward had taught her word-for-word
while making an effort to keep her tone light.

At the next intersection, Haylee was in the process of navi-
gating down steps when she noticed Polly hide behind Song's
legs. An open wagon loaded with supplies clattered to a halt.
"Hello, Mister Reece," Song called out.

"Good day, Mister Zhao," the driver returned while
tipping his hat. Still reeling from the discovery of Polly and
the pendant, Haylee was totally caught by surprise when she
looked up and into eyes she knew! It was Josh...but not Josh.
How is this possible? The blood drained from her face, and she
lost her precarious struggle to maintain balance. Fifty pounds of
dry goods tumbled from her grasp. One bag fell behind her and
the other on top. Pain seared through her chest. *Be a man! Be a
man!* she told herself while keeping it all inside.

Reece Keener jumped from the wagon to assist the fellow
now buried under his inventory. Song and Polly rushed forward to help too.

As the heavy weight was lifted from her, Haylee breathed
in a raged breath. Song reached out a hand to help her up.
Grasping it, she couldn't stop herself from crying out as he
hauled her to her feet. She made gulping sounds as she gasped
for air; her arms instinctively wrapped themselves around her
middle; her back hunched to minimize the incredible pain.

In a small voice, Polly commented, "At least the bags
haven't busted open."

Keener turned toward them after plunking down the bag
of sugar in the back of his wagon. "Are you alright?" he asked.

Unable to speak, Haylee shook her head back and forth
as tears gathered at the edges of her eyes. Song spoke up,
"Mister Keener, if you would be so kind as to take our provisions, we will take Mr. Hal to see Miss Maybel." To Haylee, he

spoke softly as he placed a guiding arm around her back. "It's very close. Lean on me if you need to."

Haylee nodded her understanding. She bit her lip again, this time to keep herself from whimpering with each step. Polly ran ahead to announce their arrival.

49.

EMIS

Maybel held the doors open as the trio entered. "Take him to Emis's room." She nodded toward the back of the building.

Haylee groaned as Song guided her to sit on the edge of the bed. Emis, used to being called on to tend to wounds before the doctor came, walked in carrying a bottle in one hand and a steaming pitcher in the other. Polly followed on her heels carrying clean towels. Haylee eyed the woman. A long dark dress came down to just above her ankles. Silk striped stockings could be glimpsed beneath its hem. The heels of her house slippers ticked over the floor as she came across the room. "Tell me what has happened." She spoke with a thick accent, addressing everyone in attendance. Her eyes were already assessing the patient.

Song spoke up. "Mister Hal stumbled while carrying our flour and sugar. One of the bags fell on top of him."

As Emis stepped close to her, Haylee caught the scent of powder and flowers.

Emis systematically checked her arms, collarbones, neck and head. Preoccupied, she commented off-handedly, "Your

hands do not have callouses that one would expect... Take in a
deep breath if you would, Monsieur," she directed.

Haylee's breath caught in the middle of her inhale and
froze. Emis reached out to probe her chest. Even in her haze of
pain, Haylee flinched away—worried that Emis would discover
her secret. Emis paused, looking puzzled. "Song, help me get
his shirt off," she said.

Just then, Edward and Reece entered the room.

Eyes wide with discomfort and embarrassment, Haylee
croaked, "No!"

Emis turned to face the people crowding the small space.
"Shoo, shoo, all of you go!"

Reece approached Emis on his way out. "Should we fetch
the doctor?"

"Non. Not yet," she replied. "It does not look like the lung
was punctured. I will be able to tell you in a few moments...if
you will kindly leave us." Reece made a small bow as he exited,
closing the door behind him.

"Now, Monsieur Hal, I think you have cracked a rib with
your fall. I brought whiskey to deaden the pain, but this is for
after I have made sure it is only your bones that have been
injured. It will be painful, but you're going to have to let me
take your shirt off."

Growing another shade paler, Haylee closed her eyes,
nodding. She screamed as Emis moved her arms while maneu-
vering her shirt. Hearing a muttered curse, Haylee was only
vaguely aware of the sound of cloth ripping. She was beyond
noticing Emis's expression as the other woman observed the
wrapping around her chest. She felt herself sinking into blackness, welcoming it.

"No! No! You are not to faint on me." She heard a stern
voice as if from a great distance. A nasty, stinging odor brought
her up from the blackness like a fish on a hook. Emis put the

smelling salts back into her pocket as Haylee blinked into awareness. "Better," Emis commented.

Pulling a chair close to the bed, the woman instructed her patient to hold on to the back of it for support as she set about unwinding the strips. "Why are you pretending to be a man?" Emis asked.

"I needed to be able to move around freely. It seemed the only way." Haylee spoke quietly as she watched the top of the woman's head; her hair was parted in the middle and pulled back into a bun that looked very smooth, almost like plastic. Haylee smiled wryly as she remembered that plastic didn't exist yet.

Emis chatted while she worked to take the girls mind off of the pain.

"Have you been in town very long?"

"No."

"I came from France with my daughter, who you already met. Where did you come from?"

"A place you've never heard of. It's far away…"

As the strips were removed, Haylee's breathing improved.

"You might be surprised, I know of very many places on this earth. One of my hobbies is studying Atlases."

Haylee tried to smile. "It's called Elverta. It's near Sacramento."

As the last of the wrapping fell away, Emis asked, "Is this better?"

Again, Haylee tried to take a deep breath. Although improved, there was still considerable pain.

"Allow me?" Emis asked, indicating that she meant to examine her.

Haylee's cheeks bloomed red as she nodded the affirmative. The woman's fingers were firm and warm. She appreciated the fact that this was the same way she checked out injured animals in her own care...until Emis found the tender spot. The resulting jolt sent Haylee through the roof.

"You're very lucky," Emis was saying as she poured a shot glass full of amber liquid. "Drink."

The burn as it traveled down Haylee's throat made her cough, which caused more spasms of hurt. Emis directed her to drink two or three more shots. "You have broken only one rib. The wrapping protected you from further injury."

As the tension in her midsection began to release, a warm feeling spread out from her belly. Haylee's eyelids grew heavy. "Thank you for your help," she murmured.

"What's your name?" Emis asked.

"Haylee. My name is Haylee."

"Well, Mademoiselle Haylee, sleep is what you need right now." Emis brought out a chemise, dropping it over the girl's head, not even bothering with her arms. She pulled her feet up onto the bed and removed her boots. "You are welcome to my bed until it's time for me to work." Haylee was asleep before Emis had finished her sentence.

Emis walked over to the bedside, taking Haylee's chin in hand. "If you had hair, you would be beautiful." She ran a finger up over Haylee's cheek, "You remind me of my maman."

~ ~ ~ ~

As Emis walked out into the main salon, she overheard Reece quizzing his younger brother.

"Why would you hire someone without checking with me first?"

She paused in the dark hallway to listen for a few moments. Her eavesdropping skills, perfected in the past, usually served her well.

"Sometimes I think you're ready to take on more respon-sibility at the store—then at other times I worry about the decisions you make."

Emis entered the room, placing a hand on Reece's arm as she pulled out a chair to join them. "You are too hard on your brother, Monsieur Keener. You forget that he has only quinze ans. Excuse me…he is only fifteen years old."

Edward threw her a smile. She inclined her head in acknowledgement.

Reece turned toward her with a quizzical look. She responded, "Hal is going to be fine. He has only one cracked rib. He needs a few days of rest then he should be able to go back to work." She sent a meaningful look at Edward. "As long as you don't make him try to carry a hundred pounds."

"I didn't hire him for his brawn. He is good with numbers and he can write. I thought he might be useful working on the mountain of invoices that Reece never seems to get to." He looked at his brother. "You keep saying that if we could keep our income consistent with our supply expenses, we'd have a much stronger loan application when we approach the bank."

Reece stared at his younger brother in shock. Holding out his hand, they shook. "I am eating my words, Ed. In the meantime, we have a load of stock to move."

The Keeners thanked Emis, promising to return to collect Hal in a few hours.

❧50❧

TRAVELER

Haylee awoke to a blurry face several inches away from her own. Polly.

"Why do you have dimples in your ears?" the little girl asked. "Are you a sailor? I saw that you have one in both of your ears. I thought sailors only wore hoops in one ear."

"What?" Haylee mumbled fuzzily.

Emis popped her head in the door. "Polly, I sent you in to get your reader, not to wake our patient."

"He was already awake."

"No matter, it is time for you to go into the kitchen with Song."

"Why do you always make me go in the kitchen?!"   ·

"You know Miss Maybel's rule about children."

"Humph!"

Haylee heard a clattering down the hallway.

Emis walked all the way into the room, looking Haylee over. "You look a little better. Edward has come for you. He is waiting outside. I will help you dress." She walked over to the bedside table, poured another shot, and held it out to Haylee.

"You can take the bottle with you. It will get you through the next couple of days."

Emis rewrapped Haylee's chest, though not quite as tight this time. As she was buttoning up the front of a fresh shirt, a knock sounded on the door. Before Emis could answer, it swung open. Martina strode in.

"Maybel wanted—" Recognizing Haylee, she stopped in mid-sentence. "It's you! How is Alfred? Where is he?"

"Aaaahhh." Haylee attempted to focus her thoughts. "He's a little better. I took him to Powell Street."

"But that is a sanatorium for sailors. Al is no sailor!"

"Dr. Powell said that he could help Homer."

"Homer!" Martina's voice rose.

Haylee sighed, "He told you his name is Al—but his birth name is Homer. Homer Scott."

Martina let rip a profusion of fast Spanish that Haylee did not understand.

Emis had moved to helping Haylee put on her boots. Having finished tying her laces, she asked, "What happened to Al?"

Martina replied, "What happened!? What happened!? This gringo says that Al took a fall from his horse and hit his head. When I saw Al, he could not speak, he did not know me, and he could not even feed himself! Gringo says he is family to Al and that he would look after him. Now he tells me he put him in Powell Street!" She turned toward Haylee. "His wife sent you! You've come to take his pile!" Martina screamed making a lunge for Haylee. With surprising speed and agility, Emis blocked Martina's way, grabbing a handful of hair and pulling hard to stop the raging female in her tracks.

"Aieee!" screeched Martina. Standing up to her full height, Emis growled in the girl's ear, "I will take care of this, Martina, now go!" Emis shoved her toward the door.

"You have not heard the last of this!" the dark beauty screamed as she stalked out.

Haylee stared in shock.

Emis leaned her back against the closed door, breathing hard. She looked pale and shaken. Her voice quavered when she whispered, "I have been reading the newspaper articles— men with symptoms like Al's. Some of my callers have spoken of this also…"

Haylee tried to stand, but fell back against the bed when the edges of her vision blurred.

Emis's trembling hands flew up to cover her mouth as she watched Haylee shudder and thrash.

~ ~ ~ ~

"You must be very, very hungry," Haylee heard Emis whisper. Haylee blinked slowly, staring up at the ceiling. Recovering from her fit, she turned her head toward the other occupant in the room. Still unable to reply, she watched as Emis left the room and closed the door softly behind her.

When she realized what Emis had seen. Haylee did the best she could to scramble off the bed—not getting too far in her attempts. She was painfully struggling to move when the door opened again. Emis entered holding the wrist of a disheveled woman who stumbled in behind her.

Emis pushed the woman toward Haylee. Swaying precariously, the unkempt female looked like she was about to fall over. "What the hell, Eme?" The woman slurred her words. "This 'un's barely out 'o nappies."

"I know what you are." Emis spoke only to Haylee. "The crystal—it told me that you were coming."

Haylee, suffering from hunger and her own physical

discomfort, met Emis's direct stare. "I don't understand," she croaked.

Darting her eyes at the teetering woman, Emis replied, "I brought you food."

Unable to resist, Haylee let her instincts take over. Leaping from her place on the bed—*thwap!*—she landed on top of the woman with her hand clamped in place. There was no resistance. It was over in minutes.

~ ~ ~ ~

Emis was transported back to the last time that she'd harvested a soul…. She'd been ravenous! Without caution, she jumped on a farmer on his way in from the field.

High-pitched screams pierced the evening air. His wife had seen! As Emis raced through the forest, sticks and branches cut her face. She held her skirts high so she could gain more speed.

A racket could be heard in the distance; the smell of smoke permeated the air. The closer it got, the more terrified she became. It was a torch-wielding mob and it was out for blood… her blood.

A pair of strong arms abruptly seized her from behind. She tried to claw her way free, but she was held fast. The man whispered something in her ear that caused her struggles to cease.

He hid her away in a quiet safe place. She loved him… That he would risk his reputation for her was beyond belief.

"I promise that everything is going to be alright." He smiled, leaning over to place a kiss on her forehead. For a moment, all of her angst and terror were replaced with soft feelings. She tilted her chin so their lips could meet; she responded with a glow in her heart and passion in her veins.

Before she even knew what was happening, she had pinned him to the ground. She heard her own screams, "No! No! No!" She tried to break the contact even as he kicked and bucked beneath her.

"No!" she croaked, as her hand remained solid as an oak.

"No," she whispered as she accepted his energy into her body.

"No," she mouthed as she watched his sparkling eyes turn to glass.

Even as her back arched, her face was wet with tears.

When it was over, she kissed his unmoving lips. Pressing her tongue into his gaping mouth, she used her hands in places on his body that had never before failed to elicit a response. Frustrated and still in shock, she stood and backed away from him. "Marcel," she sobbed, "I could not stop it."

~ ~ ~ ~

When Haylee disengaged from the scraggly woman, she stood up straighter and breathed easier. The pinched expression on her face relaxed. She looked over at Emis who watched intently. Their eyes held.

Emis stood frozen in place. The call to feed sang in her blood, rang in her ears, and ripped through her soul. She remembered what it felt like to take someone's energy inside herself, to ripple with delight as it dislodged from its host. The mighty fulfillment when it became all hers. With great effort, she turned her face away. "You're a Traveler!" Emis rasped. She shook her head vigorously from side to side. "I know how far you've come."

~ ~ ~ ~

Bewildered and distracted, Haylee focused on the sound of her boots as they traversed the boardwalk. Making only cursory attempts to respond to Edward Keener's chatter, Haylee replayed the scene that had happened only moments before.

When Haylee heard Emis call her a Traveler, something inside of her clicked into place. But before she could comprehend what it all meant, Emis had pushed her at Edward, telling him. "He will be fine in a few days. Go now, I have to work."

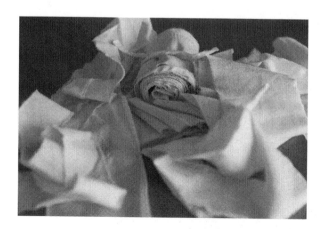

⚘51⚘

RUNNING BLIND

Emis watched nervously as Edward escorted the young woman masquerading as a man down the walkway. Clamping down on the compulsion to run screaming for Polly, she waited until they were out of sight before scrambling back to her room.

Grabbing pieces of luggage for herself and her daughter, she threw things into the satchels wildly, moving as fast as possible. A special petticoat Emis had fashioned went on under her skirt before she went to collect Polly.

She could not afford the time it would take to explain anything to Maybel before they left, so Emis put a large number of paper bills into an envelope along with a hastily scrawled note.

Making sure the hall was empty, Emis grabbed their bags. She slid her envelope under Maybel's door, thankful that the woman slept through most of the daylight hours.

Seeing that the kitchen was vacant save for Polly and Song, Emis entered. Song's eyes immediately focused on the bags. Before he could speak, she set them down and went to him. Placing a hand on his arm, she whispered in earnest. "I beg of you, help us to leave here unnoticed. I've made provisions for you with Maybel."

Without a word, Song went to Polly. Speaking to her quietly, he gently guided her toward the back door. Emis heard him say, "Remember the story of the bear and the squirrel. Now be a good girl and be very quiet for your Maman."

Emis saw tears shining in his eyes as they passed. Emis and Polly successfully entered the throng of revelers on the street, unnoticed by anyone inside the Bella Union.

~ ~ ~ ~

Polly soon grew tired of keeping up with her mother. She'd seen that look on her face before...when they had run to stay clear of the French army...and when their ship had been caught in a storm. Polly noticed heads turning in their direction as they passed people on the streets.

As the light of day faded, she watched townspeople and shopkeepers hurrying into their homes and barring the doors. Polly hadn't been out at night since they'd arrived here. She'd been told it was because Hounds and Ducks roamed the streets doing awful things. Gunfire was a common occurrence. Often in the mornings, she'd observed people cleaning up broken glass and other messes that the animals had caused. For the life of her, she could not imagine Ducks causing such mayhem. Besides, she was always on the lookout for feathers. She almost never found any.

Keeping quiet for as long as possible, she couldn't help herself from airing her concerns. "Maman! It's getting dark! Where are we going? Why are we running?"

~ ~ ~ ~

Realizing, in her panic, that she'd made an error in judgment, Emis cursed, "Merde!" Her daughter was right. The vicious criminal mobs of the night hours were a real danger.

Emis's first instinct had been to board a keelboat bound

upriver. She'd been leading them to the Long Wharf. Now, as she held tightly to her daughter's hand, she changed directions, racing back toward the ocean cove. She scanned the waterfront for familiar vessels, and the Moselle came into view. Emis knew that Captain Dupré would put them up for the night…for a certain trade.

⚜52⚜

ALONE AGAIN

Haylee watched as Edward closed and locked the shop doors. He moved back and forth, putting wooden panels in place over the panes of glass. Pulling several shotguns out from behind the counter and placing them at the ends of the aisles nearest the doors, he asked if she could manage to light a few lanterns as he finished up.

"Those guns aren't loaded are they?" she said as she moved to follow his directives.

"Of course they are." Pausing, he looked at her quizzically. "What good would they do if they weren't?"

Embarrassed by her naiveté she fumbled with the matches. As Edward continued with his chores, footsteps on the stairs announced the arrival of the other Keener brother. In all of the commotion of the afternoon, Haylee had forgotten about him.

With a lit match pinched between her fingers, she looked up into his inquiring blue eyes. Once again, she experienced a powerful reaction to this man. "Ow!" she yipped, dropping the match.

Reacting on instinct, Reece jumped to step on the burning

ember, knocking Haylee aside as he did so.

Breathless for several reasons, Haylee hunched over, hugging her ribs.

"I apologize!" Reece exclaimed. "I can't have an errant match sending this place up in flames."

"No...no. I am sorry for being careless," she croaked in return.

Reece started to put an arm around Haylee to support her, but then pulled back sharply. He looked confused and distraught, much the way Haylee was feeling. She assumed that it was because he did not like her. It never entered her mind that the opposite could be true.

Haylee was stupefied over the currents of emotions that Reece stirred within her. Upon closer inspection, she realized that he didn't look exactly like Josh, but if you stood the two side by side, you'd certainly wonder if they were brothers. Reece was taller and broader in the shoulders. Where Josh's hair was brown and curly, Reece's was raven black and straight. Their eyes were exactly the same, though: sky blue, with whirls of thought shining in their fathomless depths, framed by long, thick lashes. The timber of Reece's voice, though reminiscent of Josh's, had a depth all its own. His Irish brogue sent tingling waves of anticipation over the surface of Haylee's skin. She wanted to put her hands on him, not to steal his soul but to feel his warmth, to sink into the sense of trust and safety that she felt near him. *Am I inventing all these feeling about this stranger just because he reminds me of Josh?* Haylee wondered. Attempting to block out the disturbing comparisons, her mind betrayed her by envisioning what it would feel like to press her lips against his.

Deftly lighting the lantern, Reece called out to Edward that he'd take Hal back to the kitchen. Holding the light up high so they could both see, he directed, "This way."

Throughout the meal that Reece had prepared, both men

made small talk, but Haylee remained silent and picking at her food. She responded with one word replies or grunts. Reece continued to look like he was on edge, jumpy and cross. Finally, he threw his napkin on the table. "For God's sake, Ed!" he exclaimed as he got up. Throwing his dishes in the washbasin with a loud clank, he stalked out.

Edward watched Hal straighten up as his brother exited. "Yesterday when you came into the store, you were a regular chatty Joe. I know that you are probably still hurting, but what's going on between you and my brother?"

Looking at Edward, Haylee responded, "Mr. Keener, I wish I knew!"

As soon as Reece was out of the room, Haylee's mind cleared. *What the heck am I doing sitting here? I need to talk to Emis!*

She stood. "This was not a good idea. I should go."

"Hold on friend." Edward reached for the Haylee's arm. "If you've been in town for any length of time, you'll know it's not safe to be out at night. You can bunk with us and start working straight away in the morning."

At Hal's hesitation, Ed pressed on. "I'm sorry about the injury, but my reputation is on the line. I have a long history of working to prove myself to my brother. If you walk out now, it'll set me back five paces."

Haylee replied honestly. "I am not sure if I'll be back tomorrow, but one thing you don't have to worry about is my being out after dark."

~ ~ ~ ~

Reece drew deeply on the cigar. Filling the space in his mouth with as much of the warm flavorful vapors as he could, he took a long inhale to blend the evening air with the smoke as it traveled down to fill his chest. The habitual behavior had long ago ceased to burn and scorch his throat but caused a release of tension. With each draw, the muscles along his neck and back loosened. Next—his stomach settled. Finally, his mind cleared and his thoughts came to rest on the subject of his unease. Hal.

What is about Hal that has my hair standing on end? I can barely stand to be in the same room with him.

Reece exhaled sending out a plume of white-tinged smoke.

If he has the skills that Ed thinks he has, then my brother was astute enough to pull a needed asset into the business. He was following everything Da ever taught us about not judging people by their looks but by their actions. But...

Draw—hold—exhale.

~ ~ ~ ~

Haylee exited by the same back door Reece had used earlier. The cool air felt good on her overheated skin. Moving into the shadows, she paused to regard Reece a short distance away as he smoked a cigar. The red glow from the ashes acted like a beacon. Every instinct in her wanted to approach him from behind, wrap her arms around his waist and rest her head on his shoulder.

What is wrong with you? she chastised herself.

She slipped silently away.

~ ~ ~ ~

Lost in his thoughts, Reece did not hear a sound as the back door opened and closed. His neck and shoulders began to bunch up again as the truth voiced in his mind. *I would have thought that if I had perverse proclivities for boys, that desire would have made itself known before now...*

He tightened his free hand into a fist. Testing himself, he was relieved to note that his body did not respond when visualizing relations with other males... *So why is it that I can't stop staring at him? Why do my feet lead me to reduce the distance between us whenever he's nearby? Why do I have to forcibly have to stop myself from reaching out to touch...*

"Oh for God's sake!" Reece cursed, threw down his smoke and crushed it vigorously under his boot.

~ ~ ~ ~

The streets were alive with ruffians. Gangs. Haylee headed straight toward where they congregated. Stray bullets were a real danger. With adrenalin pumping, she moved fast from shelter to shelter. Whether the tremors came up because she needed to feed or because food was so plentiful, she could not determine. Remembering how much better her ribs felt after Emis's offering, Haylee did not attempt to censure her behavior. Picking off outliers was easy. With each one, she felt stronger and clearer of mind. Anger grew within as she gained knowledge of her victims' contemptuous activities. Extortion, robbery, brutalization, racial harassment, and murder were just a few of their proclivities. Worst of all was their motto: "We get away with it because we can."

As the third man grew still under her unyielding webbed hand, she muttered using his own accent, "Ye slimy bloke, I get away with it too."

There were too many of them to make a difference by inactivating just a few. For a change, she didn't feel remorse for her actions.

~ ~ ~ ~

Once her midsection felt pain free, Haylee raced back to the Bella Union in search of Emis. Panic struck when she discovered that mother and daughter had left in a hurry. For a few hours, Haylee ran through the city searching everywhere she could think of. It was useless. She finally realized that they could not have gotten far because her pendant would have started to heat up.

Tired yet invigorated, healed yet weary, Haylee climbed

the rigging onto the deck of Dicey. It occurred to her that some of those criminals may have arrived aboard this very ship. *Those guys make the drug wars and gangs at home look like schoolyard bullies. No wonder all the law-abiding people hide behind closed doors.*

A quick inspection of the schooner assured her that she still had the place to herself.

The bed looked welcoming, but her mind was too busy for sleep. She kept thinking back to her first meeting with Edward Keener.

Haylee had grown weary of scouring the city looking for God-knows-what. Tired and discouraged, she'd entered the Mercantile. "Hello there, sir, welcome to Keener Brothers," a cheerful young man greeted her with a smile. "Hello." She could not help but return the gesture. The boy looked to be about fifteen or sixteen. Dressed in shopkeeper's garb, he was snappy and alert. Finding herself starved for engaging human interaction, she felt uplifted by the conversation.

"I haven't seen you here before. Are you new to town?"

"Yes, as a matter of fact, I am."

"If you are bound for the gold fields and need to get set up, we have just about anything a fellow could need. What can I help you with?"

They spent a pleasurable few hours chatting. Haylee told Keener her name was Hal. She occupied herself while Edward helped other customers by wandering around and marveling at all of the beautiful 'antique' merchandise on display.

She had to catch herself from asking him to explain what unfamiliar products were used for.

Haylee learned that Reece, Edward's older brother, had moved out west the year before. "He tried his hand in the gold fields for a while," Edward chuckled, "but then he learned pretty quickly that the real business to be had was outfitting the miners. Fortunately, he knew a lot about that as that's been our family business for generations!"

Haylee laughed at his stories of home. There was real fondness in his voice as he spoke of his parents and sisters. "I couldn't believe my good fortune when Da decided to let me come out to help Reece with the store!"

Edward said he had a quick skill for reading people and the ability to put them at ease within moments. This was why he manned the Keener store while his older brother, the negotiator of the family, spent his time procuring and transporting inventory. The arrangement worked well for them— giving them each a clear domain for their work and enough space to keep their naturally hot tempers from flaring up at each other.

Haylee could tell that Edward, like everyone else who encountered "Hal," noticed that her hands were frail, her face too smooth, and that there were peculiarities in her mannerisms. But when Edward learned that "Hal" had worked in an office before, he quickly offered her a job.

"If you have time to kill, I have a task in the back room that has your name written all over it," Edward mentioned hopefully.

Laughing for what felt like the first time in forever, Haylee agreed. Later, she would wonder how it was that she'd gotten herself pulled into that. *Extreme loneliness and a friendly face*, she surmised.

She pulled the ships log toward her.

I found Polly. She has my pendant.

Emis, Polly's mother, knows things about my condition. I mean to find out what it is.

Another surprise—Reece Keener. At first, he reminded me of Josh. When Reece is anywhere close to me, I can't think of anything else. The attraction to Keener goes way beyond a sense of familiarity. It is so powerful that it nearly obliterates everything else in my mind.

Thank goodness he thinks I am a man! If he were to look at me as a man looks at a woman…

I have to stay focused for Josh, for Glori, and for my dad!

Sincerely, Haylee Louise Garrett.

❧53❧

THE SEER

Aboard another craft in the cove, covers rustled as a naked woman moved to slide out of bed.

A heavy hand whipped out to grasp her wrist. "Not so fast, ma chèrie."

"You want more, ay?" came the feminine reply. Not wishing to rescale that hairy, jiggling mountain of flesh or gasp for breath from within the depths of his pungent cloud d'odeur, Emis donned the mask of a contented courtesan. "You are a like a magnifique stallion, François. You must give a girl a chance to recover before beginning again."

"Non. I have a need for another of your services."

Understanding, her eyes grew wide. "Non! I will not read for you!"

She was yanked roughly forward. A knife blade pressed painfully at the base of her neck. "You will, or you'll not live to see another day, mon amour."

The point of the knife pierced Emis's fair skin. Warm red liquid slowly dripped down, making a circular arc around her breast. He leaned in close; she could smell the liquor on his breath. "And that pretty little flower in the other cabin…who knows what will happen to her if her maman is not around to protect her?"

White-hot fury filled Emis. She swore that she would never be subject to another's power. As much as she despised what she'd been forced to participate in and what she'd had to endure to return to 'normal,' she wished at this moment that she had the tremendous power of the Traveler. Visions of Haylee wielding it filled her mind. *This putrid excuse for a human being would be laid flat before me,* she thought. Hatred infused her mind. She gritted her teeth as she ground out, "Very well."

Releasing her, he chuckled as he reclined back against the headboard, his fingers lacing behind his head. A mean sparkle glittered in his eyes. "A mother protecting her only child is so easy to manipulate. You might fare better if you rid yourself of the girl." François raised a bushy eyebrow. "Child slaves, especially pretty puppets, are in high demand in certain parts of the world. I will make you a handsome offer."

Wiping her blood with his undergarments, she threw them in his face. A constant torrent of curses flowed as she yanked on her clothes. "You will have no fairy tales or pretty platitudes! Keep your whiskey at hand, François; in all likelihood you will not find what you learn to be to your liking."

"I'll take my chances, whore. You are going to tell me if you see anything of consequence between Captain Pillarton and my son. I guarantee that I will know if you are lying," he spat.

Before she quieted her mind, Emis berated herself for seeking out a fellow countryman. *I should have known better!*

A tingling sensation across the back of her shoulders signaled Emis's entrance into her meditative zone. Hazy bits of information, floating free, began to swirl and gather around the room. Gossamer things that only Emis could see settled into place. She cleared her throat so that her voice could become a conduit between the unseen and the physical world.

"I see another voyage before you. Fair skies and favorable winds. Your wife, she wishes to contact you. Your sister's health is failing. Your son has had a successful trade voyage in the East and is even now on his way home with his hull and coffers full. ....I see no contact between Pillarton and Jean Luc."

Emis's eyes flew open. "You bastard! How could you teach your son to murder men and then send him out to do your dirty work?"

Captain Dupré moved as if he wished to wring her neck, but Emis held up he hand. "There's more—" Resuming her receptive demeanor, " You will leave this port tomorrow…" she hesitated before continuing. "Your Lord will be pleased with what you have brought him."

Emis waited patiently for the next waves to settle. "You have contracted a disease in your travels François. It is the cause of the pains in your back."

François Dupré frowned; leaning forward he began to rub the spot she spoke of.

"There is nothing the doctors can do," Emis continued. "You have about two years before the pain cripples you."

"What!" he blurted out.

"If you continue to imbibe half-seas over, your time will be much shorter than that." Emis stopped. She regarded the stunned look on the captain's face with some satisfaction. Then that expression began to bloom on her face. Emis was accustomed to following the waves of knowledge for other people, but never for herself. As events from her future began to unfold before her mind's eye, she cried out, "No…oh no!…no…no… no!"

From inside her thoughts and everywhere outside, she heard, "Travelers work in pairs. If you violate the oath of your ancestors, the consequences will be dire."

Upholders redemption will be yours when asked.

In human time 1849, the message on the monitoring device changed to one that had not appeared previously...Warning.

"We have never witnessed this message." Elin and Nile spoke as one.

"The Upholders must be awoken," Darion commanded.

"We will intervene only if it is necessary," Tethalana stated. "If the Upholders are awoken, all will be lost—including ourselves."

Everyone paused to stare at her. She raised her eyebrows, urging them to understand her full meaning...

.54.

PLANS IN MOTION

Rousted from a sound sleep and shoved hastily and unceremoniously off the docked ship where they'd spent the night, Polly was understandably cross. When she noticed that they were heading back up the hill rather than to the Long Wharf at Branham Place, where her mother told her only the night before that they would board a keelboat, she asked why they were doing something different.

Not liking the reply, the quiet of the early morning was broken by Polly's cries. "I hate you! I hate you! I want Song," she blubbered as her mother tugged her along the street. They stayed to the outer edges where the mud wasn't so deep.

Emis stopped, grabbed Polly by the scruff of her dress, and then slapped her hard across the face. For a stunned moment, mother and daughter stared at one another, one's face trembling and about to crumble, the other surprised but resigned and steely.

"Polly, I don't have time to coddle you!" Emis ground out. "Be quiet and do as I say. Do you understand?"

Nodding even as the tears coursed down her cheeks,

the little girl did her best to do what it was that her mother so urgently wanted her to do.

It was a relief to see the Bella Union coming into sight. It felt safe there to Polly, mostly because of Song. At the side entrance, he opened the door to Emis's soft knock. Polly shot through it, clinging to her familiar caregiver.

Feeling her tremble and press her face into his shirt, Song hugged her while murmuring words of comfort. He raised eyes, full of concern, to Emis.

After a hurried conversation, Song nodded his understanding and pulled the girl inside, shutting the door firmly behind them.

~ ~ ~ ~

A pair of eyes stared out of a dark alleyway, noting the transaction. Reflections from the street lamps reflected in their depths.

Emis adjusted and straightened her dress. She visibly stood up straighter. As if with a clear purpose, she once again traversed the streets.

The first rays of the warming sun began to peek over the horizon by the time Emis and her silent tail left the business district. Only one set of gaiters made noise along the boardwalk. The second set of footfalls kept to the dirt and mud. From time to time, Emis would pause and glance over her shoulder. Unable to locate the cause of her concern, she would continue.

Her journey ended at the base of the steps leading up to a fine brownstone house. The observer watched the woman pace back and forth a few times before gaining the momentum that took her up to the top of the steps. After a few moments, the bell ringing and door knocking roused the occupant of the home. Lights turned on before the door was yanked open by an irritated man wearing a hastily tied robe.

They regarded one another briefly before Emis's urgent tones drifted across the street. Once they were both inside, more lights turned on.

It was some time before Emis emerged from the house. By that time, the streets were busy with traffic, and people were busy conducting their affairs. Her hair was wild and her clothes not quite straight. She paused on the top step to tuck a thick bundle of papers into the bodice of her dress. Meanwhile the man standing behind her in the doorway wore a relaxed expression. In his hand was a lit cigarette. He eyed Emis as she made her departure.

Making sure she knew which direction Emis was heading, Haylee crept up to the house to read the small sign by the door: Anthony Pratchett, Lawyer

Back along the boardwalk, Emis wove her way around pedestrians as she made her way toward her next destination. It was not a surprise that she came to a stop at the Keener Brothers storefront. Reece was busily moving heavy products outside the front door for display. Haylee's eyes glittered dangerously from their hiding spot as they noted Emis standing a bit too close and laying a hand coyly upon his arm. Their conversation ended in Emis's laughter, as the two entered the store, closing and locking the doors behind them.

Haylee had to firmly restrain herself from following them. *She can't...I won't let her!*....She pressed herself back against the wall. *What am I doing?! How can I be jealous? I hardly know them.*

~ ~ ~ ~

The sound of jangling chains, creaking thorough braces, and straining horses drew near to her hiding spot.

Edward Keener pulled hard on the reins while speaking firmly to his animals. One of them took longer to settle; it favored a foot. Setting the brake and jumping down from his seat, he began removing the tarp that covered a wagonload of store supplies. The ends of many bolts of cloth stacked in rows, barrels filled with shovels, augers and picks, powder horns in burlap bags, crates with the words 'fine wines & spirits' painted on the side, an assortment of earthenware vessels, boxes filled with washing and shaving soap, and small casks of lamp oil became visible.

Tipping his hat to passersby, Edward continued his activities. As Haylee observed, she took her mind off its previous subject and concentrated on what a dedicated, hard worker Ed was. *This must be the day of the week that Edward and Reece trade jobs.* She liked how Reece methodically worked to develop Ed's skills. She thought more about Edward. He was open and friendly. Perhaps not having to take the lead in managing their business made him more relaxed than his brother. The way Edward interacted with Polly showed that he was comfortable with children and had an easy sense of humor. She liked him. She truly felt bad about letting him down with the job situation. She'd known at the time that setting down any kind of roots was impossible, but the desire to do so, and to connect with other human beings, was persistent and strong.

Edward squinted as if a bright light had shone in his eyes and paused in his labors. Haylee knew he'd spotted her by the way he straightened up and smiled. Halfway across the road, he held out his hand. "Hal! You came! I was beginning to wonder if you'd skipped town." They clasped hands in a manly greeting.

On the verge of denying his statement, Haylee went along. "Well, I had to help prove to your brother that you weren't wrong about me."

"Excellent!" He clapped her on the back while escorting her toward the store. "Let me open up and get you started in the office while I finish with the wagon."

The store was cold and dark as they walked through.

They were almost to the back of the building when they heard shouts and a crash from below.

"What the—?" Edward exclaimed as he raced toward the steps that led down to the storeroom. Haylee was right on his heels.

⚬55⚬

TALKING WITH A GUN

Emis stood in the corner of the office brandishing a revolver in one hand. Reece lay at her feet, unconscious. A head wound at his temple oozed a red flow that reached the floor and pooled near his ear.

"Reece!" Edward hollered as he raced to his brother's side.

Startled by the intruders, Emis brought her free hand up, aiming at them. She was shakey and her eyes were shiny. The women's eyes met and held. "What are you doing here?" hissed Emis.

Edward dug around in his pocket. His hand came out with a wad of white cloth. "Reece, buddy, can you hear me?" he inquired softly. He shouted over his shoulder, "What is going on here!? Emis, why?"

Emis blinked rapidly, eyes darting between the Keeners and Haylee.

Haylee realized that someone was going to end up dead if everyone didn't calm down. "Ed, I think she's here for me."

Emis glanced down at Reece, taking note that the cloth in Edward's hand was soaked through. She took a few deep breaths, then nodded as if a conclusion had been reached.

"She's right," Emis stated.

Haylee saw the question clearly written on Edward's face. *She?* Her cheeks began to feel hot.

"I am done running," Emis declared. "I am tired of doing things I don't want to do. You're all going to do exactly as I tell you, or I'm going to start shooting. It is as simple as that." Cocking the revolver's hammer, she aimed it right between Haylee's eyes. "At this close range, I am sure I won't miss."

"Edward, get up and tie Haylee's hands," Emis commanded. Again, the questioning look appeared on Edward's face as he located the strapping he'd use to follow her directions. Stepping close enough to begin his chore, his frightened eyes scanned her face. "Haylee?" he whispered.

"Tie them tight." Emis said. "She's much stronger than you can imagine. I don't want her getting loose,"

Haylee looked pointedly at Reece and whispered to Edward under her breath, "I think it's just a head wound. His color is good and his breathing is easy. He's already stopped bleeding. I'm going to try to distract her. Keep watching for an opportunity to make a move."

"What does she want with you…Hal?" he whispered back.

"That's enough!" Emis commanded.

Haylee looked at Edward. "I'm sorry I lied."

"Isn't that touching," Emis commented dryly as she stepped closer to verify that Haylee's bonds were secure. "If you know what's good for you, Haylee—and for them—you will stay right where you are."

Emis continued. "Now, Edward, it's time for Reece to join the party. Get the whiskey from over there." She gestured with the gun to the shelves behind the desk. "Pour it on his wound." Giving Haylee plenty of space, Emis redirected the gun to Edward's back.

"What do you want, Emis?" he yelled.

"Don't worry, honey, you can't give it to me." She looked down at Reece. "But he can. You're about to find out. Now go!"

Reluctantly, Edward did her bidding.

Reece's scream surely could be heard out in the street. "Easy, brother." Edward squatted at his side, handing him the hanky and directing him to hold it on his head. "You've taken a blow to the head."

~ ~ ~ ~

Bleary eyes struggled to focus. "I am aware of that," Reece snarled with a gravelly voice. His gaze scanned the room, pausing on Emis and the revolver…and then to the boy with bound hands. His instantaneous feelings of protectiveness at the sight worried him.

Not seeming overly bothered by the gun-wielding prostitute, Reece struggled to his feet with Edward's help. Resting his hips at the base of his desk, he used his free hand to steady himself.

"I came here to make an unusual request," Emis began. "It was declined."

"Hey!" complained Reece, "you can't just walk up to someone and ask them to adopt your kid."

All eyes turned to Emis. "Well I can and I did," she replied.

"That's not something you can spring on someone and expect an instant 'yes' or 'no' answer," Reece commented dryly. "What I wanted to know before you clobbered me was why?"

"Right," Emis said. "I came to you, Keener, because you are a decent man. You found Song for me and you care for your brother well. I have no choice." Nodding in Haylee's direction, she continued, "The fact that she's here means that I have run out of time. I must make provisions for Polly before it's too late."

Reece's head swung so quickly in Haylee's direction

that he winced in pain. When their eyes met, she raised both eyebrows while making a feeble attempt at a smile. He scowled darkly.

~ ~ ~ ~

Waving the gun again, Emis told Edward to step away from his brother. She looked at him quizzically, then glanced back at Reece. "I could tie you down or leave you loose," she muttered. "Which way will have the greatest impact, I wonder?"

She walked over to the storeroom doors, saying, "No one is to try anything funny." Closing them and turning the locks, she continued. "Everyone pay attention now. You're about to see something that you'll never see again." Aiming her firearm at first one Keener then the next, she said, "You two stay right where you are. I like you both real well, but I promise you that I'll lay you flat if you move." The men exchanged glances.

Stepping close to Haylee, but keeping her eyes on the Keeners, Emis began to speak in low tones that the brothers could not hear. "Have you asked yourself since the last time we met, how I knew what you would do to that woman?"

Haylee stood up straighter. She had not asked herself that question. Since that night, she'd only focused on that fact that Emis had said that she knew how far she'd traveled, that she'd called her a Traveler, and that she had something Haylee would want. *How did she know what I would do to the woman?* Haylee wondered.

"Oh yes," Emis whispered, "I know precisely what you're experiencing and your great desire to control it, stop it, and reverse it."

Haylee's heartbeat increased as she listened. Could she believe what she was hearing?

"I know you've done things to hurt people, and I know the depths of your despair."

"Because you are a Traveler too?" Haylee questioned.

"I was."

Haylee's heart constricted with hope…and fear. "Was? So there is a way to stop it!"

Emis smiled knowingly. "Indeed there is."

"Tell me how!" Haylee yelled, her voice tinged with desperation.

The smile on Emis's face widened. She turned her body and raised her voice so that the two men could hear.

"There is something Haylee wants from me. Something she has traveled a very great distance to find. Even she does not know what it is that connects us together. You are all going to help me put an end to the nightmare. But first, I must make you believe that what I am about to tell you is true. As reasonable men, you have to see something to believe it."

Haylee, not sure what Emis was about to do, started to shiver.

Moving Haylee and Edward toward the center of the room, Emis stood between them, holding the gun on Reece. She continued, "A very long time ago, a group of women were put into bondage, charged with the task of upholding an oath to a race of ancient Gods."

Everyone in the room listened closely to Emis's words.

"Every so often, maybe every hundred years or so, one of these women turns into a monster. A Traveler that feeds off of other human beings."

She paused to look at Edward and Reece. "You think this a fairy tale, I can tell." She nodded in Haylee's direction. "Look at her face." Haylee's expression was one of repulsion and fear. "Obviously she does not think so. I wonder what she knows that you do not?"

Emis continued. "We are Travelers, Haylee and I. She wants what I have; something that will make it stop."

Haylee's eyes grew wide, and hope rose up in her.

"Before she can even think of stopping it, I will have what I want!" She turned forcefully to Reece. Shaking his head, he replied, "Emis, this is absurd. We need to sit down like rational people—"

"You had your chance, Keener," she spat out. She aimed the gun straight at his heart.

"No!" Haylee and Edward cried together.

"There is a hunger that lives inside a Traveler, a hunger so deep and all-consuming that it cannot be denied. It begins with a trembling in the belly and rattles through the bones."

Try as she might to resist the effects of Emis's words, the outer edges of Haylee's vision began to blur. She shook her head from side to side.

"If it has been too long between feedings, the trembling can be quite severe."

"Emis stop!" Haylee cried in desperation.

As Haylee began to tremble and quake, the Keeners grew more anxious.

"It is her hands that are the instruments of destruction for her hapless victims."

Haylee's hands began to flex in time with Emis's inflections. With fear showing in her wide eyes, Haylee backed away from Ed.

"She has superior strength when the time to feed arrives. No bonds can hold her. She ceases to think like herself. She thinks now like an animal, going for the closest thing that will satisfy her need."

—*Thwap!* The bonds that Edward had tied fluttered to the ground like bits of string. For a brief, fear filled moment, Emis wondered if she'd made a grave miscalculation. She wondered if Haylee did have any of her right mind left...if she would turn on her.

The men stared in disbelief at Haylee's hands and the change that had come over her.

But Emis's words held true. Haylee jumped on the closest prey…Edward.

Edward flailed under her like a trapped bug, arms and legs waving. Reece, no longer mindful of his head injury, tried to jump on top of Haylee to save his dying brother. A shot rang out that stopped him before he could complete his leap.

~ ~ ~ ~

Haylee paused, momentarily startled by the gunfire, but an instant later, she resumed her gruesome task. Arching her back as the essence of Edward entered her being, she closed her eyes to savor the moment of ecstasy. *Ahhhh— he's sooo fresh!*

The beauty of the moment was short lived as she disengaged. Edward's blank stare caused her to crumble. "Oh God!" she sobbed. "Not again!"

Shuffling around on hands and knees, she saw Reece lying again on the floor surrounded by another pool of blood. Emis crouched over him as she pressed on the wound in his side; her revolver lay forgotten on the floor.

"Get off him!" Haylee screamed, leaping across the distance to knock Emis away. With frantic hands, she tore at Reece's shirt so she could see what was underneath. Thankfully, the bullet had only grazed the surface of his skin. Ripping off her own shirt, Haylee pressed it into his flank.

She leaned over the top of him. "I'm sorry! I'm sorry!" She cried. "He's not dead, Reece. Ed's not dead!" His eyes cracked open; he peered at her quietly before rasping, "What did you do to him?"

Haylee, Reece, and Emis stood in the kitchen of the Mercantile living quarters. The first two wore looks of forlorn despair. Emis appeared chipper. Reece stared blankly at the two women as he attempted to process what he'd seen. If he had any doubts whatsoever, all he had to do was walk into the next room to look at his brother. He was torn between rage, grief, and fear. The only thing that kept him together was Emis's confident assurance. "If you do what I ask from here on out, I will tell you what needs to be done to restore him to exactly as he was before." He silently cursed himself, *Are you fooling yourself? You are hanging your little brother's fate on a crazy entertainer who also happens to be a demented monster?*

Emis brought out the stack of papers that she'd offered to him earlier. Reece froze, looking from the papers to her face and back again. He raised an eyebrow, incredulous. "You think I am going to sign that now?" he ground out. *This woman just orchestrated a crime against nature and ruined my life. If she thinks I'm going to sign for custody of her daughter, she's a fool!*

Emis returned his stare calmly. "Oh," she smiled, "I forgot a pen." She rummaged around until she found one. Reece's hands rested on his hips as he regarded her actions. As she moved back in his direction, holding out the writing instrument, her voice was direct and cold. "I gave you a chance to do this before Haylee took Edward down. If you had signed it then, your brother would be perfectly fine right now, so you only have yourself to blame for the state he is in."

Reece's skin grew pale, and he swallowed audibly.

Emis continued. "As I see it, I am the only person who knows how to bring him back. You are welcome to live with him like that. I can walk out this door right now and find another guardian for my daughter. Good luck if you think she" — Emis nodded in Haylee's direction — "will be able to figure out how repair your brother." Emis paused for effect. "You are going to sign this, Reece Keener, and you are going to sign it right now, or you, your brother and this Traveler can go straight to hell." She chuckled. "It shouldn't take you too long; you're already half the way there."

Reece glared at her for a moment before setting his mouth in a grim line. He snatched the documents and pen from her hand. "Damn you!" he thundered.

He despised being used. Even more than that, he was angry at himself for allowing himself to be boxed into a corner with no exit. That is not how one survived in a place like this. For the life of him, he could see no other alternatives. Signing his name with an angry flourish, Reece turned around, shoving the items back into Emis's hands. *Bloody hell!* he thought. His resentful scrutiny moved over to Haylee. *Who or what is she? A man-girl who 'traveled so far.' Where, exactly, did she come from? Will she do that again? How do I know that I won't be the next meal on her plate? And what does happen if I end up with Polly? Is she one of these things too?* Reece's head felt full of crazy-making thoughts. If he weren't made of sterner stuff, he'd be chugging gin and hightailing it for the hills. *Damn my own eyes if I can't keep them off of Haylee. Now that I know she's a woman—is she really a woman?—I can't stop thinking about how attractive she is, even with the short hair. I can't believe that I didn't see it before. I wonder what it would feel like to—*

"Agh!" Reece muttered in frustration as he stomped out of the room.

~ ~ ~ ~

Emis smiled wickedly. "You've chosen well, Haylee. Reece Keener is a fine specimen." She glanced over her shoulder toward the empty doorway.

"What are you talking about? I haven't chosen anything," Haylee responded waspishly. Emis chuckled. "Oh, but you have. Reece is your mate. When you take him—" At Haylee's wide look of terror, Emis modified her speech. "Not with your webs, but as a woman takes a man—he will please you. He has the stamina to meet the appetite that you don't even know that you have." Emis knew she'd hit her mark by Haylee's reaction.

"He would never…" Haylee gulped. "He despises me. I can see it in his eyes."

"He does now. But when you bring his brother back to him…he will forgive you. Then he will love you. He has even less choice in the matter than you."

Triumph glittered in Emis's gaze. "I have something to show you." She lifted her skirt. Reaching into a deep pocket tucked into its recesses, Emis brought out an object that filled the palm of her hand. It was a true cerulean. The crystal was two inches long and one inch in diameter. Catching the light in the room, it returned glints of color.

At the sight, Haylee turned pale. She did not know how she knew it, but this was what she was sent here to retrieve! Her own pendant had led her first to Polly and then to this.

Like a person dying of thirst and seeing a tall glass of water in front of her, Haylee lunged for the crystal.

Emis made no move keep it from her.

Upon contact, Haylee was thrown across the room violently.

Hearing the crash, Reece rushed back in to find Haylee cradling her head and Emis straightening her dress.

Looking unsympathetically at Haylee, Emis said, "Now you know. It cannot be taken by force. It must be given…in a very specific way—and for that you must wait."

⚘56⚘

A CAPTURED MOMENT

Two days later, the odd foursome traversed the busy streets. Reece and Emis sat on the bench seat of the supply wagon. Edward was sprawled out in the back with Haylee watching over him. The two in the front argued bitterly. "I don't know why you are insisting on this." Reece complained resentfully. "We have more important matters to attend to."

"I know very well what you think is important! What we are doing is for Polly. Just shut up and keep going!" Emis responded with her own irritation.

Stopping the wagon in front of the Bella Union, Emis stepped down, saying quietly, "I'll only be a minute."

Reece looked over his shoulder. "How's he doing?"

Haylee met his eyes, sighing. "No change." She hated answering that question with the same answer so many times. Haylee stood up to stretch her legs. Looking down at her new clothes—she preferred to continue dressing as a man—she brushed clinging straw chaff from her pants. Hopping down from the wagon bed, she wandered to the front of the conveyance. Stroking the noses of the horses, she let herself relax into their thoughts. She wondered how Lovey and Titan were getting along. Surprised to discover that one of these horses held a mental picture of her two four legged friends, Haylee smiled as she received a good report about their comfort and appetites.

Reece, dressed in his Sunday best, sat stoically on the bench, arms crossed over his chest. He observed the gentle exchange between Haylee and his steeds.

Haylee's eyebrows drew together as she leaned back to look questioningly into one of the horse's eyes. "Awww," she murmured sympathetically.

"Reece, would you come down here for a minute?"

Haylee could see conflicting emotions on his face as he met her eyes, then glanced away. She was certain that when he looked at her, he was vividly reminded of her attack on his brother, and she couldn't blame him for avoiding that. But there was something else there, too. Something close to longing...but she had to be imagining that.

"What is it?" He wanted to know.

Running hands down the horse's flank to his foot, Haylee bent his joint so Reece could see the bottom of the hoof. He looked shocked as he watched the animal cooperate with her.

"Ailbe has a small rock stuck between his shoe and sole. Can you dig it out with your pocketknife?"

With hands on hips, he regarded her for a few moments, shaking his head before taking the hoof in his hand and focusing on the task. "How did you know Ailbe's name? And how to say it properly?"

She shrugged her shoulders. She could not possibly admit that Ailbe had told her, so she replied, "Edward must have told me."

Realizing that he was in a position where he could not easily put distance between them, Haylee tried to talk to him.

"Reece," she reached out to touch his shoulder. He jumped like he'd been bitten, which made the horse jumpy too. "Sorry!" She stepped back as he sent her an impatient glare.

While he got back to work on the hoof, she tried again. "All I wanted to say is that a lot of what Emis said…that night…was true. I was just an average girl…"

Shaking his head, he mumbled, "Haylee, you could never be just an average girl."

Pretending that the statement didn't send ripples of warmth into her heart, she continued. "I was an average girl living an average life with my dad on a farm until just a couple of years ago. Then stuff started to happen."

He dropped the hoof, patted Ailbe's flank, and then leaned against the wagon to continue listening.

"Strange and frightening things like what I did to Ed." She glanced to where Edward lay in repose. She saw Reece close his eyes and keep them closed, but he didn't walk away in disgust like he usually did, so she kept going. "I didn't understand what it was at first, but then when I did, I still couldn't stop it. I hate myself for doing it." The tears came then and her voice cracked. "I did it to my best friend and to my stepmom…and I probably would have done it to my dad if I hadn't been brought here." She paused for a moment with a hand covering trembling lips. She turned away saying, "I just wanted you to know that I am suffering for what I have done. It's way worse when you are the one directly responsible for damaging so many people. Emis is the only hope I have for making it right. There is no other option for me; I have to do what she says."

Haylee crawled up to sit on the back edge of the wagon where she sat snuffling.

~ ~ ~ ~

Reece watched her with a heavy heart. Part of him wanted

to comfort her. Yet he was afraid that if he made a move in that direction he wouldn't be able to control things from going in a very different direction. Another part of him wanted to wrap his hands around her neck and squeeze. Still another recognized her remorse, saw her fear, and realized that they both, in their own different ways, were being forced to dance to Emis's tune.

~ ~ ~ ~

A short while later, Emis and Polly came out looking freshly scrubbed and pretty.

With everyone loaded back into the market wagon, Emis kept Polly tucked close to her side. "What's wrong with Edward, Mama?" Polly wanted to know. Reece pursed his lips while Emis glanced in the back of the wagon. "He's sick, ma chère. He will be alright soon."

"Why are we going to have a daguerreotype made?"

Emis straightened her dress as she replied. "This is a very special day for you, my love. Today you have a new papa."

"What?" Polly clapped her hands. "Did you marry Mr. Keener?"

"No!" said Reece simultaneously with Emis's, "Non."

Emis shushed Reece as she continued. "Mr. Keener has agreed to be your guardian should anything happen to me." Seeing her daughter's concern, she continued. "It is nothing Polly. This is something adults do to protect their children. Since Reece is our friend, he's happy to act in this capacity." Emis looked pointedly at Reece. "Aren't you, Mr. Keener?"

Glancing over at the little girl, he nodded as he lifted the corners of his lips in an attempt to smile.

Polly certainly doesn't look like a monster. I am sure I would have heard if either she or her mother were involved in anything untoward. Song would have mentioned it. What am I going to do with a kid if I end up with her? Even if I am rather fond of her. Why is Emis so insistent on this?

The quintet parked their vehicle in front of the St. Francis Hotel. Another argument broke out.

"We can't just leave him laying out here," Reece stated in exasperation.

"We can't take him inside!" Emis complained.

Haylee's brows knit together. "I don't think anyone will kidnap him."

Both Reece and Emis glared at her.

Emis planted her hands on her hips. "Just throw the blanket over him. People will think he's dead."

"Emis!" responded Reece and Haylee.

"We should have brought Song. He could have watched over him." Everyone looked at Polly, thinking she was right.

In the end, they opted to cover Edward with a blanket. "Sorry, Ed," Reece murmured, shaking his head.

They tromped across the street to Ms. Julia Shannon's photography studio.

The proprietress greeted them as they entered.

As she filled out paperwork to start a file, she asked, "Is this a special occasion?"

"Yes," said Emis at the same time Reece said, "No."

Seeing the hurt in the little girls' eyes, Haylee elbowed him in the ribs.

He grunted. "Damn it, Haylee, that hurt!" His ribs were still tender from the gun-shot wound.

She motioned to Polly with her eyes and a head nod. Once he understood her meaning, a sheepish look came over his face. "Yes, this is a special occasion," he revised.

The photographer looked perplexed when no one offered further information. She escorted the tense group into her camera room and looked confused about how to pose them. Pointing to a tiny couch in the middle of the room, she said,

"Please sit or stand as you see fit."

Ms. Shannon busied herself with setting up her equipment while her subjects figured out their grouping arrangement.

Emis was the first to approach the couch. Scooting to the far right, she held out her arms to Polly who came to stand beside her. Reece and Haylee chose to stand in the back, far apart from each other.

Ms. Shannon cocked her head to one side as she regarded the shape of the group. "Mr. Keener, please move farther to your left."

When Haylee moved to create a greater distance between them, Ms. Shannon moved her closer.

They were required to remain still while she worked the camera. Standing this close to Reece, all of Haylee's hairs stood on end. His scent filled her head. Desire and longing made her want to lean her body against his. She hardened her stance to keep from embarrassing herself.

Something vaguely remembered nagged at Haylee's thoughts.

The flash exploded; their eyes danced with stars. The moment in time had been captured.

As the group disassembled from their stance, Haylee remembered...this photograph. She'd held it in her hands in the attic at home. The realization caused her to stumble. Without thinking, Reece reached out to break her fall. At the contact, all thoughts left both their minds. His arms, of their own accord wrapped themselves around her, pulling her against his body. Their gaze locked. It felt as if time stood still.

Emis's droll observation broke the spell. "Oh please! I know where you can get a room."

~ ~ ~ ~

On their way to deliver the girl back to Song, the adults

were quiet.

Polly chattered.

"That was fun! I think when I grow up I want to be a photographer like Mrs. Shannon. Maman, do you think Song would like to see our daguerreotype? Will I work at Mr. Keener's store now that he's to be my papa? Can Song come with me?" Emis lovingly stroked Polly's hair.

"Yes, Song will go with you to Keener's"

"Wait a minute!" snarled Reece. "You didn't say anything about Song in our deal."

"Shut up! Stop being an ass!" Emis responded in kind. "Maybel works him like an animal. She only lets him watch Polly if I pay her...handsomely, too I might add! If I don't..." She noted small ears listening and changed what she was about to say. "You know very well that he will be a boon to you and Edward. He makes Polly feel safe. That's all. We'll talk about this later."

~ ~ ~ ~

Back at the Union, with a heavy heart, Emis knelt before her daughter, holding her close. "Polly, I want you to always remember how much your Maman loves you. That you are the best daughter any Maman could ask for." Emis hated good-byes. This one would be the hardest one of her life. She attempted to maintain a calm demeanor, but couldn't quite keep it all inside.

"Maman, why are you crying?" Polly, wearing a frown, reached up to wipe away her mother's tears.

"Because I am so happy that you have a new Papa. You are a lucky little girl. Once Mrs. Shannon is finished with our daguerreotype, Song will go pick it up. Then you will always have a memento of this happy day when we were all together and when you got Papa Reece."

Polly wrapped her arms around her mother, hugging her tight. "I love you so much, Maman."

"I know, Chère, this is what makes me strong."

Moments passed. Emis was reluctant to release her precious babe. Rapidly, she ticked through her plans, trying to find another alternative. Arriving back to where she thought she had the greatest chance of success, she fortified her resolve. Taking a deep breath to keep her voice from quivering, she held Polly at arm's length. "Now go help Song."

As she watched her daughter skip down the hallway, tears flowed freely down her face. "When you remember me, my little one, I hope you know that I did the best I could for you. I hope you don't look back on our time together and feel disappointed in me. In a few days' time, the Keeners will come to take you to your new home." Emis kissed her fingers and blew a gentle, loving caress to her girl. "Be happy. Farewell, my sweet."

Once outside, Emis found a quiet alleyway in which to let the bone rattling sobs consume her. Dogs from several blocks away howled with the mournful sounds.

·57·

REECE'S CONFUSION

It had been decided, mostly by Emis, that Haylee's living quarters on the abandoned schooner would be the best place for them to conduct their next order of business.

With Reece's wounds, it had been a struggle to load provisions onto the Dicey. Even more of a struggle was figuring out how to get Edward on board. In the end, they decided to send the two women up the rope ladder first to guide his hands. Reece brought up the rear, guiding his feet. Everyone but Edward huffed with exertion.

Once aboard the vessel and they'd regained their breath, Reece clapped his hands. "Ok! Let's get this show on the road."

Emis responded with a passionate fury that surprised them all. Strings of unintelligible words barked from her while she drove him backward with a jabbing finger to his chest.

Once spent, she continued in a quiet voice. "Keener, you have no idea how close to the edge I am." She massaged her neck as she moved her head from side to side. "I promise you this, there are many roads to hell. If you don't stay out of my way, we'll all be going there together." She swung on Haylee with a finger pointing in her face, "That goes for you too!"

"Now all of you, leave me alone! I have to think."

To Reece, she said, "Go see to your brother's needs. I'll call you when I want you."

Turning on her heels, she marched below deck. The sound of a slamming door resounded clearly in the silence.

Reece and Haylee stood regarding each other wearily. Hurt, again, by the familiar and frequent sneer of revulsion that crossed his face, she turned in the opposite direction and ran.

~ ~ ~ ~

The evening air was brisk by the time Haylee tiptoed down the ladder. Passing by the room that Reece shared with Edward, she couldn't help but overhear Reece's pleas to Ed to "snap-out-of-it." She paused at the doorway, which was open just a crack. Leaning on the wall outside, she shook her head, letting the sadness that she always carried wash over her. For the first time since it happened, she let herself open to all that was Edward. Closing her eyes, she smiled wistfully at the visions of racing through the woods with his sisters. All four of them were beautiful and cunning. Each one so different from the other. He loved and missed them very much. Edward wanted the entire family to join him and Reece in the west. Reece, the eldest of all the Keener children, was cautious. Edward could mimic him exactly as he said, "We won't be sending for any family until we are well established with enough stores to support them all."

Haylee watched Reece snap his fingers near Edward's ears and eyes as he knelt in front of his blank faced brother. Not even a startle reaction was forthcoming. Next, he lightly patted the boy's cheeks. "Ed, come on! You've got to be in there some-where." His voice was tinged with anxiety.

Haylee quietly pushed on the door, staring down at the

brothers. Hurting with Reece, her voice was sad when she spoke. "He really isn't 'in there.' Because he is inside of me," she stated simply.

Red-rimmed eyes turned to glare at her. Normally he would have yelled at her to get away, but this time he asked, "What did you do to him?"

Shoving her hands deep into her pockets, she looked down at the toe of her boot as it scuffed the planks on the floor. "I wish I could tell you. I wish I knew myself."

Breathing in deeply she continued. "Your sisters are Deirdre, Einin, Ryanne, and Briged. Edward wants to move them all out here at once."

At his look of surprise, she said, "You're wondering if he told me about them while we worked at the store. He didn't." She braved onward. "He's envious of the bond between you and Briged. You listen seriously to her opinions. Ed was excited when your Da let him come out to join you instead of her, even though she is older and, in his mind, would have been the better choice."

Reece stood, turning toward her. Incredulity was written in his expression as he finally began to comprehend what Haylee was trying to communicate.

Grabbing her shoulders, he squinted into her face as if he could peer inside. "Does he know what happened to him? Can he see me and hear me right now?"

Haylee tried to not think about how good he smelled or how much she wanted to hold his face and kiss away his worry lines. She attempted to back away, but he held her firm.

"No, thank God!" she said. Her eyes darted from side to side as she worked to access the information he wanted. "It's more like he's gone to sleep. I have his memories of what has happened before. He doesn't have any new thoughts happening right now."

"What are you?" he demanded, giving her a little shake.

"I know you think I'm a monster. I think I am too!" Tears gathered in her eyes. "I assure you that I didn't volunteer for it!"

Releasing her abruptly, he began to pace. "Damn it!" He punched a fist into his opposite hand. "You're going to be able to bring him back...just like he was before?"

"Emis said it's possible. I have to believe it's true."

~ ~ ~ ~

A chill passed over him. Reece raked his fingers through his hair. He was a reasonable man. A man interested in facts and science. A man who, until now, believed that with smart business acumen, hard work, and determination, he could achieve the goals he'd set for himself and for his family. Until this girl walked into his life.

When he'd thought she was boy, he'd begun to question if he'd gone queer. When he'd watched her jump on top of his brother, instantaneous jealous adrenalin had flashed through his veins...until it registered that Ed was in trouble. Then violent anger had exploded within, making him want to break her, choke the breath from her. The shot had rung out and everything had gone blank until he'd awoken to her again... this time an angel hovering over him with concern, ministering to his wounds, behaving like she cared. *How is it possible for one woman to cause such strong and conflicting emotions?*

Looking again at Edward sitting in the chair he'd put him in, so still, so unanimated, so blank, broke Reece's heart. Thoughts of sitting down to write to his parents, telling them that he'd let them down, that their youngest child was damaged beyond repair, made his throat constrict. He was used to being in charge, in control, used to making things happen, and now he was at the mercy of these two strange women. It was damn frustrating and more than a little unnerving.

Although his primary focus was his brother's situation, Reece couldn't help but feel curiosity about Emis and Haylee. *What the hell were they?* In spite of his mental and emotional turmoil, Reece believed that Haylee didn't know much more than she'd already told him. Emis may well be the only one with answers. Calming himself with an effort, he returned to questioning Haylee. She seemed sincere in her desire to help and willing to talk. For the first time since this all started, he was ready to listen.

"How long has this been going on?" he asked. Haylee sat down on a barrel in the corner of the room farthest away from Edward. Her mind wandered back to the day things had changed drastically. Her eyes flew open wide as the thought settled in. Two years. It had started right after her eighteenth birthday…and today she'd turned twenty. She looked away from him. "I try really hard not to think about that. But it's been going on for two years."

"So you've done…what you did to Edward…before?"

Eyes on the floor, she nodded. "Too many times." Tears gathered at the edges of her eyes.

Reece massaged his forehead. "Do you know why you do it?"

Still not looking at him, Haylee shook her head from side to side.

"How often do you do it?"

She stuttered, "Every few weeks. You should…be safe from me. At least…for a…little while."

"Unless Emis leads you down a primrose path," he stated dryly.

"I guess." She nodded.

Propping a hand under an elbow, he grasped his jaw with the opposite hand, staring, perplexed, at Haylee. He closed his eyes. He didn't want to feel anything for her! He didn't want to comfort her or be drawn to her in any way. Yet he couldn't seem to help it. Going down on a knee before her, he resisted touching her but bent forward in order to make eye contact. "Haylee, I will try to help you if I can."

Reece had no way of knowing that Josh had uttered those very same words to her.

The waterworks let loose, "Oh God!" she cried as she brought up her hands to cover her face.

Reece could not stop himself from gathering the miserable girl into his arms. His surprise and alarm at his uncontrollable actions were instantly replaced by feelings of tranquility and rightness.

❧58❧

EMIS REMEMBERS

While Reece and Haylee were having their heart to heart discussion, Emis was busy composing two letters. Both would set events into motion satisfactorily.

Finally…finally, a sense of quiet blanketed her like the calm after a storm. It had been so long since she'd felt this way that she set her pencil down, leaned back, and closed her eyes just to bask in the goodness of the feelings.

When she was ready to move, a small hint of a smile showed around her mouth. "Until tomorrow, my love," she whispered.

It was time to set the rest of her plan into motion.

Emis followed the sound of voices down the passage. She stood in the open doorway for a moment, watching Reece hold Haylee. She nodded with confidence thinking, He'll do it.

"Ahem." She announced her presence, sending them springing apart. "Haylee will come with me." She looked pointedly at Reece. "Get a good night's sleep. At first light, I will knock on your door. You will wait ten minutes then join us on deck."

When Reece opened his mouth to speak, Emis held up a hand to stop him. "You're to do exactly as I say…nothing more." Glancing at Edward, she said, "Make sure he is sufficiently cared for so that he will be alright for the bulk of the day."

Reece cast a worried glance in his brother's direction. Emis continued with softness in her voice that had not been there before as she met Reece's eyes. "If all goes according to plan, he'll be your Ed again by tomorrow night."

Haylee's heartbeat accelerated as she prepared herself for what came next. She tried to smile bravely at Reece. Their eyes held.

59

UPHOLDERS REDEMPTION

"Follow me," Emis directed as she went back to the cabin she'd taken. "It's time to get you out of those men's clothes."

"What?" Haylee exclaimed. "What do my clothes have to do with anything?"

Emis spun on her, tense and angry again. "You will do as I say. Follow the directions I give…and don't talk or all bets are off! I don't have to do this. If you want to spend the rest of your life this way, you might as well tell me right now."

Haylee shook her head and bit her tongue.

In Emis's room, the older woman made her strip down. She'd prepared a lavender scented bath and silently proceeded to wash Haylee's short hair, pouring warm pitchers full of water over her head. Emis wrapped her in a towel. A beautifully scented powder was poofed all over, sending out clouds of fine dust that hung in the air like a dreamy cloud. Next, Haylee was outfitted in some of the prettiest, softest, women's sleeping wear that she'd ever laid eyes on. Her confusion had given way to stoic observation as Emis worked away.

"There is a ceremony that we Travelers perform for one

another." Emis spoke in low tones. She looked into the mirror and noticed Haylee's eyes growing wide. She heard her intake of breath—preparing to prattle on with questions—Emis raised an eyebrow. "If you begin to speak, I will stop and you can just go in blind." Emis waited to see if Haylee understood. Mutely, the girl nodded.

Emis continued. "It is my job to prepare you to perform the same job for the Traveler who will come to you. It is my job to trigger your journey back to your own time stream."

The bowl of soup that Emis set before her at the small table reminded Haylee how hungry she was. Emis spoke as Haylee ate. "You too, need to have a good night's sleep. Once you are finished eating, I will accompany you to make sure you have everything you'll need for the morning."

~ ~ ~ ~

In the captain's cabin, Emis paced with her hands on her hips. Brows furrowed and wearing a frown, she appeared to be lost in thought. Haylee, growing cold and suddenly very tired, wrapped a blanket over her shoulders as she perched on the edge of the bed to wait. Clearly, whatever was going to happen would not occur until the morning.

Emis stopped moving; her head snapped up. "You have the pendant box?"

Surprised, Haylee thought for a moment. She wasn't sure. She could not remember seeing it for some time. "I don't know," she said as she got up, pulled out her saddlebags, and began rummaging around.

Throwing her hands up, Emis commented with exasperation, "You have to have it, you ninny. Where one goes so does the other."

Haylee looked at her blankly.

"The pendant and its box. They stay together. Surely

you're not able to go far without them?"

Haylee's hand clasped over the pendant, pulling it out. With a look of confusion on her face, she stated, "No one ever said anything about the box."

Emis huffed. "It really doesn't matter. The pendant and the box will stay together regardless."

Haylee continued the search in her luggage. "Emis, if you had webs…like me…does that mean you also jumped through time?"

"I told you no talking!" Emis yelled.

"Come on!" Haylee yelled back. "I am completely igno-rant…you know things! It's not fair to keep me in the dark!" Haylee located the pendant and the box and brought them out for Emis to see.

Emis nodded tiredly. "Tomorrow. You'll get what you want tomorrow. I will knock on your door at first light. You are to wait five minutes. Meet me on deck…bring both of those with you."

Emis turned back saying softly, "Good night, Haylee Garrett." She inclined her head. "Sleep."

~ ~ ~ ~

In spite of the tension aboard the Dicey, all of the residents slept. Dreams that spoke of worries, fears, and hopes whispered to them all…except for Edward.

By the time the knocks sounded at the doors, the occu-pants of the cabins were already awake and apprehensive about what lay ahead.

Haylee was the first to arrive on deck wearing the long green dress that Emis had laid out for her. Even though she knew she had more things to worry about, she couldn't help but feel exposed by the plunging neckline. She kept trying to pull it up higher. Spotting Emis kneeling near the edge of the deck, perspiration and prickles nettled her skin. She approached the stiff form waiting for her. Haylee held up the necklace and the box, showing Emis that she had brought them.

Pale and serious, Emis inclined her head. "Come to me," she said with effort. Haylee saw that Emis held her arms crossed over her chest. She clasped folded papers in one fist; the other hid something within. When Haylee got near, she could see that Emis trembled. "Closer," Emis directed. Haylee stood about twelve inches away, facing the woman.

Speaking as if her jaw were wired shut, Emis began, "State your full name."

"Wait!" Haylee cried as she remembered that Reece was to follow in only a few moments.

Rolling her eyes, Emis asked, "What?"

"I need to ask questions. Can I do it when the ceremony is finished?"

"Doubtful." Emis trembled. "Two…you may ask two questions. Make it fast."

"Did my mother do what I do?"

"No. The seeds lie dormant for a century or more."

What the heck does that mean? Haylee's thoughts raced as she composed a second question.

"Can I go back to a regular life once this is over?"

Again rolling her eyes, Emis responded, "To a degree. Now silence! State your full name."

Suddenly Haylee's breath came in short gasps. She felt incredibly cold. Something about this felt wrong, but she didn't know enough to do any differently. "Haylee Louise Garrett."

Emis strained to lean forward, her trembling increasing, and sweat dripped from her hairline. "Haylee Louise Garrett, hold the pendant box in front of you and say these words, 'The Traveler wishes Upholders' Redemption.'"

As Haylee repeated the words, Emis uncrossed her arms,

revealing what she held in each hand—the folded papers and the large crystal. Haylee froze at the sight.

It glimmered in Emis's hand. Its blue inner beauty radiated outward as it answered its calling. This was the first time that Haylee was able to study the crystal. As she did so, something ancient and strangely familiar shifted inside of her. A voice, as if from its center, whispered in her mind, *Are you ready?* In a wave of relief and joy, she closed her eyes as she responded, *YES!*

Opening her eyes, Haylee stared at Emis. Emis showed more signs of strain and made grunting noises. "Bring the box closer to me so that I can reach it."

Haylee leaned forward with arms extended.

Emis reached out an unsteady hand, pointing the crystal at the box. Haylee was astonished to see that as the crystal came in close proximity, a small indentation appeared in its smooth surface. The indentation matched the size and angles of the crystal's point exactly.

When the two came into contact, the box disappeared from Haylee's grasp. In its place was a podium-like device that encased both of her wrists. It looked to be made of the same type of swirly material, except its shape was now was very much like a stockade. The base of it appeared to come up from the deck of the ship. Where it ended, Haylee had no idea. The upper end—the holes that surrounded her wrists—were at the same height the box and crystal had been when they made contact. Since Emis was kneeling, Haylee was bent over at a forty-five degree angle. She was shocked when she looked at her hands. They were frozen in place with her fingers spread wide, her webs fully exposed.

Haylee sucked in a frightened breath. It didn't hurt at all, but her hands and wrists were completely immobilized. Tug as she would in any direction, the apparatus was solid as stone.

Emis's eyes darted over Haylee's shoulder. "Right time,

Keener." Her voice was thin. Hand shaking almost out of control, Emis reached over the restraining device and dropped the crystal down the bodice of Haylee's dress while tucking the folded papers in the same place.

"What?" Haylee asked in confusion.

Emis strained forward. It looked as if she were about to kiss Haylee. She made painful sounds.

Emis stared at Haylee's open webs. Haylee knew with a strong wave of certainty that the ceremony had taken a terribly wrong turn. She panicked. "Emis! No! What are you doing?"

~ ~ ~ ~

Reece paused at the top of the ladder to stare at the two women. Haylee's back was to him. She wore a dress. His heart constricted at the sight. Even the rear view of her arrested his breathing… Emis knelt in front of her. The sun coming up behind them gave off a glow that was striking. The sound of alarm in Haylee's voice made his feet move.

Before he could reach them, Emis had pressed her face firmly into one of Haylee's webs. The fingers clamped down, sending Haylee into throes of feeding behavior.

Seeing it for the second time was no less terrifying than the first. Reece's hands flew up to grasp the hair at the top of his head. He cursed. *Should I try to knock Emis free?* Almost as quickly as it began, it ended.

Haylee's grip released.

Emis tottered blankly in place for a millisecond.

Haylee crumpled to the deck as much as the device locking her wrists would allow.

The clink…clink…clink of a chain letting out and picking up momentum sounded before Emis's body jerked violently backward.

"No!" Reece cried out in alarm. A splash went up as Emis

hit the water.

A second splash followed as Reece dove in after her. He didn't seem to notice the bracing chill of the water. Strong scissor kicks surged his body ever downward in an effort to seize hold of Emis's wrist. It was no use; her descent was too fast. He screamed with rage.

Green shafts of light refracted within the moving water. Emis stared blankly, her face turned upward like a flower seeking the sun. Strands of dark hair waved good-by in slow motion. Slack hands on reaching arms undulated gently. Streaks of bubbles spun on an upward course.

The dark depths of Yerba Buena Cove accepted the life surrendered until all that was left was a recollection of the woman that was Emis.

⚭60⚭

WINGING IT

"Haylee…Haylee." Something cold splashed on her face and neck. She couldn't move her arms. "Haylee, can you hear me?" Reece's worried voice broke into her thoughts.

Instinctively, Haylee moved her face away from the cold. Cracking her eyes, she saw Reece looking concerned. She wanted to reach out to him. Her inability to move brought her back to full awareness.

Reece, soaking wet, kneeled at her side.

Her wrists were still locked in place, hands frozen open, webs reflecting in the light. She tried to pull herself free; nothing budged.

"I'm stuck!" Taking note of the haunted look on Reece's face, Haylee recalled what Emis had done. Her own eyes grew wide. "No! Oh God! Why did she do that?" Haylee struggled and flailed, doing everything she could think of to free herself. She kicked at the thing. She screamed in frustration, in fear, and in sorrow.

Reece joined in kicking repeatedly at the base. Eventually they wore themselves down until they were too tired to fight.

The restraining object did not move an inch.

Hunched over, Haylee leaned her head on one of her arms. "Emis should not have done that. The ceremony is not supposed to be that way," she commented softly.

Reece lay sprawled on the deck. "How would you know how it's supposed to go?"

She shifted her body so she could see him more clearly. "That's a good question. How do I know that?"

Reece lifted his head so he could meet her gaze.

Haylee examined her thoughts. "When I looked at the crystal, something happened." Her eyes widened. "The crystal! She put it down my dress!"

"What?" Reece sat up.

"Right before she...put her face in my hand." Haylee's face scrunched as stabbing pain pierced her head. "Ahhhh!"

Instantly, Reece rose to return to her side. He stayed clear of her hands. "What's wrong?"

"My head! It hurts," she cried. Haylee wanted to drop her head into her hands but was unable to make the movement. Squeezing her eyes closed, she let the tears escape; there was no way to stop them. When Reece attempted to reach out to her, she flinched away, "Don't touch me!" she yelled.

Not knowing what else to do, he ran below deck for water and a cold cloth. Hearing her cries from above, he sprinted through the cabins, searching for headache powder. Locating a box in a sailor's trunk, Reece poured some in a glass, swishing it with water as he dashed back up top.

It was extremely tense and unnerving watching Haylee suffer. Reece's stomach clenched in a tight knot. He wracked his brain for anything else that might provide relief. For a while, it had gotten so bad that he feared she would die, stuck in that thing. Not being able to save Emis, then not being able to help Haylee, and having a vegetative brother below deck had him imagining that he had traveled into the bowels of Hades…and landed right here on the deck of the Dicey.

Once Haylee had crested the peak of that wave and started to come down on the other side, he figured out that his nearness and a gentle hand rubbing her back did help.

He hadn't realized how much he liked looking at her face, with the light of clarity in her eyes, until he'd seen it again.

Thinking of Emis, his chest—or his heart— he wasn't sure which, constricted as the edges of fear closed in.

~ ~ ~ ~

Reece was completely dry by the time Haylee was recovered enough to communicate. She slept on her knees with her head resting on her outstretched arms. He'd spent the last few hours staring at the webbing between her digits. They weren't as frightening to look at now…he just made note to keep a safe distance from them. Dark circles showed beneath her eyes when she raised her head.

"Has that ever happened before?" he asked as he sat on the deck.

"No." She shook her head. Haylee felt sick to her stomach as she tried to put her thoughts into words for him. "Usually," she compressed her mouth while giving him a meaningful look, "when the…essence of a person comes into me, it feels like a gentle meshing with what I already have in there." She paused, thinking, her eyes searching for answers somewhere in the clouds. When she had what she wanted, her gaze returned to his face. "Emis was like a lightning storm hitting me straight on."

"Can you see her thoughts?" he wanted to know.

Haylee furrowed her brow while shaking her head. "I can feel something in there—I think that's why my head was hurting—but I can't get to it."

She grew quiet for a few minutes before continuing. "The crystal and papers in my dress—Emis put them down my dress. They'll need to be retrieved." Her cheeks began to bloom, "and as you can see, my hands are a little tied up."

"What?" He half laughed while getting to his feet.

Haylee gave him a beseeching look. Shaking his head he muttered, "Leave it to Emis."

Haylee rolled her eyes.

He approached with his hands shoved in his front pockets, stopping inches from her. He investigated all around her feet. "Well...it doesn't look like anything's fallen out during all of your thrashing about."

"Will you just get it!"

"That's a rather compromising position you're asking me to take. After all, I am a man of honor."

"Ah!" she complained as she kicked out in irritation. "Reece! Come on! My back is starting to hurt! The sooner we get this over with, the sooner we can help Edward."

Kneeling down, he began to feel around the waist of her dress. He discovered where they were quickly enough but extracting them would be another story. He stood up, taking a step away. She looked at him. "Couldn't find them?"

"Oh, I found them alright."

"Well?"

"They are both right by the waistband of your skirt." His mouth made a straight line. "As I see it, I either have to reach up there from the bottom of your skirt...or down through the neck line. Unless you want me to get my knife and cut them out?"

Already feeling the flames on her face, she squeaked, "Go down through the top."

"Apologies," he smiled limply when Haylee closed her eyes and turned her face in the opposite direction.

It really wasn't that bad. Reece was as gentlemanly and

quick as possible, but the feel of his arm sliding along her torso sent flames from her face all the way down to her womanly center.

The instant that Reece's fingers came in contact with the crystal, a blinding flash and a wave of power sent him flying across the deck.

"Reece!" Haylee screamed as she watched him violently crash into the mast.

He lay in the spot where he landed, immobile.

"Reece! Reece! Answer me!"

Haylee's bodice was in tatters, and the crystal lay pulsating, unnoticed at her feet.

"Help! Help us! Somebody help us!" Haylee shrieked and flailed.

As time passed, with no help forthcoming, her frantic voice grew weaker. Haylee no longer had the strength to fight against the device that held her place Exhaustion and dehydration set in. She'd begun to hallucinate.

~ ~ ~ ~

"It is time," Elin and Nile spoke in unison.

"Agreed." Tethalana and Darion nodded.

"This would be much simpler if we could take physical form," Tethalana complained.

"You know that is forbidden," Darion chastised.

The two continued, "Since the container is in its expanded form and the girl is in contact with it, we can use it to make the corrections you wish, Tethalana."

"Very good. And her mate?"

"We are not completely certain, but we believe that we can realign the crystal using the same method to accept his genetic coding. However, once this is done, it cannot be reversed. Every descendant of that strain will have access."

Tethalana took her time to digest and consider this. Grimly she responded, "Understood."

Darion chuckled, but with irony. "That Emis almost outwitted you."

"Almost doesn't count," Tethalana threw over her shoulder. Facing the youths, she gave them instructions to reinstate the rhythmic verbalization that the girl's ancestors used to convey the information they needed. Her access to this would be delayed so that her brain would have time to recuperate after the pending ordeal.

Elin and Nile began their work, pressing buttons and murmuring among themselves.

"You'll have to include a time stream return trigger for the male that the crystal will recognize,"Darion said.

'Yes, yes," they nodded in unison. "It will be the same as all the Travelers have used."

Tethalana looked on silently. "We've never had one Traveler harvest another," she commented.

"And a Traveler has never been mated while in her travel stream." Darion commented dryly.

They all stopped to regard him.

A smile broke out on Tethalana's face. "That energy fragment will be stronger than most... We will use that to delay the trigger. Haylee will have the gift of time."

~ ~ ~ ~

In her blurred, feverish visions, Haylee saw her animals and her dad. Josh put in an appearance. Reece told her that he'd fallen in love with her. She slept fitfully off and on.

In one of her dreams, she saw two children. They looked see-through, like ghosts. They were on their knees, talking at the base of her restraining device. Perhaps they were touching it as well.

A tall woman in a long, white dress appeared, also ghostlike. Her shoulder-length hair was silver-white and her kind eyes were surrounded by wrinkles. She stood straight and tall before Haylee. They regarded one another quietly for a few moments before the woman joined all of the fingers of her right hand to form a point, touching them to her forehead, chin, and heart. Holding her hand in front of her chest, she spread her fingers wide, like a flower blooming. From the center of her palm, tiny lights floated up into the air. "I honor your service to the Upholders." The woman's rich voice reverberated throughout the open space.

Perplexed, Haylee watched her walk over toward Reece. Haylee wanted to call out to the woman to help him, but she was unable to speak. She watched her do the same motions with her hand and send the floating lights to him.

Both Haylee and Reece rested more easily after that.

~ ~ ~ ~

Reece groaned as he cracked an eye open. He turned on his side and groaned more loudly. Feeling sore and groggy, he slowly got up on his hands and knees. *What happened?*

He remembered the blast as he brought his hand up to his aching skull. He took stock of his body, checking to see if anything was broken as he rose up into a sitting position.

Across the way, Haylee hung in an awkward position behind the thing that held her captive.

"Haylee! Are you alright?"

Reece limped over to her. Her dress was torn, but thankfully, she looked unharmed. *How is it possible that the explosion blew me away and nothing happened to her? How is it possible that I am alright too?*

His eyes could not help but be drawn to the exposed skin under her bodice and the rounded curves visible there. The crystal lay in plain view on the planking next to her.

Unbelievably, Haylee was standing on the papers that had previously been lodged in her clothing. He had a vague memory of her screaming out his name.

Careful, so as not to wake her, he removed his shirt and draped it over her for modesty.

Reece was leaning on the mast that had broken his fall, reading Emis's letter, when Haylee finally awoke.

~ ~ ~ ~

Relief flooded through her as Haylee watched Reece, who was across the deck, in silence. In his hands were Emis's letters. The mass of hair on his bare chest startled her. Her eyes could not resist following the tapered path of the dark curls... that disappeared blow his belt. If her gaze was a touch, it would have gently explored the lines and contours of his well-defined muscles. Haylee noted his scowl. She looked down to see that his shirt was covering the front of her. Knowing that he must have seen her exposed was humiliating.

Her back hurt, her throat was sore, and her wrists were abraded. Other than that, things were about where they'd left them. *Was that blast from the crystal? When it threw me the first time, it didn't seem like it had as much force.*

Reece shuffled the papers to read the next one, his scowl had turned into a grimace.

Are those papers waving in the breeze, or is he trembling? Haylee wondered. When she couldn't stand the silence any more, she asked, "What does it say?"

His face was pale when he turned toward her. With worry in his eyes and strain in his voice, he replied, "It says that the crystal burns the webs away." He came over to her. "Are you alright?"

"Yes, I think so—you?"

"Fine," he said distractedly as he returned to read. "With

each burn, there is a phrase that must be spoken."

She stared at him silently for several prolonged moments. Nodding, she said, "Well...now we know. Did she say what has to be done to bring Edward back?"

"No."

Haylee's face fell.

He continued. "She said that if you survive the burning..." —now he looked green— "we will find another letter with instructions for that." Their eyes met again then both fell to the crystal. "If I can't touch the damn thing, this whole plan of Emis's is rubbish!"

Haylee cocked her head to the side as a feeling came to her. "I don't think it will do that again."

"And you know this...how?"

She just shook her head in silence.

Taking the matters into his own hands, Reece knelt down next to the blue stone. He rolled up Emis's letter and used it to move the crystal a few inches. Nothing happened.

Next, he pulled a hanky out from his pocket, wrapped that around his hand, and repeated the experiment with the same results. Finally, he braved a touch with his fingertip. Again nothing.

Glancing up at her, he nodded before reaching out to take it into his hand.

The moment the crystal had full contact with his skin, it buzzed a little as it settled firmly in his palm. Reece's eyes flew to Haylee. "It moved!" A contorted expression passed over his face.

"What just happened?" "When...." he hesitated. "I just..." His face relaxed. "When I said, 'It moved,' those words felt like they amplified and echoed in my chest.

Once they'd both settled down over the strange behavior of the crystal, they resumed their mission to follow Emis's instructions.

Indicating her understanding, Haylee began taking deep breaths. "Let's get this going."

Is this why I am locked down? Haylee's core quivered. *So I can't run away?*

"I'm ready," she stated with much more bravery than she felt.

Reece, however, did not look ready. He stood in front of her webbed hands, gazing down at the crystal in his hand.

Its color was quite beautiful, a clear blue at the outer edges. Toward its center, the color deepened into indigo. Unlike other crystals, this one had no inclusions or cloudy spots. He turned it over, rubbing a fingertip over the smooth-as-glass geometric surfaces. He startled when a light from its center sparked on then began to pulsate. "It feels like it's starting to heat up!"

Reece blinked rapidly. His chest rose and fell as he sucked in lungfuls of air.

He reread the paper again, and Haylee could see the internal battle written on his face.

"Look, I know you're not crazy about this idea. Believe me, neither am I, but the longer you take the more scared I am!" Haylee said with a strained tone.

Reese's chest continued to heave.

"Do it for Edward, Reece," she said, *and for Glori and Josh… and for me.*

A curt nod of assent was his only response. With the crystal in one hand and Emis's letter in the other, he mouthed the words he was directed to say.

Reece and Haylee locked gazes."Throughout the ages of men we have always traveled…" He held the crystal out before him.

Those words! They reverberated inside her head, echoing and bouncing around, making her feel dizzy. The sensation was like nothing she'd ever experienced. It was like each letter and syllable branded itself into her gray matter with incredible clarity.

He lowered the crystal to the space between the pinky and ring finger of her left hand. As soon as it came into contact with the web, Haylee screamed.

Reece froze.

"No!" she growled, breathing heavily, "Don't stop!"

Steeling himself, he pressed forward, reading the next words. "Of men, with men, but more than man alone."

Haylee could not possibly have heard through her screams, yet the next phrases had the same effect. She knew and felt each and every word.

Shaking and sweating, Reece noticed that as soon as the crystal met the apex between her fingers, all signs of the webbing disappeared. No bleeding, no remnants of skin, and no scar. Haylee's breathing was labored. She spoke between heavy gasps.

"Only six more to go..." She regarded him.

"Haylee?"

"Emis told me last night that once this gets started, it can't be stopped." She made an effort to appear calmer than she felt in order to encourage him to forge onward. "We can make this take days, but I'd rather get it over with. Go!"

"Remnants of our story hidden in legends and lore."

The touch. The burn. Screams that sent daggers into Reese's heart.

Smiling weakly, she nodded, "five."

"Aaaaaaaaahhhhhhhhhhhhhhhh!"

"Travelers passing their tools; one to the next."

Both of their faces were streaked with tears. "Haylee, I can't..."

"You can't stop," she whispered, hanging her head between her arms. "You can't stop...for Edward." She lifted her eyes when he did not move. "Please, Reece."

He took a few deep breaths in a row before raising the crystal again.

"Aaaaaahhhhhhhhhhhhhhhhhhhh!"

"Tools dispelled at the ceremonial passage."

Throwing down the accursed things he held, he went to her. Propping her up, he stroked her hair. She weakly begged him to continue.

"No. We are going to wait. You have to rest."

He moved a barrel over for her to sit on and found a blanket to cover her.

Cursing, he repeatedly kicked at the thing that held her locked in place. "What the hell are you?" he yelled.

Haylee fell into a fitful sleep. He left her briefly to check on his brother. Nothing was different there. Storming into Emis's room, Reece searched for the second letter. He took out his rage on anything that stood in his way.

Later, after feeding Haylee crackers and some apple slices, he helped her drink some water. Smiling at him, she wiggled the web free fingers of her left hand. "Look, I can move that one; it looks normal again and it doesn't hurt at all."

Without saying a word, he tucked a strand of hair behind her ear.

"I have a plan," she whispered.

"What is it?" he asked quietly, thinking how much he admired her spirit.

"On the next hand, you just go boom, boom, and boom. No breaks between the fingers, just get it all over with in one fell swoop."

"Hell no!" he stood up.

"Look, Reece, I don't know how much more of this I can take. If it were you on this side of this thing, wouldn't you want it that way?"

He just stood there staring at her, shaking his head. "You're sure?"

With watery eyes, she nodded. "Yes, just get it over with. I'm begging you."

"Aaaaaaaaaaahhhhhhhhhhhhhhhhhh!!"

"One sister to the next. Performing their duties as the Promise decrees."

"Aaaaaaaaaaaaaaaahhhhhhhhhhhhhh!"

"Carrying the lineage forward…"

Haylee threw up the water and food that she'd eaten. Reece hesitated.

"No…keep going," she said weakly.

He did.

"Aaaaaaaaaaaaaaaaahhhhhhhhh!"

"To the day…"

"We're almost there, Haylee."

"Aaaaaaahhhhhhhhhhhhhh!

"When the Promise is fated to unfold."

As the last web burned away, the contraption binding Haylee's wrists turned from a solid into a cloud of blue, green, and gray. Haylee fell through it, dropping to the deck like dead weight.

Staring in shock, Reece blinked as he watched the colorful cloud condense, smaller and smaller, until it solidified…into a decorative box perched in the palm of Haylee's hand.

Exhausted and laboring, Reece sank to his knees then crawled to her side. He made sure she was still breathing. He cried tears of relief. He picked up a hand, spreading out her palm and fingers. *It looks like a hand…just a hand and nothing more. After all that, how can it possibly look like that?*

There wasn't even a twinge of uncertainty as he brought it up to his face and kissed her palm. Scooping Haylee up into his arms, he carried her to the captain's cabin. He sat down on the edge of the bed with her still in his lap. The early evening light whispered over the planes of her face. Holding her close to his heart, he lay back on the bed, refusing to release her. Amazed at her strength and endurance, he placed a gentle kiss at the corner of her lips. His own exhaustion overtook him then. He closed his heavy eyelids.

Sleep began its work to repair and restore the spent duo.

❧61❧

WATERS OF LOVE

The consciousness of dreams carried them out on a receding tide into deeper waters where half images played out.

Like two warriors seeking affirmation of life after a great battle, they reached out to each other, fingers entwining. They shifted body positions so that gaps were closed. Breathing harmonized.

Waves of stillness, together, gave way to movements. Hands caressed, sighs aroused. Tenderness and touches led to the peeling away of restricting cloth. Quietness settled in again.

As the night wore on, slumber stripped away worries and inhibitions. Freedom to seek hearts' desires sparked masculine lips to seek feminine. Hands caressed. Soft, slow strokes turned muscles taught. Pulses quickened up a tempo like ancient drum rhythms. Covers that had grown too warm were thrown aside.

Haylee moaned. Her hands reached out, clutching, pulling, and seeking something that she could not name.

Reece's body moved with hers, matching the hypnotic dance that had begun. He nuzzled his face into her neck, nibbling and kissing the tender skin.

Every instinct in his half sleep state demanded that he push forward!

Something stopped him.

Their eyes flew open. Suddenly they were both fully awake.

She stared at him, and he at her. Shocked by their positions and predicament, they remained still for a few moments.

Reece's eyebrow arched; the edges of his mouth crooked upward in amusement.

For only the briefest moments, he had thoughts of preventing a child. Logic decreed that Haylee could not have prepared the herbal soaked sea sponge he'd observed women using…if she would even know to do such a thing.

At the moment, he was consumed with the joy of finding himself on the verge of loving this beautiful woman who was so gloriously accessible.

Haylee was amazed that this man who she was so strongly drawn to was holding her in his arms and looking at her with acceptance shining in his eyes. He made her feel free, and cared for…and not alone. She had no thoughts of hesitation whatsoever. Returning his smile, she thought, *Yesss,* as she pulled him in closer.

A full moon rose in the night sky, pulling hard on the salty body of water, causing waves to rise up and crest. Liquid, air, and force of motion formed white peaks that glittered in the darkness before they fell to pound against the shore. After a time, the motion calmed; the tide receded and all was still. The sea and the sleepers once again drifted under a smooth glassy surface.

~ ~ ~ ~

Waking up abruptly, as if startled out of a sound sleep, Haylee sat up in bed. She flicked her hands, holding them up with fingers spread wide, just to make sure. The webs were gone. Reece mumbled at her side, throwing out an arm to pull her back in close. Haylee inhaled deeply to fill her head with his intoxicating scent. Memories of their night together made her grin. A liquid warmth in the center of her womanhood responded to her thoughts. A smile played about her mouth as she let herself be pulled back under the warm covers.

❧62❧

LETTERS FROM THE DEAD

Eight months later...

Reece sat in his office, now on the second floor of Keener Brothers Mercantile. He could hear the sounds of brisk business going on below as Edward and Song assisted customers. Polly's laughter drifted to him. It was good to hear that sound after all this time.

In his hands, he held a crumpled piece of paper. Soot smudges marred the outer edges. Eventually he'd put it back in his strong box.

His eyes scanned the words, that, by now, he'd committed to memory.

I allowed you to see secrets that have been closely guarded by my ancestors through time because I know of your fears that Polly will develop into a horrible creature. Polly is just like any other girl, except that she has a piece of heirloom jewelry. She will never become a Traveler. I chose a good family for her to grow up with when I picked you and your siblings.

Every member of our line carries that pendant — it contains a small portion of the primordial crystal within. Another oddity of our kind is that we only have a single female child. Once we've given birth, we only have seven years left to live.

Travelers are very few and far between. Their only place in the past is to carry the large crystal forward—until the moment comes to hand it off to the next Traveler. Other than that, I cannot explain why we do what we do, but know this—the savagery of the behavior we are compelled to act upon shreds the heart of the women who are struck with the affliction. The Redemption Ceremony and the subsequent ability to return some of the souls we've taken, is a concession granted to us by the Upholders. But it comes with a cost; one year less for each soul returned...

Once the Ceremony is complete, and the Traveler has recovered— she must return to her own time stream. You will speak the words that spark that event.

You may have heard…in France, I was once quite famous. I read the future for those I choose. I leave you with this: when Polly reaches her ninth year, there will be more children in your life. Their mother will be a tall sturdy woman with eyes that are blue like yours. She will be a good companion to you and a fine mother. You will spend many happy years together.

Your businesses will grow and you will have much to be thankful for. Through all the goodness I foresee for you Reece, I also see a dark area. My advice to you is to release it when it comes. A life lived with heavy burdens carried in one's heart is weighted and tinged with unnecessary grief.

If that darkness is Haylee, then my words above are meant tenfold. The desire you felt for her was part human nature, but also something more… When a Traveler crosses the path of her mate, there is an intense attraction between them. Nothing can keep them apart—until they've produced their offspring. If you loved Haylee before you sent her back, your seed has already become a part of our lineage. I am truly sorry about that.

If my plan was successful, the Travelers will be no more…

Reece thought back to the many conversations he and Haylee had had about Traveling. She understood that the two crystals brought her here. She was more than frustrated that the way to get back didn't seem to be automatic...or under her control. He knew he should have shown her the letter. Let her read it with her own eyes, but...he just couldn't.

Reece leaned forward, placing an elbow on his desk, and massaged his throbbing forehead. His lips formed a compressed straight line. His fingers pressed insistently on his temples in an attempt to loosen the tightness that knotted there. His thoughts went back to that morning on the Dicey. The morning he'd read this letter for the very first time. The morning Haylee had brought Edward back.

The two brothers shared an emotional reunion. Mostly Reece was emotional; Edward was bewildered by his brother's actions and confused as to where he was.

Not long after, Reece recognized Haylee's distress. Pale and swaying precariously, she reached out for his hand as her legs gave way. He caught her before she reached the floor. Wearing a worried scowl, he scooped her into his arms.

She was so weak, she could hardly move. She looked haggard and gray; huge circles formed under her eyes. He couldn't shake the knot of worry in the pit of his stomach. After everything they'd been through, he wished they could have been celebrating, instead of wondering at her plight.

Her recovery had been long and painful. But he'd been with her day and night, taking heart in every small improvement; encouraging her to be strong.

When she was better, Haylee had insisted on going to Alfred Pool, who she always referred to as Homer. They'd argued bitterly over that. Song had been the one who carried her limp form home that night.

Again, Reece worked to nurse her back to health. This time

was taking longer than the time before. Edward and Ailbe were the ones who figured out Haylee's connection to animals. Edward and Song had convinced Reece that there was a healer in Chinatown who might be able to help Haylee. At his wits end, he'd agreed. When they were bringing Haylee out to the wagon, Ailbe suddenly became agitated. Reece wanted to switch him out for another horse, but Edward stayed his hand. "Hold on, Reece. If there's one thing Haylee's taught me, it's that animals have more going on than we give them credit for. Let Ailbe have a look at her to see what he does."

Both Keeners were surprised to see what looked like sadness in the horse's eyes. Ailbe gently sniffed around the girl, nuzzled her face and hair, and made a series of deep, soft murmuring sounds deep in his chest. It was clear when Ailbe had finished his inspection because he settled back into his harnesses, clearly waiting to set out on their journey. Edward let the horse have his head, as he seemed to have a specific destination in mind. Ailbe had brought them to a stable that boarded horses. Reece rolled his eyes. "He probably came here because there's a female in heat."

"Probably," Ed smirked, "but I am still willing to suspend my belief until I have more information."

Ailbe began making a series of loud horse calls, startling the two men, as they'd never heard him do that before. Answering calls came from within. Haylee, who had been hovering in a state of half sleep, perked up at the ruckus. "Lovey!" She smiled weakly.

A happy reunion ensued when she was greeted by Lovey and Titan. Snuffles, smiles, and three way woman to horse conversations went a long way toward reviving her.

Reece had been more than willing to bring the other two equines back to their own stables.

Reece knew Haylee felt strongly about going back to restore

her stepmother and her close friend Josh. He had the words to do that for her, but he simply could not do it. In the months since that day on the Dicey, she had indeed discovered that she was with child. Reece let go of his worry that it would inherit the Traveler's curse. However, he couldn't release the tension he carried over Haylee's limited life span as a result of her pregnancy... For the moment, the rightness of being with her was all that mattered. They were happy; happy to spend their days together and even happier about their nights. Reece enjoyed seeing her hair grow longer and looking at her wearing proper dresses...even though she complained bitterly about their cumbersomeness. She promised daily that if she was here long enough, she'd do something to improve women's wear. Comments like that cut at his heart. He had every intention of keeping her right here, with him, deeply loved and protected. Haylee continued to hope to leave.

Reece remembered the times when he'd sat at this very desk, hesitating over writing letters to his parents and sisters. Should he write to them about Haylee and the babe? It was hard to imagine keeping something so important from them, yet something always held him back.

Business was booming, and he was on the verge of closing a deal on property that would be the next Keener Brothers Mercantile. He had smiled when he imagined the clan bringing their boisterous personalities, humor, and music to town and thought, *maybe I'll tell them once the baby is born.*

Polly had done well, considering all that she'd been through. True to her mother's words, Song was a great help in keeping the girl grounded and comforted as well as a considerable asset to the Mercantile. He'd taken on many of Reece's responsibilities with inventory transportation, giving Reece more time to work on expansion and to spend time with his women. The little girl had become Haylee's constant shadow. Haylee kept her busy with schoolwork in the office while she worked on filing and invoices. The girl, like Edward, had an affinity for people.

Recently, she'd started touching people in a way that made Reece apprehensive. She'd take a person's hand or grab their elbow to lead them toward something in the store that they wanted to see. After he'd watched her do this a dozen times or so, he stopped fretting. Every person that Polly interacted with paused, like they'd forgotten to take the next step in their walk. An odd expression would cross their face before they took a deep breath. Upon the exhale, all their worry lines would disappear. A beatific smile would break out on their faces. For a time, it was as if all their cares vanished. Folks started seeking Polly out, reaching for her hand as soon as they walked in the store. She was turning into quite the little sales person.

The sound of the two female voices laughing or singing in the office put smiles on the faces of all the menfolk. Reece overheard more than a few conversations about the baby once Polly knew about it. The little girl would prattle on about how she would be a big sister once it was born, since Reece was her papa. Sadness always played across her face when the topic of motherhood came up. He could tell that she held herself back from asking if Haylee was her mama now. Haylee seemed to know what Polly was thinking. But rather than talking to her, Haylee would simply pull the little girl in close and give her long tender hugs. It seemed to help.

Reece wiped at the tears that made tracks down his face.

His mind wandered to another day in April. Haylee'd been so excited when the baby moved for the first time that morning; she'd raced from the bathroom in her long white sleep shirt. "She moved, Reece!" Haylee had trilled as she grabbed his hand and placed it on the spot. He eyed her with a tolerant smile. He realized that this was the first time Haylee had referred to the babe as "she." Part of him fervently wished for a boy. A tiny flutter under his hand had the corners of his eyes wrinkling as they shared a smile.

"She's a strong one, our little Serena," he replied with mirth. It did not miss his notice that he'd accepted that it would be a girl. It was Haylee's turn to look at him questioningly. "Serena is my grandmother's name." He shrugged his shoulders.

Haylee smiled and whispered, "I like it," before kissing him on the cheek. They decided to close the store and take the whole family on a picnic.

Haylee and Song had great fun preparing the food while Reece, Ed, and Polly harnessed up the horses and loaded the wagon. Haylee had a specific place in mind. They arrived there by early afternoon. It had been an idyllic day spent napping and reading in the sun, playing games with Polly, and making up feats of bravery for the men to challenge each other with. Not long before it was time to pack everything up, Haylee had come for him, taking his hand and gently leading away from the others. At the base of a sizable rock outcropping, she told him the story of when she'd first arrived here. He'd heard it before. Although he tried to accept it as truth, a part of him still had trouble fully believing…until she pulled out the little stash of items that she'd hidden within the rock.

When he had held the coins and paper money in his hand and read their date, '1977, 1980 & 1985,' he finally stopped disbelieving. His heart sunk when he saw her tears. Haylee sniffed, looking down at her feet. They'd had this conversation before. He could tell that she held her tongue. Tipping her chin up he'd asked, "You would still go back if it were in your power?"

The knife in his heart gouged again as she nodded her head sadly. "You would choose to leave me then?" He moved his hand from her chin to the back of her head so he could hold her face and rub his thumb along her jaw.

Her mouth trembled as she replied, "It's not that I would choose to leave you." She covered his hand with her own. "Now that I know that I can repair the damage I've caused, I can't stop thinking about how to get back so I can do that. How would you feel Reece, if Edward had to permanently remain the way I'd left him?"

She was right, of course, but he didn't know those people... "What about how sick it makes you and what of the babe?"

She dismissed this, "We didn't know that she was even there when I restored Edward and Homer—and she survived."

Reece's breath had caught in his chest. If she returned the two that were uppermost in her mind then that would mean... He closed his eyes, not even wishing to think it. It had been on the tip of his tongue to tell her about losing years from the precious time that she had left. He was fairly certain that Emis had not told Haylee that particular bit of information. If he'd spoken those words out loud, then she'd know that Emis had given him the key to her return. *No! I will not do it!* He'd thought.

Then the fire had broken out. Reece rubbed the charred edges of the paper, remembering when he'd desperately grabbed it from the teeth of the flames, frantic to save it. The memory of that night was so clear, it still felt like it had just happened yesterday.

It may have been caused by someone dropping a lit match when going for a smoke, or a stray ember from a cook stove, or even something more sinister—a group of ruffians spilling a lamp or firing a stray shot while shaking down some poor soul with the wrong colored skin.

With the first smell of smoke on the air, there had been panic in the streets. Having watched the quick and haphazard way that buildings had gone up, Reece had known a catastrophe like this was inevitable. He'd prepared for it. Immediately upon hearing the cries, "Fire! Fire" Reece implemented his plan. Polly was sent to watch at the front of the store, staying well clear of adults who would be in a panic. She was to shout out the names of the shops that had caught aflame—so they would know how much time they had left before they had to evacuate. Shotguns were placed on top of the counters in case they were needed. The rest of the adults worked as quickly as possible to move key items of stock into fire safe storage.

They had just enough time to make a quick run through both floors, grabbing anything of personal importance to put into the vault.

As they stepped outside, a cacophony of frenzied activity assaulted them in the streets. Edward broke into a full run to the stables to lead their animals to safety.

Explosions not far off signaled that buildings were being demolished in order to break the fire line. Towering walls of flames greedily ingested its dry tinder feast. Above the din, Reece had yelled to Song to follow him and for Haylee to get Polly away from the crowds.

A great gale of wind from the inferno blasted the people who went into action fighting the fire. Heat scorched their eyes, timbers crashed. Scalding water from heaved buckets rained down upon the workers; burning exposed skin. People screamed as flames jumped onto them. Animals released in the frenzy trampled everyone in their path.

Reece had grabbed a speaking trumpet to yell with a raspy smoke-ravaged voice instructions that would save lives and make headway in their campaign. Some people had enough wits about them to respond to his directives. Many more were wild with panic—all reason having escaped them. Sometimes Reece wished he could have been one of them, crazy with fear, doing something insensible…something that would have gotten him killed.

A mob had gathered at the edge of the activity, shrieking and moving like a swarm of bees. Reece saw that Haylee and Polly had gotten caught up in it. They were being carried along in its path like leaves trapped in a fast moving stream. Haylee struggled mightily to extract the little girl but could not make progress.

Time seemed to move like molasses as he watched a two-story burning building begin its downward descent directly on the spot where Haylee and Polly thrashed.

"No!" he'd roared as he tried jumping over and through the crowd to get to them. "No!" he howled as the wall of flames tilted sickeningly, gathering speed as it came down.

Gasping in horror, he spoke the words that he promised himself that he would never ever speak…"The Traveler Returns."

Reece swiped again at the tears that were still wet upon his face. Emis had been right. He carried darkness within him; for Haylee, Serena….and for the information that Emis had given him in her letter that he failed to share. He picked up his pen and began to write.

My Dearest Haylee —

EPILOGUE

It was a beautiful, sunny day. The rolling hills were covered with a fragrant carpet of grass and wildflowers. Dotting the mounds of earth were oak trees and scrub redbuds. The warm, sweet, heady scents of spring uplifted everyone's mood. Josh laughed as the girl wound bits of his hair around her fingers. "Come on, Serena, leave it alone." He playfully brushed her hands away.

Shifting his weight, he adjusted the straps that were digging into his shoulders. He continued his narrative.

"My family moved to the Los Angeles Basin in the 1930s. I came up here to go to school because we have business ties here."

"Thank goodness for ties," the third member of their group said. "If you hadn't gone to Berkeley, we would have never met."

"Right," he smiled, looking down at their entwined fingers. He gave her hand a gentle squeeze.

"Where are you taking me?" he wanted to know.

"You'll see. We're getting close…I think." She peered around, working to get her bearings.

As they hiked along the trail, he couldn't bring himself to

tell her that he was already very familiar with this place.

Josh thought about how much he loved her; her mind, her enthusiasm, and all the wild stories she had to tell. He loved her smile. Today, those expressions were tinged with something else…worry perhaps? *I want to spend the rest of my life watching her, he thought. I wonder when she's going to finally cave in and let me put a ring on her finger?*

"Oh Josh! I think I see it!" Releasing his hand, she raced ahead to an outcropping of rocks a short distance away. Laughing, he jogged along behind her, causing the heavy backpack to bounce in time with his footfalls.

A delighted giggle broke out from behind his head. "Horsey!" Serena chirped.

"Neigh! Neigh!" responded Josh. He elongated his gait to give her more of a rolling motion.

He watched Haylee in the distance, searching for something in the rocks. He hadn't told her yet about the grant he'd won from the Université de Lyon…it included a cute little two bedroom house in a neighborhood with lots of young families. He grinned.

She found what she as looking for; he could tell by way she stiffened then reached out with a purpose. She was on her knees, looking somber as she poured over an assortment of things in her lap. "What's up?" he asked, when Josh arrived at her side.

Replacing the items back inside the metal box they'd come from, she set it aside so she could help remove Josh's backpack with the child in it. He glanced over at the container. He could see the edges of what looked like a stack of old papers.

Haylee adjusted the expanding part of the backpack frame so it could stand up on its own. From one of the side pockets she fished out a sippy cup and a Tupperware container filled with Cheerios. She opened them and handed them to her daughter.

Coming back toward Josh, pain was clearly visible on her face.

"Do you remember when I told you about my time jump?"

He rolled his eyes, "Not this again."

"It's not my imagination, Josh. I can finally prove it to you here."

Taking in a patient breath, he sighed. "Alright, I agree to suspend all logical arguments and sit here quietly with my hands folded nicely while you show me proof." He nudged his glasses farther up on his nose.

She nodded with a grimness that suggested he should be concerned.

Forty-five minutes later, Josh was wearing an expression of dazed confusion. She'd brought him to the place where she said she first arrived in 1849; a place where she'd stashed all of the items she had on her person at the time.

Of course, on the night that Haylee had been transported, she hadn't had a watertight metal container with her. Someone else had put that box there. Along with a sizable stack of letters and legal documents was a small but significant bag of heavy gold rocks.

Weighing it in the palm of his hand, he shook his head.

You'd think with all of the extraordinary things I have witnessed with Hay, I'd be used to this by now.

If all of that wasn't enough to liquefy his brain and have it oozing out of his ears, the paper clutched in his other hand could have done that all on its own. It was a document he'd heard about but never believed existed. It was part of the trust that his family had administered for well over a hundred years. Management responsibilities were the primary reason he'd chosen to come up here to go to school. The trust governed an enormous piece of open land that was now completely sur-rounded by houses and business parks–land that they had been hiking on."

A clause in the verbiage stated that if a specific document were produced between 1985 and 1992, the instructions upon it were to be followed to the letter. If the document never surfaced, then the remaining heirs of the trust could sell or dispose of the property however they saw fit. Proof of its validity would be provided.

The paper read: *"If this document is presented by my wife, Haylee Louise Garrett Keener, on or before the year 1992, then the entire tract of land known as Wild Cat Canyon is to be transferred into her ownership for the express purpose of providing for her and for my daughter."*

It was signed by Josh's great great great great great grandfather, Reece James Keener, and dated June 8, 1869.

Josh's stunned gaze traveled first to the cherubic angel with a gooey fist buried in her mouth, a child he'd claimed as his own.

His eyes then moved to Haylee a short distance away. She'd taken the stack of letters with her across the field. Her back was to him; her shoulders were slouched. He watched her body shake as she made an effort to muffle her sobs.

⚜The End⚜

A Sneak Peak: Haylee and the Last Traveler

They stood near the edge of the bed where Glori lay as the late afternoon light faded into tones of muted orange, pink and gold. Haylee held a shoebox. Inside were several items; a two inch long blue crystal and a decorative jewelry box.

Gene glanced at the contents. "That little case was your mom's."

Haylee drew her eyes away from Glori's impassive face to her father's. Then she looked down into the box. "Josh and I found it with her things in the attic."

Gene nodded. He raised a hand as if he wanted to touch it, but Haylee turned away and extended her arms. "These are dangerous, Dad! DON'T - under any circumstances - TOUCH THEM!"

"Haylee…." Gene looked confused, "I've handled that box before."

"Not when they are together, you haven't." Exasperation stamped itself across her face. She stepped away from the bed and went to stare out the window. "The first time I touched that crystal, it shot me across the room. When Reece touched it, the blast nearly cracked his skull wide open. Something happened…back there….that made it so that I can hold it. But I don't want to take chances to see what it might do to someone else."

She turned to her father. "I need it to bring Glori back. When I'm finished, I'm going to go down fast. I'll need you to do a few things for me. Catch me before I hit the ground. Take me to my bed and let me sleep it off….it might take a few days. Hide this box in my room. There's a good place at the back of my closet. Make sure that neither you nor Glori go near this thing."

About the Author

Since 1997, Redfern has been a professional artist and photographer. Her college years were devoted to obtaining a degree in business administration and marketing.

While attending California State University, Sacramento, Redfern began researching vampire myths—separating out facts from fiction. Haylee had begun to emerge...

In the summer of 2012, Redfern worked with author Lisa Boulton to illustrate and publish a children's picture book, *Toby Bear and the Healing Light*. That experience paved the way for Haylee to reawaken and come fully to life.

Redfern lives in the darling gold rush town of Nevada City, California with her husband, son, two dogs, two cats and a fish named Rocket.

Extras:

Homer's Story

http://bit.ly/1saAAuY

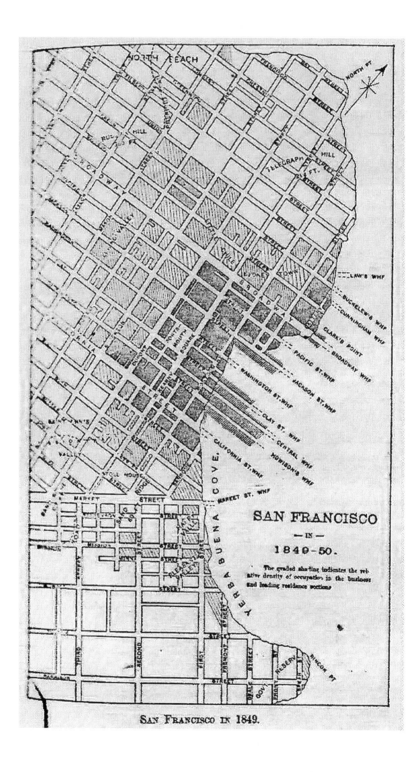

SAN FRANCISCO IN 1849.

Dear Reader,

When I first set out to write this story, I was determined do it in e-form only...save trees, no need for inks, cutting machines or shipping activities. (Yes, I know, e-readers consume energy too.)

I changed my mind because I enjoy the kinesthetic aspect of holding a book in my hands, turning the pages and marking the spot where I left off. I like passing books along to friends, checking them out of the library and buying them. I also discovered that although there are millions of people reading e-books, there are still plenty of us who want physical books too.

This book is a partnership between us. It is a labor of passion and dedication that took nearly two years to complete. It is hundreds (maybe thousands) of decisions made to spend time focusing on writing, editing, formatting and creating art pieces rather than a million other things. It is also *your* decision about what to read and taking the time to do it...instead of the million other things *you* could be doing. It is *your* imagination and emotions that fill in the spaces and build the framework.

Stories and the characters that exist solely within words are nothing more than sheets of paper and ink — or dots on a screen — if the readers aren't there to breathe life into them.

If you enjoyed *Haylee and the Traveler's Stone*, here's what you can do next.

If you loved the book and can spare a few moments, a short review would be very much appreciated on Amazon.com and or Goodreads.com.

Be the first to find out when my next book is coming out: join my e-mail list at http://bit.ly/1pnZzyu.

Images & Artwork Attributions

All of the art pieces for the cover design and interior pages were made using a collage-type process. Multiple Public Domain and Creative Commons licensed images were combined with Photoshop techniques and, in some cases, digital hand painting.

Cover Design, Photography and Collages: Lisa Redfern
Interior Design and layout: Megan Greene

Cover and Background Elements
Fractal_175-1113vv-nv.jpg: graphicstock.com
    Commercial License Usage purchased from http://www.graphicstock.com
Blonde girl.jpg:
Knut Niehus, http://www.visualphotos.com/artist/2x16868/knut_niehus
    Commercial License purchased from http://www.graphicstock.com
Elbaite-cktsr-11b.jpg: Rob Lavinsky, iRocks.com
    Creative Commons Share-Alike 3.0
Textures-grunge-nebula-1.bb-jpg: graphicstock.com
    Commercial License Usage purchased form http://www.graphicstock.com
Vector10052012007.jpg: graphicstock.com
    Commercial License Usage purchased from www.graphicstock.com
Aigue-marine Pakistan 180308.jpg : Vassil,
http://commons.wikimedia.org/wiki/User:Vassil
    Public Domain Image
Monitoring Device: Collage by Lisa Redfern
3interior KCPL Bldg Kansas City MO.jpg: Charvex, http://commons.wikimedia.org/wiki/User:Charvex
    Public Domain Image
Cows that Talk: photograph by Lisa Redfern
    Own Work
Oscar the Cat: Super flyffy cat (5364339790).jpg: Takashi Hososhima
    Attribution-Share Alike 2.0 Generic
Cowboy Boots IMGP9050.jpg: Nikodem Nijaki
    Creative Commons Attribution-Share Alike 3.0 Unported
Pigs: photograph by Lisa Redfern
    Own Work
Old Tractor: John Deere 3130 2.jpg: Johan Viirok
    Creative Commons Attribution 2.0 General License
Tissue: Sunset glory landscape: Fiona Storey
    Public Domain Image
Tissue: Kleenex-small-box.jpg: Evan-Amos
    Public Domain Image
Corn: Assorted grains: Fir0002
    GNU Free Documentation License, Version 1.2
Eggs: Eggs_(2241173285): Jeremy Noble from St. Paul; United States
    Creative Commons Attribution 2.0 Generic

Hall: Stanton_Hallway: JonRidinger
     Creative Commons Attribution 3.0 Unported
Doris's Trunk: Grandpa's WWII Trunk: photograph by Lisa Redfern
Imaginary Kiss: First-kiss-as-bride-and-groom.jpg: Arestheblue
     Creative Commons Attribution 3.0 Unported
Stone Circle: Harrespil Okabe.jpg: Creator Unknown
     Public Domain Image
Medical Bag: Debbie Reynolds Auction - Rex Harrison "Dr John Dolittle" signature
costume with top hat, shoes, prop parrot, and doctor bag from "Dr Dolittle".jpg: Doug
Kline from Los Angeles, CA, USA
     Attribution 2.0 Generic
Trestle: photograph by Lisa Redfern
     Own Work
Melded Pennies: 1909 US Penny.jpg: United States Mint, http://www.coinnews.
net/2009/11/09/pcgs-trueview-coin-imaging-at-baltimore-show/
     Public Domain Image
Keys: Keys_with_pink_background: Eviatar Bach
     Creative Commons CC0 1.0 Universal Public Domain Dedication
Match Flame: New Flame: photograph by Lisa Redfern
Heart Candles: God is Love.JPG: Wingchi Poon
     Creative Commons Attribution-Share Alike 3.0 Unported
Pendant Box: Collage by Lisa Redfern
Italian - Pyx with Arabesques in Quatrofoil Frames - Walters 71314 - View B.jpg:
Walters Art Museum, http://en.wikipedia.org/wiki/Walters_Art_Museum
     Public Domain Image
Roman - Pyxis - Walters 4776 - View A.jpg : Walters Art Museum, http://
en.wikipedia.org/wiki/Walters_Art_Museum
     Public Domain Image
VW Bug: 1957 VW Bug: photograph by Dianne Peterson
     Own Work
Running Shoes: Shoes sport-right.png: Walké Retouched by Karta24
     GNU Free Documentation License
Graduation Cap: LinusPaulingGraduation1922.jpg: National Library of medicine
     Public Domain Image
Walnut Orchard: photograph by Lisa Redfern
Messed Up Bed: Unmade bed.jpg: maxronnersjo
     Creative Commons Attribution-Share Alike 3.0 Unported
File Folders: Hangmappen: Basvb
     GNU Free Documentation License, Version 1.2
Pumps: Red High Heel Pumps.jpg: Hattfjelldal Ministerialbok Dåp 1860-1878.djvu:
Den norkse kirke
     Creative Commons Attribution 2.5 Generic
     Almighty1 at en.wikipedia
     Public Domain image
Backpack: Embroidery work done on a backpack: The embroidery work of Gyuráki
Sarolta (User:Asarolt)
     Creative Commons CC0 1.0 Universal Public Domain Dedication

Genealogy: Hattfjelldal Ministerialbok Dåp 1860-1878.djvu: Den norkse kirke
　　　Creative Commons Attribution 2.5 Generic
Pin Cushion: photograph by Lisa Redfern
　　　Own Work
Chair: ART DECO: UweBesendoerfer/MichaelPopp/kultsesse
Commercial License Usage purchased from www.graphicstock.com
Traveling: abstract-space-background-for-design-913-146.eps: artist unknown
　　　Commercial usage license purchased from www.graphicstock.com
Burned Beans: Baked Beans: photograph by Lisa Redfern
　　　Own Work
Wagon Train: The Mormon pioneers coming off Big Mountain into Mountain dell.
png: Harry A. Kelley
　　　Public Domain Image
Camp Fire: Fires_wood_flames_burning_embers_coals: Jon Sullivan
　　　Public Domain Image
Horse Tack: _MG_2293: Alex Proimos from Sydney; Australia
　　　Creative Commons Attribution 2.0 Generic
Martina: Teodor Axentowicz 1.jpg: Teodor Axentowicz 1879-1934
　　　Public Domain Image
Homer's Art Book: Wernigeroder Wappenbuch 001.jpg: Anonymous
　　　Public Domain Image
Gum: photograph by Lisa Redfern
　　　Own Work
Feed Bags: Coffee beans at Longbottom - Hillsboro, Oregon.JPG: M.O. Stevens
　　　Creative Commons Attribution-Share Alike 3.0 Unported
Ledger: Ledger of the fur trader Dedo from Leipzig, 1876-1885: Collection Kuhn
　　　Public Domain Image
Bandages: photograph by Lisa Redfern
　　　Own Work
Captain's Cabin: Collage by Lisa Redfern
Civil War Naval Museum, USS Hartford Captain's cabin.jpg: Kevin King, https://www.flickr.com/people/15775662@N00
　　　Creative Commons Attribution 2.0 Generic License
Deck of sailing ship at Port Los Angeles, ca.1905 (CHS-1491).jpg : USC Digital Library, http://digitallibrary.usc.edu/cdm/ref/collection/p15799coll65/id/2378
　　　Public Domain Image
Grand Turk(33).jpg: JoJan, http://commons.wikimedia.org/wiki/User:JoJan StateLibQld 1 161763
　　　Creative Commons Attribution-Share Alike 3.0 License
Sailing ships docked at Eagle Street Wharf, Brisbane, ca. 1888.jpg: State Library of Queensland, http://en.wikipedia.org/wiki/State_Library_of_Queensland
　　　Public Domain Image
Handwriting: created and photographed by Lisa Redfern
　　　Own Work
Mercantile: Old Western Store at Malakoff Diggins SHP.jpg: jcookfisher
　　　Creative Commons Attribution 2.0 Generic
Desk: StateLibQld 1 158274 Government Printer's Office, Brisbane, 1921.jpg: State Library of Queensland
　　　Public Domain Image

Livery Stable: October 1974. DETAIL OF NORTH ENTRANCE - Black Horse Livery Stable, Grant Street, South Pass City, Fremont County, WY HABS WYO,7-SOPAC,2-4.tif: Boucher, Jack E, Library of Congress Prints and Photographs Division Washington, D.C. 20540 USA http://hdl.loc.gov/loc.pnp/pp.print
> Public Domain Image

California Travel Advrtisement: California Clipper 500.jpg: - G.F. Nesbitt & Co., printer
> Public Domain image

Homer's Story: Collage by Lisa Redfern
WWFowler.jpg: Creator Unknown, Proceedings and transactions of the British Entomological and Natural History Society
> Public Domain Image

Vlaho Bukovac - Mrs Richard Le Doux - Google Art Project.jpg: Walker Art Gallery
> Public Domain Image

Mikkola ja Talvio by Järnefelt.jpg: Eero Jarnefelt 1863-1937
> Public Domain Image

James Campbell - Waiting for Legal Advice - Google Art Project.jpg: Walker Art Gallery
> Public Domain Image

Wernigeroder Wappenbuch 001.jpg: Creator Anonymous, http://daten.digitale-sammlungen.de/~db/0004/bsb00043104/images/
> Public Domain Image

John william waterhouse the lady clare study.jpg: Art Renewal Center Museum
> Public Domain Image

Map of San Francisco: sf1849.jpg: http://www.sfmuseum.org/
> Public Domain Image

Squirrel in Vet Office : Collage by Lisa Redfern
Doctor's office equipment.jpg: Subsconci Productions
> Creative Commons Attribution-Share Alike 2.0 Generic License

UCHSHealthCenter9.10.09ByLuigiNovi2.jpg: Nightscream, http://commons.wikimedia.org/wiki/
> Creative Commons Attribution 3.0

Squirrel on tree.jpg: John Sullivan
> Public Domain Image

Slumgullion Stew: photograph by Lisa Redfern
> Own Work

Teen Today: Mock Magazine Layout by Lisa Redfern
Cybill Shepherd: Noxell Corporation-makers of Noxema
> Public Domain Image:

Author's Online Resources

A set of color art pieces created especially for Haylee and the Travler's Stone e-trilogy can be viewed or purchased at http://lisa-redfern.artistwebsites.com

Background Research & Resource Notes - http://bit.ly/1lyJFk3

Animal Studies | Archival Sources | Backstory Hint |Books | Myths | Genetic Research | Gold Rush | Human Culture | Mythology | Plants | Psychology |San Francisco History | Science | Videos

Author's Pinterest Boards - http://bit.ly/1uD90tt

Book Business | Haylee - Background Research |Haylee - Book Cover Studies |Haylee - Book Trailer Studies Haylee - John William Waterhouse art inspiration | Haylee - Market Research | Book Art & Building | San Francisco 1849-1850s

Author's Website: www.redfern.biz

✑ Coming Soon from Little Mountain Publishing ✎

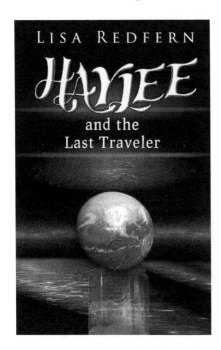